The Gypsy Woman Spoke:

"You belong here. This is your destiny . . . this land . . . this joining of your English blood with ours happened before, many years ago. You have come to fulfill a purpose—nothing could have stopped you. It is fate. There will be trials and much heartache you will suffer, but like the tempering of the blade in the fire, suffering will bring strength and reward.

"But, you must beware . . ."

PASSION FLAME

JEANNE MONTAGUE

Published in England as *Touch Me With Fire*

ACE BOOKS, NEW YORK

PASSION FLAME
Published in England as *Touch Me With Fire*
Copyright © 1981 by Jeanne Montague

An Ace Book

Published by arrangement with Macdonald & Co. (Publishers) Limited

ISBN: 0-441-81806-4

First Ace Printing: January 1983
Published simultaneously in Canada

Manufactured in the United States of America

Ace Books, 200 Madison Avenue, New York, New York 10016

With thanks to
Julia and Rosemary

Chapter One

1783

THE SKY was a stretch of relentless blue, dotted by small fluffy clouds which came scudding across from the black, forbidding range of mountains hunched in the distance. Autumn held the land, and the coaches had been traveling for days, leaving the shelter of the low hills of Budapest away to the north, crossing the Great Hungarian Plain. The country was flat, mile upon mile of straight track bordered by locust trees and Lombardy poplars. The swaying acres of wheat fields seemed endless, broken only by gaudy patches of sunflowers turning their golden faces toward the south.

Outriders flanked the vehicles, scarves covering their noses against the dust, hats rammed down over their ears, cloaks flapping as the strong gusts slapped them across their horses' flanks. The leading carriage rolled like a ship at sea through the red-gold fields; while in its wake came a massive stagecoach which bore the servants, followed by a hired wagon carrying boxes and luggage. In England, travel had been bad enough—rutted cart-tracks in the country, the thoroughfares in town

1

paved with granite cobbles which rattled the framework
of a carriage, but the state of the roads on the Continent
made it essential to use six horses to every conveyance
instead of four.

Lady Francesca Ballinger stared bleakly from the
window of that large, elegant structure, slung on giant
leather springs, which headed the cortège. After four
months of constant traveling, she was still not used to
the swaying, jolting movement. She had hated leaving
England, filling her eyes, her senses, with the beauty of
the spring, even enjoying the light, soft rain, as they
drove through the sleepy hamlets clustering along the
Dover Road. Boarding the ferry, she had been torn in
two, morbidly convinced that she would never see her
homeland again. Now, surrounded by an alien landscape, her vital, lovely face was sullen, full red lips
pouting, green eyes stormy beneath the brim of her
absurd, highly fashionable little hat, as she reflected
gloomily on her fate.

She had been destined to make this journey since
babyhood and, not for the first time, she cursed the fact
that she was the Earl of Marchmont's only child and
that he was filled with intractable ambition for her. This
had compelled him to have her trained, educated and
groomed for one sole purpose—that of marrying the
Margrave Carl of Govora—a man whom she had never
met. His estate was situated in the Carpathian Mountains, a remote, wild region. The earl had been an
ambassador there, years before, just after Francesca's
birth. He had met the newly widowed Duchess Renata,
acting as regent for her two-year-old son, and together
they had planned the match. The margraves were nobles
of rank equivalent to an English marquis, and this particular family was rich and powerful, in league with the
dominating Hapsburg Empire which controlled most of

Europe. Marchmont saw the advantages and determined that his daughter should enter into a binding alliance. The duchess had wanted to spread her net to England, and Francesca's generous dowry of ten thousand florins had swayed the balance. It was agreed that Francesca should undertake the long journey when she was old enough for the marriage to be consummated.

It would have been wiser if he had sent her earlier, before she gained any knowledge of the world, and men. She was now sixteen, with a mind of her own, headstrong and impetuous. It had been abundantly clear for some time that she was going to be a beauty and now this promise had been fulfilled. Many who knew them were struck with wonder that the earl, so conventional and austere a man, had produced such a gorgeous self-willed creature.

"What right had father to bargain my life away?" she fumed inwardly, slim hands locked fiercely together in the lap of her billowing silk skirt. But even she, so rebellious and hot-tempered, had been unable to defy him when, alarmed by her increasing popularity among London society and fearing that she might be compromised by one of the beaux who flocked to her, he had been adamant in his decision to dispatch her to her betrothed without further delay. The earl had got his way, but Francesca's lips curved into a small, pensive smile as she reflected on the fact that she had also scored a major victory. He was totally unaware that one of the men selected to accompany her in the role of body-guard, Sir Mark Harcourt, had been paying court to her for some time, and that she felt a warm, answering attraction. There was much to recommend him to the heart of a young, beautiful girl, filled with a reckless desire for living. He was tall and slender, with wavy fair hair pulled back into the modish pigtail, tied with a black ribbon bow. His eyes were hazel, humorous, adoring, and he was something of a dandy in his tight, tailored breeches and velvet jackets, a froth of Mechlin lace at his throat. With him, she had explored the outer fringes of love for the first time, and it was enough to make her aware of the deep sensuality of her nature. He wrote verses praising her, his wooing gentle, persuasive, and she was flattered and touched by such devotion. Unbeknown to anyone, with the exception of her maid, Hetty Trouncer, the couple planned to elope before they reached Govora.

Oh, yes, Hetty would help, she was a willing party to any madcap adventure which her mistress might suggest. Francesca glanced across at the maid where she sat on the opposite seat, heartened by her cheerful, oval face, the smile in her sparkling eyes, her warm, optimistic personality. How very different she was from Mrs. Lavinia Wagstaff, her bird-witted chaperone, the last in a long succession of nurses and governesses who had helped bring up the young girl. Francesca had never known her mother, who had died when she was born, though from her she had inherited compelling emerald eyes and hair which cascaded over her shoulders, thick and curling and of that very dark red color which seems to ripple with lighter gleams. Lavinia was lazy, snobbish and loved to gossip; a middle-aged widow who still clung to the now outmoded high, powdered wig and the huge oval hoops of yesteryear. A large, overpainted lady whom Francesca found it very easy to hoodwink.

It was not so easy to deceive the other occupant of the coach, Dr. Ranby, her erstwhile tutor and religious advisor. Employed to teach her the difficult foreign languages essential for her new position, he missed little that went on around him. But they had always got on well for, beneath his shell of dignity, he had a streak of genuine kindness and was fond of the enchanting, wayward Francesca, willing to help her in every way—a stranger in a strange land. Always dressed in dark, sober clothing, he had pleasant, regular features, graying hair receding from a fine brow, and thoughtful, observant eyes.

Francesca gave a sharp, impatient sigh, pulling the pins from her hat with its circlet of ribbons and roses and shaking her hair free. She tried to settle back against the plush seat, shutting her eyes, longing for the oblivion of slumber, but her thoughts continued to whirl, pictures of her old life rising behind her closed lids . . . the earl's magnificent residence in the most select quarter of London . . . the rolling estate of Tallents in Devon . . . scenes of the carefree existence she had once know. She thought about the journey which had passed in a haze of discomfort, incarcerated in the stuffy coach. Francesca had argued and stormed, wanting to take a horse and ride with the men, but her advisers would not hear of it. It would be most unseemly for a future margravine to act in such an unladylike manner. What would the winds and hot sun do to her complexion? Lavinia had added, plump, ringed hands raised in consternation. Did she want to reach her bridegroom looking like a gypsy?

They had stopped at posting inns along the way, Paris and Vienna had proved an exhausting round of soirées and balls, organized by distant relations, at which she had been positively lionized, the attention rather going to her head. Because of this, she and Mark had never really been alone for a moment and there had been no opportunity to discuss their elopement. In fact, Francesca had a sense of plunging disappointment at his tepidity—it was almost as if he was deliberately avoiding the subject. She felt sick with jealousy when she saw how much he was admired by the bewitching ladies who descended upon him at functions. It was obvious that he was no stranger to European highlife.

Racked by conflicting emotions, she was almost glad to leave those civilized cities behind, though progress was painfully slow. If they covered twenty miles a day they considered themselves lucky, as they followed the road which wound along beside the Danube, where white castles nestled among the thickly wooded hills which swept down to its banks. They stopped to rest in charming villages with timbered, painted farmhouses, neat cottages and solidly spired churches. The inns were clean, the food good, and there was a highly organized system for changing horses. As they traveled deeper into Hungary, such pleasant respite vanished; the country-side becoming much more bleak, lovely in its own way, but alarming too. That gloomy mountain range coming ever nearer was oddly menacing, as if its lofty crags and pinnacles harbored a thousand real or supernatural foes.

Francesca felt a start of fear; she and Mark must act without delay. She could not banish from her mind the niggling thought that he seemed reluctant to make a move. There was the question of her dowry, of course, which old Colonel Launey was guarding closely, hardly ever taking his eyes from the heavy leather bag which contained several pouches of silver coins and valuable jewels. Even now, it was tucked behind a cleverly contrived sliding panel under the seat of the coach. He checked and rechecked it—usually managing to find a different hiding place daily. When visiting noble houses, he had taken the precaution of placing it in the strong-room. Deep in the earl's confidence, he was determined that both money and bride would be delivered to their destination without mishap, and Francesca was uneasily aware of his shrewd eyes constantly watching her from under beetling brows. One of her father's cronies, Launey was a retired soldier, a great hulk of a man, still sporting a fiercely military mustache, his dark blue broadcloth coat cut like a uniform.

As if conjured up by her worried thoughts, his grizzled head appeared at the window as he slowed his mount's pace to speak with her. Normally, he rode in the van, raking the distances, alert for trouble. Serviceable pistols winked in holsters on each side of his saddle and his sword hung at his hip. Launey commanded the outriders as if they were a troop of cavalry, and the mere sight of them had been enough to ward off the attentions of surly, unwelcoming peasants, and had certainly insured a civil reception at the lonely farmsteads where they rested when night closed in. Launey spoke fluent German, a relic of his mercenary service, and was a most comforting presence in almost any circumstance, but he was getting old and certainly too stout. Sometimes his gray look of exhaustion alarmed Francesca, but he refused to travel in the coach, becoming offended at the mere suggestion.

Yet after exertion, his face would occasionally turn purple, eyes popping as he struggled for breath, and then Francesca felt bitter rage against the earl! What right had he to drag an elderly, sick man out of retirement and, playing on his loyalty, demand that he lead such an expedition? Ranby was a tower of strength, though Lavinia had done nothing but complain ever since setting foot on the ferry, perking up only in the establishments of the nobility. Hetty had proved to be an endearing companion, with an adventurous interest in everything, although Lavinia did not approve, thinking her too young and flighty to carry out her responsibilities properly. Ladies' maids should be middle-aged and strait-laced, not rosy-cheeked young flirts with dancing brown eyes.

The procession began to ascend a gradual incline, the flat plain dropping away behind them as they entered a densely wooded area, flashing with streams running down from the mountains. The track grew rougher, the sturdy horses picking their way along the winding path leading into the foothills.

Launey, his florid face beaded with the sweat which trickled from under his cocked hat, said gruffly; "We're here, m'dear."

"What?" Francesca shot up in her seat, a bolt of alarm stabbing her. It could not be . . . not so soon!

"No . . . no . . ." he rumbled. "Not Castle Costin—we have crossed the frontier."

Jerked back into the headaching stillness of late afternoon, her tongue felt furred, her clothing sticking clammily to her skin. She had not been able to wash properly or change her underclothes for almost a week. Matters of small moment to one suffering as she did, doomed to an arranged marriage unless rescued by a reluctant lover, but of sufficient importance to add to her irritability.

Launey jogged beside the open window, his yellowed teeth flashing in what he fondly hoped was a reassuring smile. "We've some way to go yet, madam, but we're certainly in Rumania now, though it will be a couple of days before we reach the Margrave's castle—his lands stretch for miles, so they tell me."

Relief made her feel lightheaded. There was still time to escape. Francesca felt an itch of curiosity to look out upon this territory, such vast expanses owned by the man to whom her father had promised her. Hetty was leaning from the other window, shouting back over her shoulder. "Ooh, just get an eyeful of this, ma'am!"

The prospect was breathtakingly beautiful. As they breasted a rise, a wide panorama was spread out before them through a break in the trees. They were on a rocky ridge with lovely views of dense forest which fell away to the plateau below. The river was a silver streak glinting far away on the plain. Sunset-edged evening was drawing low purple shadows across the ragged outcrops. It had a wild, savage beauty frightening in its harsh intensity, the snow-capped peaks glowing blood red. Francesca's heart contracted and she shivered, unable to shake off a strong premonition of disaster, even when Mark's horse jumped at the window as the whole party paused to give the horses a breather.

"What a place for hunting!" he enthused. Mark made a dashing figure on horseback, and knew it. It showed off his broad-shouldered, narrow-waisted build to perfection; even during the rigor of the past weeks, his valet had kept his linen unblemished, his suits brushed and pressed, his high boots gleaming. Francesca feasted her eyes on him. He was so handsome, her Mark—such a fine gentleman, soon to be her husband.

Launey circled round to join him and they indulged in talk of the chase, while Francesca and Hetty climbed stiffly down, glad to stretch their legs on the short, springy turf. The men dismounted, and servants took bottles of wine from the food hampers, filling glasses. Launey stumped cheerfully about, bellowing orders.

"The countryside abounds with game," Mark remarked with satisfaction, fancying himself as a huntsman. "I was told so in Budapest and my own eyes have proved it. Herds of deer roam these forests, wild boar and pheasants, too."

They were walking a little apart, leaving Hetty to bring up the rear. Francesca had already confided in her and, knowing her part, the maid was charming the susceptible soldier. Francesca and Mark leaned against a rocky promontory, sipping their wine and pretending to admire the view. Behind them, the servants and guards were taking a rest, the horses cropping the sweet grass in the shade, harness jingling.

"Perhaps your skill as a hunter will sustain us when we make our break for freedom, beloved," Francesca murmured, giving him a sideways glance from under her sweeping lashes. She pressed her breast against his arm, feeling the returning pressure. "You realize that we must go tonight, Mark. It is our last chance."

Was it imaginings born of her overwrought nerves, or did she really feel a slight stiffening of his arm? She leaned closer. "You do still want to marry me, don't you, Mark?" Her direct gaze embarrassed him, and his eyes slid away from her wide, clear ones.

"How can you doubt it, darling?" His fingers closed on hers, and she darted a glance across the clearing, afraid that Launey might notice, only to see that he was engrossed in her pert maid. Mark's thumb was caressing her palm, reminding her hotly of times in the past when his impudent fingers had explored her more intimately. His voice was a whisper in her ear. "I'faith, I grow so heated when in your adored company that I quite ruin the cut of my breeches and have to carry my hat before me."

A blush deepened the peach-like bloom of her cheeks. "Then we'll run off tonight, shall we, Mark?"

"We must be patient, my angel, and prudent. I have a modest sum of money with me but. . . ."

"Who cares about money?" She swayed against him, her heart racing with eagerness. "We can ride like the wind for Budapest. There, we can find a priest and be married. We can work and support ourselves. I have many gifts—I'm a fine needlewoman, and you could give English lessons. When my father learns that we are wed, he will let us go home. I have a small inheritance invested there.''

She was talking wildly, and his dubious expression brought her to her senses, for she had been trained for no other role than that of mistress of a great house. True, this required skill and knowledge, but as for earning a living by menial tasks—it was entirely out of the question. Mark had no intention of demeaning himself by becoming a lowly schoolmaster, and he had serious doubts as to the earl's reaction to the balking of his ambitions. It was more than likely that the earl would cut Francesca off. She had enough common sense to recognize these hard facts, but desire was in her blood, blinding her.

If only she could get her hands on the dowry! Her brain was working feverishly. Launey was the stumbling block, and had she but the means, she would have drugged his wine. Dismissing this idea, she played with the notion of having Hetty seduce him, certain that the maid would fall in with this and they could sneak the bag away while he slept. She brooded and plotted, staring unseeingly at the untamed view, her fingers locked with Mark's.

Several members of the party had gone crashing off into the undergrowth, seeking a place to relieve themselves. They disturbed a covey of partridges who rushed out, squawking in panic. Launey, anxious to impress Hetty, gave a shout and ran toward his horse, intending to prove the accuracy of his shooting. Then he suddenly stopped in his tracks, roaring in strangled incoherence like a wounded bear, and dropped to the ground in an apoplectic fit. The servants crowded round him as Francesca pushed her way through, throwing herself on her knees at his side, tearful, guilty, convinced that God would punish her for her wicked thoughts about that staunch, kind old man.

The strongest of the men hefted him into the coach. Their guides told Ranby that there was a homestead nearby. Whips cracked, harness creaked, wheels turned, and the vehicles lumbered into motion. Lavinia was throwing hysterics, gasping for her smelling salts. Francesca let Hetty soothe her, seated on the opposite seat, the massive, helpless Launey stretched lengthwise, his heavy head lolling on her lap. His hands lay on his paunch, every vein distinct and covered with blotches which she had never noticed before. She mumbled words of comfort, but it seemed that he was scarcely within earshot, wandering deep into that dream world from which he might never return. She tried to tell herself that he was resting and regaining his powers, while knowing with forlorn certainty that his soul was slipping away. His dark, indifferent eyes were turned upward to her face.

"We'll soon have you refreshed and well again," she tried desperately. He gave no sign of hearing. "Is there anything you want?" Still no word or even motion. She went on with a great effort. "Shall I put Dr. Ranby in charge?"

Her eyes felt swollen with tears and she stroked back the graying hair from his brow above his half-closed eyes. His tongue crept slowly along his lower lip and withdrew. "Yes . . . Ranby . . . don't trust the guides." The hairs in his nostrils stirred with the force of his breathing, and after a moment he spoke again. "The money . . . look to the money. . . ."

They reached the tumbledown dwelling, a poor farm rented by serfs from their lord, feudal in conception. The servants were housed in the barn, grumbling and complaining, the sick man laid in a room at the back,

and Francesca was given the hayloft. A sorry-looking
old man and his slatternly wife were the tenants, and
the sparse accommodation was bargained for by one of
the guides, a man named Arpad, small-boned, sallow-
skinned, with quick, shifty eyes.

He was appointed spokesman because he knew a little
English, bobbing and ducking, maddeningly obsequi-
ous, bowing to Francesca every time he neared her.
Even from four feet away, she caught his rank odor, a
ripe mixture of dirt, sweat and garlic. "Madame will be
safe here, dry and warm in the straw, not the same as
silken sheets but . . ." he raised expressive hands and
eyes to the smoke-blackened beams of the dingy kitchen.

"Is there no doctor in these parts?" Francesca asked
curtly, disliking this filthy, squirming person. She was
perched gingerly on the edge of a wooden bench near
the trestle table, sipping at the bowl of broth which had
been dumped down unceremoniously by the housewife.

Arpad's mouth dropped open, displaying black,
broken teeth. He shook his greasy, unkempt locks.
"No, madame. No doctor. But the woman, she knows
about herbs. She will cure the fat one."

It was getting steadily darker, and Francesca slipped
out into the yard to find Mark. He was overseeing the
off-saddling of the horses, and it was easy to speak with
him there, among the coils of rope, rusty chains, tools
and hay of the stable.

"We'll leave just before dawn," she said, eyes
shining. "I have the money bag. Will you be ready, with
horses?"

He drew her against him in the shelter of a stall. "Of
course, dearest love."

Her heart sang as his lips found hers, kissing her
deeply, thoroughly, possessively. She ran to the loft on

winged feet, throwing herself down on the heap of straw which was her makeshift bed. "Hetty, lay out my riding habit, we are away at daybreak."

Hetty's features registered surprise and alarm. "You and Sir Mark? Are you sure 'tis the right thing to do, ma'am?"

Francesca silenced her with a sharp look, and ordered her to pack a few essentials. She put on her green velvet riding costume; it had a long sweeping skirt which could be hitched up at one side, and a tight-fitting smart jacket. It showed off her slim waist and the high, proud line of her breasts to perfection; the low vee-neck was softened by a loosely tied cravat and elaborate scrolls of gold braid decorated the deep cuffs and the borders of both jacket and skirt. Scarlet leather boots encased her feet, and a three-cornered hat completed this dashing ensemble. The effect was very worldly, or so she hoped, needing to feel confident. Sometimes, when with Mark, she found herself in the position of decision maker, and did not much care for this, wondering if he really was the strong, virile lover of her dreams. But now was not the time for doubts—tomorrow was her wedding day.

"What of the rest of us, ma'am?" Hetty hovered at her elbow, very worried, eyes scared in the light of the single rush whose feeble glow did not penetrate the corners of the dilapidated loft.

"Dr. Ranby has money, and will insure that you either go on or return to Budapest. I think he will decide on the former, as some explanation will have to be made to the duchess. No doubt, search parties will be dispatched, but even if they do catch us, we shall already be man and wife." Francesca tipped some gold pieces from her purse into Hetty's hand. "Take these, and stay close to Ranby. He will look after you. We'll meet again soon, never fear."

Lavinia was fully occupied helping Ranby to nurse the colonel, which suited Francesca admirably. She settled down to wait for the hours to pass, impatiently wishing away the final barrier between herself and her lover.

Outside it was dawn, but the faltering sun had not yet risen out of a tangle of night clouds, blue-black over the eastern sky. With her valise in one hand and the heavy money satchel over the other shoulder, Francesca crept through the silent cottage. In the barnyard a rooster was crowing, his strident call awakening the echoes and setting the mangy dogs barking. She sped across the muddy yard, thinking that she heard the farmer stirring, but putting her faith in the hope that they would assume she was going for an early canter.

Mark was in the hay sweet stable. He turned at the rustle of her skirt and crushed her to him, kissing her over and over until she was breathless. "Sweetheart, I've not slept a wink for thinking of you!" He murmured into her hair, his tongue darting into her ear and then between her lips. She felt the probing heat of it and surrendered to his caresses. Hearing the voices of the laborers tramping out to commence toil, she tore herself away, saying shakily, "We must leave, my love. Plenty of time for that when we have covered a few miles."

He gave her a fond glance, then helped her to mount, her long skirt draping the beast's flanks gracefully, her gloved hand holding the reins. She had strapped her bag to the back of the saddle, while the dowry was hitched to the pommel. Mark had pistols with him, and his own simple belongings were rolled into a bundle behind him. They clopped through the farm gates without hindrance, riding boldly, as if enjoying the fresh air. But once out of sight of the house, Francesca turned to grin at Mark. She made her horse sidle; her knee bumped his and he turned his smile full on her.

"We've done it!" She was jubilant, unable to believe their incredible luck. "We're free, darling . . . free!"

She laughed wildly, bobbed her heels into the chestnut's sides and galloped off. Francesca let him go, bending low over his withers, hanging on to her hat, her mouth whipped by her lace collar and strands of hair. Mark inclined forward in the saddle to urge up his steed, careering after her. Trying to recall the way, she guided her animal down the narrow trails which meandered through the dense mass of beech and oak trees.

The woods were rustling with small furry creatures, while birds had already started to carol a hymn of praise to the sun. There was that slight dampness in the air which hints at hidden mysteries; the forest was flaked with a clear, glassy dazzle; the lightening sky was pale turquoise, streaked with pink. The odors were enough to make her dizzy: wet earth, with a spongy, mossy smell, the strong scent of fox or badger, the sharpness of wild garlic pummeled beneath their horses' hooves. Francesca's throat ached with loved and happiness. The world had never looked more fair. The hump of hoofbeats on turf, the creak of leather and jingle of harness exalted her, as they put miles between themselves and pursuit. They slowed their foam-flecked mounts to a trot, for they had a long way to go. The Great Plain must be traversed though, traveling light, it would not take them as long as it had the cumbersome coaches. They paused in a clearing where deer poised, watching them before bounding away.

"Are you certain this is the right path?" A shaft of sunlight tipped Mark's lashes with gold as he looked at her. "I should have thought we'd be descending into the plains by now, if we're following the same track as yesterday.''

Francesca frowned, looking about her, sitting her beast easily while it dropped its head and began tearing at the ground. "I must admit that I don't know. I could have sworn we came this way, but I cannot see an opening in the trees. Perhaps I was mistaken.''

"It would be very easy to get lost here," he commented, and swung down, coming round to help her, his hands resting either side of her waist and remaining there once she was on her feet. Francesca was stiff. They had been riding for some time and it was getting hot, the sun climbing steadily across the vault of bright blue.

Hetty had packed rye bread and beef in the saddle-bag, along with a bottle of red wine. They sat at the base of a tall pine, their backs against the trunk, and Francesca unwrapped the food from the napkin which enclosed it neatly. They munched in companionable silence. Mark pulled the cork and raised the bottle. "To you, my angel, to your beautiful face and most perfect body," he said, then tipped it to his lips.

Hand in hand, like two adventurous children, they went exploring, Mark holding the leading reins of their mounts. Francesca was sure that she had never been so happy. Mark was not only her lover, he was also her dear friend, with a quick, intelligent mind and sensitive eye which noted everything, each view, every wild flower or flashing bird. As they walked, he quoted verse, finding her a captive audience for he was possessed of undoubted charm. His love of old ballads and poetry and his fine talents as a mimic had made him popular in the salons of London, and now he proved a wonderful source of fun. But she would have enjoyed anything that day, breathing in great lungfuls of wine-clear air. The sun beat hotly through the arch of trees which reminded her of the vaulting of some huge cathedral, and they heard the near sound of water, coming out where a sparkling stream frothed over boulders, winding between low banks.

It widened further along, flowing into a reed-edged pool. There, in the leafy gloom where the brook ran deep, they drank, then watered their horses. The coolness was tempting and Francesca dabbled her hands and wrists in it. " 'Tis so warm. I must swim," she announced, glancing at Mark from the corner of her slanting green eyes. "Will you come in, too?"

He lay at ease among the verdant grass, resting on one elbow, watching her in pleased contemplation. He shook his head. "Not I, darling, I cannot swim. I'll rest here and feast my eyes on the glorious sight of my naiad taking her bath."

Francesca could sense her cheeks glowing with more than just the sun's heat, and a tingle of excitement ran up her spine. She wanted to undress before him, though feeling a little shy she averted her face, and turned her back. Her hands were trembling as she sat down, lifted her skirt and worked her feet out of her boots. One of them stuck, she was used to Hetty's assistance, so Mark came across to help. His hand seemed to burn through the soft leather as he gripped her ankle and tugged, while she braced herself. They laughed and made a joke of it, but all the time the tension was mounting between them, each very conscious of it. There was a hard wariness in his face, and he smiled only with his lips; his eyes were keen as they slid from her face, down her throat to her breasts with a look which made her arms and back tingle.

Slowly, he took his hand from her stockinged foot, and sat back on his heels, staring at her in a way which gave her a momentary thrill of sheer fright—she instinctively recognized man the predator, a being with muscles far superior to her own. They were quite alone, he could do with her as he willed. If she were to find him repulsive and beg him to stop, she would be unable to prevent him from having his way with her. But suddenly her eyes collided with his openly assessing gaze, and she was only aware of the increased beating of her heart and a crazy stab of anticipation.

"I'm waiting, my jewel," he said in husky undertones which made her shiver. "Undress for me—slowly—so that I may savor every delight of your divine, maiden body."

As if mesmerized, she did as he requested, her movements languid, immeasurably graceful, tantalizingly hesitant. Her velvet skirt whispered to the leafy forest floor, to be followed by her jacket. Then, wearing only her diaphanous chemise with its round neckline and belled sleeves, and a single flouncy petticoat, she unbuckled her garters, bending to peel off her white silk stockings. She unfastened the bow of the drawstring at her waist and the petticoat dropped down, to lie in a discarded heap with her other garments. She stood for a moment, her body covered by the knee-length shift whose transparency clung to her summits and defined her valleys with lovely exactitude. Mark had grown very still; the whole forest was caught in a hushed waiting. Francesca reached down and, gripping the hem with both hands, pulled the garment off over her head.

"My God!" she heard Mark exclaim, very softly. "You are so beautiful."

She could not look at him, aware as she was of the wealth of hair falling almost to her waist, and her naked skin over which a light breeze played, making the fine down rise on her limbs. She was perfectly proportioned, with narrow shoulders, full breasts, a minute waist and

rounded hips. Her thighs were long and slender, her
knees dimpled, her calves shapely, leading to slim, fine-
boned ankles and neat feet. With a light, nervous laugh,
she flicked him a glance, arrested by the burning fire in
his eyes.

Francesca had the sudden urge to cover herself but,
having gone so far, had to carry it off with what she fer-
vently hoped was an air of worldly panache. Resisting
the desire to hurry, she picked her way along the bank,
seeking a suitable place to climb down, longing to
plunge deep into the screening water. The pool was icy,
filled by the brown, peaty stream which broke and
frothed round white, gleaming stones, all the way from
the mountains. The cold silk sand flowing under her
soles and burying her to the ankles made her catch her
breath. She stood thigh-deep in the amber, slow-
running water, and Mark sat on the bank just behind
her, staring and staring.

"You are a veritable Leda, dearest. Would that I were
Jupiter disguised as a swan! Like a goddess from the
fountains of Fontainebleau—yet not a stony Venus, for
your buttocks are stippled with gooseflesh, and your
delectable nipples upturned like the hopeful noses of
little pets, yearning to be fondled."

There was something about this spate of fulsome flat-
tery which jarred. Francesca found it slightly irritating,
even disturbing. She had overheard him using similar,
though not so intimate, phrases to the Parisian ladies. It
smacked of insincerity. She scolded herself for petty
jealousy, of course he meant every word! Was he not
her own true love? She half-turned, smiling at him
through the veil of her hair. The sense of power was
intoxicating, far stronger than the wine, this knowledge
that the sight of her body could cause such havoc in the
male. He could not tear his eyes away, the tip of his

tongue coming out to lick over his lips. She tossed back her hair and laughed, then dived into the water.

The shock of cold was exhilarating, reminding her of swimming parties in the cove which led down from Tallents. Carefree days in high summer, when she had learned to master the white-flecked waves, though never naked, as now. Her governess had insisted that she wear a long gray cotton bathing dress which trailed on the ground, as modest as a nun's habit. She reveled in this newfound freedom of complete nudity, and struck out boldly for the center of the pool. There she teased and tormented Mark with a display of ravishing visions: smooth white skin against the dark water, slim arms and legs moving in leisured, seductive sweeps, the alluring siren promising sexual gratification—in her own time!

"Mark . . ." the laughter in her voice echoed among the enshrouding trees. "Mark, do you want me?"

"You know that I do, little witch!" he growled. "Come out . . . come to me now . . . now!"

She swam close to the bank at his feet, looking up at him with sly invitation, her breasts visible as she stood on the bottom. "You come in and get me!" she challenged, impudently splashing him with shiny droplets.

He lunged for her, but she darted out of reach. "Damn it, Francesca! You know I'm no swimmer!"

He looked angry enough to kill her, and her laughter rang out again, followed by contrition. Poor Mark. It was wicked to treat him thus. Her own blood was pounding in answer but, even so, she hesitated, wading slowly towards the edge saying, "Hand me your cloak, Mark."

He wrapped her in it as she emerged. In the tremulous shade the light was dappling his face, spreading patches of green lace, running into his eyes, slanting across them, spilling out again to his mouth; she almost gave up the struggle, unable to stop staring at his lips, wanting them to explore every inch of her. Nevertheless, she rubbed her limbs dry and, taking up a fold of the voluminous woolen cloth, attempted to soak up the moisture from her dripping hair. She pulled on her chemise, the linen clinging to her damp skin. She felt too vulnerable naked, in the open, and her petticoat soon covered her legs.

"Why are you dressing?" There was a frown about his eyes, and he caught her by the wrist, hauling her up against him.

"The water was cold," she answered, leaning her head on his chest, feeling his hands tremble as he held her. "I am chilled to the marrow."

"I'll warm you, love." He bent his head, moving his lips over her bare neck, the slight rasp of his unshaken jaw sending pleasurable shocks through her. He had never looked more handsome or appealing, eyes alight with adoration, the soft breeze which rustled the treetops stirring his golden-brown hair.

They sank down on the mossy turf. She was cool to touch, the water still running from her locks. He stretched at her side, turning to take her in his arms, and in her nostrils was mingled the fresh, clean smell of her own skin and the stinging fragrance of the wild flowers crushed beneath them. It was so peaceful, so quiet, almost as if they were the only couple alive in the world. Mark pulled her slowly against his warm body, his lips taking hers in a demanding kiss. Francesca pressed closer, her tongue darting into his mouth, her body on fire for more than just kisses. And yet a small voice of doubt still whispered in her brain, and a quick mental flash of her father's disapproving face abruptly brought her to her senses. Supposing she allowed Mark to possess her before their union had been blessed by a priest, and conceived a child? The shame of it would kill the earl. They must wait until they were married although, even then, it was quite likely that her father would disown her.

As tactfully as she could, she stayed the hand which was trying to push up her petticoat, raising herself on her elbow, looking down at him and attempting to put these confused feelings into words. "Mark, dearest Mark . . . we must wed first. It would not be right."

He grew very still, his smile fading, a hard expression creeping into his eyes. "What mean you? Is this some teasing game?"

"Oh, darling, don't you see? I want to be your wife before I give myself to you," she stammered, filled with a sense of failure and rejection, hurt by his withdrawal. She kneeled at his side, anxious for some soft, reassuring word. "I must be able to stand proudly with you, and declare to the whole world that we are one. It will spoil everything if we have to hide and be ashamed. And there is my father to consider. . . ."

He shrank impatiently from her gentle touch and she was appalled by his flash of cold fury. "A little late to think of the niceties now, my dear," he sneered, averting his eyes and sitting apart from her, arms resting on his knees, staring gloomily off into space. He was still breathing hard, disappointed, with his moist curls and sullen mouth, adding unkindly, "Why so concerned about the earl all of a sudden? We have the dowry, haven't we? A tidy sum on which to live for a while!"

Cold realization began to dawn on Francesca, and she regarded him through narrowed eyes, her body held taut, back stiffening in growing anger. "The money! Is that all you care about?"

"Not entirely. You are most desirable, even though at

the moment you are acting like a silly virgin!" He spat out the word as if it were an insult. Rage flashed through Francesca, overriding guilt and an aching feeling of loss.

"I thought that was what you wanted," she replied tartly, standing up and shaking her skirt, adjusting her bodice and pulling the cloak primly about her. "Would you prefer to discover that I had been bedded by every spark in town?" Then an unpleasant suspicion struck her, and she paced towards him, arms akimbo. "To what are you accustomed, Mark? The attentions of Court ladies seeking one of lower rank to titillate their jaded appetites? Or perhaps the painted jades of Dog Alley, who pleasured you for a fee?"

"Curb your waspish tongue, madam!" Gone was the polished gentleman, and she found herself confronting a rather shabby soul lurking beneath a suave exterior, one crossed in his plan to despoil her in order to smooth a pathway to her fortune. Now he must start over again, woo her with further words of love, take on the shackles of matrimony! True, she was charming—but her chief attraction had always been her wealth, for the gambling debts he had gathered meant he owed too much money to too many people. Annoyed by the thwarting of his carefully laid schemes, physically frustrated in his plans to take her, Mark now found her innocence cloying and, accomplished dissembler though he was, he could not keep the mask from slipping.

Francesca was furious, knowing that he had cheated her. At one moment he had been a tender lover and the next, this cold, unfeeling scoundrel! She knew that no matter how softly he spoke to her in the future, his blandishments would fall on stony ground. She would never trust him again.

So engrossed were they in their silent antagonism,

they were taken completely by surprise when, with shouts, the flash of steel and the pounding of hooves, a crowd of men broke through the trees, some mounted, others on foot. Horrified, Francesca swung round, her eyes alighting on the guide, Arpad, who was grinning insolently and shouting:

"The fair young English woman—*angol no*! You did not know that Arpad had his eye on you, did you, my beauty? Ah, yes, Arpad saw you slip away with the smart milord—and followed you here. You left a trail a blind man could follow."

He was almost dancing with enjoyment at her expression of shocked alarm, chuckling and wheezing as his ruffianly companions threw themselves on Mark. A dozen or so in number, they were exclaiming in a strange, guttural tongue, while Arpad lunged for Francesca. Spurred by fright, she feinted neatly, avoiding his grasp, only to find herself facing a huge, formidable figure who seemed to be the leader of the group. One massive hand shot out and grabbed her wrist so brutally that she gave a gasp of pain. He jerked her up close to him until she was within inches of the most villainous countenance that she had ever beheld. His skin was swarthy, his hair black and greasy, and a long rat-tailed mustache trailed down on either side of his sneering mouth. She was powerless in that steely grip, for he had the shoulders of an ox, a great expanse of chest and a corpulent belly. He stared down into her terrified eyes and she caught the fetid odor of his breath. He wore a shaggy sort of cape composed of sheepskin which stank evilly and, on his head, a bonnet of moth-eaten fur from which a heron's feather drooped.

His bloodshot eyes, sunk in deep fatty wrinkles, looked her over with greedy interest. Francesca had never instantly hated anyone with such violence, her flesh crawling with loathing at his touch while his followers laughed loudly, nudging one another. A savage crew, some in rags, others wearing bizarre clothing, they bristled with weapons, daggers stuck in colorful sashes, swords swinging at their hips. For a fraction of a second, she was aware that Mark was yelling in the background, straining in the arms of his captors; then one of them, losing patience, snarled something which she could not understand, and smashed his fist into Mark's face. The blood gushed from his broken nose. Mark doubled over with a grunt; she had never seen so much blood, drenching his shirt front and cuffs, as his hands went up in a vain effort to protect his damaged face. Blind rage and indignation galvanized her into action. How dare they treat them thus? Damned brigands! Mark might have hurt her, but he was a fellow countryman and she would not stand by and see him take such cruel punishment.

Her hand flashed up and her nails clawed at the big man's face, leaving long livid scratches. Before he could recover from his astonishment, her arm swung again, hitting him with such force that his head jerked back.

"Unhand me, you damned varlet!" she stormed, a blazing virago, emerald eyes flashing, her flaming hair seeming to spark. She had enough presence of mind to address him in German, neither knowing or caring if he would understand.

"Vixen!" he bellowed, his grip crushing the bones of her wrist. "Were you not such a valuable prize, I'd make you yell for mercy!"

"But Zoltan . . ." Arpad was hopping anxiously at his elbow, like a sparrow facing a vulture. "Sir, beloved leader, she is not to be harmed—those were our instructions. Le Diable said we were to capture her so that he may hold her to ransom."

"Damn Le Diable!" Zoltan roared, and his comrades looked up from rifling the baggage, ready for trouble. "Why should I obey him like a craven cur? The woman is in my hands and she's worth money, either from the duchess or at the Turkish slave auctions. I'll not give her to Le Diable!" Someone had found the moneybag, and gave a whoop as its neck was torn open and the contents cascaded to the grass. Without loosening his grip on the struggling girl, Zoltan's fierce eyes raked his unruly band. "Leave it!" he grated and they shrank back.

Arpad fell to his knees, groveling among the leaf mold, retrieving the scattered wealth for Zoltan. Mark lay unconscious nearby, unaware of the feet that trampled and kicked him. There was so much blood that Francesca feared him to be dead. In savage desperation, she fought, spitting, clawing, her hand pummeling Zoltan's face and chest repeatedly while he rumbled with laughter, mocking her.

"That's right, fight me! The Turks will pay a high price for a spirited wench . . . it serves to make the conquest more sweet!"

She could feel the strength draining out of her, tears of rage coursing down her cheeks, her body throbbing from the vicious onslaught, unable to draw back, her ribs crushed in his vise-like grip. A scarlet haze shot with bright stars was floating before her eyes. She knew that she was going to faint. She was abruptly released as, with a clever twist, Zoltan brought her to her knees before him. He towered over her, while his cronies gathered in a rough circle, their harsh voices excited and pleased. She watched them through half-closed lids; one made some remark in German, accompanied by a crude gesture and they all laughed.

Francesca opened her green eyes wide and glared up at the colossus above her. "Bastard!" she hissed.

"Don't you dare touch me again!"

For answer, Zoltan's open palm slashed her across the face, once, twice, and she was knocked nearly unconscious. Francesca opened her mouth and yelled. Suddenly the glade seemed to explode, carved up by the flaying hooves of a great black stallion which reared over her tormentors, scattering them. Zoltan, dumb with surprise, was attacked by the rider who leaped from the saddle, felling him with a single blow to the jaw. Two of the other men went flying, and she heard the sharp impact of a fist hitting bone as Arpad received a staggering punch in the face. The crazily spinning trees were blotted out by the huge shadow of a man who reached down a hand and pulled her to her feet.

There were grim-faced men in the clearing, and she heard the sharp click of pistols while her attackers raised their arms above their heads sullenly, eyes swiveling from Zoltan's scowling features to those of the man who was staring down at him with an expression of cold, haughty rage.

"What is the meaning of this, Zoltan?" he demanded, while the others cringed. "Durst thou disobey my commands yet again? I warned you, the last time I caught you mistreating a prisoner!" His voice was deep, resonant, its timber sending a chill down Francesca's spine.

She was trembling violently, hardly able to stand, not yet believing that she had been saved from the repulsive Zoltan. Even in her bruised and shocked state, her first impression was of height, strength and darkness. Her heart sank within her, for the stranger was menacing in his awesome fury, and she quickly realized that he might be as bad as Zoltan. These men were ravaging animals! Why should he be any different? His appearance was certainly as outlandish as theirs. He wore the same baggy breeches stuffed into the tops of boots fashioned of coarse hide, an enormous wolfskin coat which reached his calves, a shapeless hat of the same fur covering his head, and he was armed to the teeth! He was long-limbed and powerfully built, much taller than any man there, standing at least twelve inches over her five feet four. The face beneath that strange headgear was thin, hawklike and saturnine, framed by black, curling hair, and the smoldering eyes were a curious color, like sherry with the sunlight pouring through it. He had a look of uncompromising ruthlessness which marked him as an adventurer and gambler, a man free from bonds and ties.

Francesca was gripped by a strange, painful giddiness as she stared up at that dark, hard countenance. Slowly she released her pent-up breath, feeling a queer, choking sensation as his eyes fastened on hers. Blind panic rushed up to overwhelm her. Whatever happened, she must escape this alarming man.

"Le Diable . . ." Zoltan muttered, wilting before him. "I meant no harm. A jest, nothing more."

A tanned, sinewy hand shot out to lift Zoltan to his feet by the collar, big though he was, and Le Diable glared into his shifty eyes. "Scum!" The word snaked from his scornful lips. "Lying dog! You thought to cheat me, to turn your men against me, seeking fat pickings and very little fighting!"

Zoltan's face purpled and he shook off the restraining hand, drawing himself up, aware that the men who had followed his disreputable leadership were assessing him, their loyalties divided. Le Diable's supporters were alert for trouble, most of them carrying knives and guns, one even had an axe stuck in his belt.

"Who are you to speak to me thus? I am Zoltan, cousin to the Duke of Little Egypt. I have many stout fellows who will run to do my bidding at a snap of my fingers." He glared about him truculently.

A sardonic smile touched Le Diable's lips briefly. He stood back, legs apart, thumbs hooked in the broad leather belt which spanned his slim waist, one dark curved eyebrow raised slightly as his somber eyes went slowly, insultingly, down over the paunchy, shabby figure before him. Francesca had never witnessed such withering scorn before. The air of arrogance and command about him made her heart pound with alarm. He was obviously used to leading men. And what men! A debased bunch of bandits!

"I doubt the duke will condone your mutiny," he answered levelly. "You bring shame to your tribe!"

Zoltan bellowed like a goaded bull, there was a flash of steel and Francesca screamed as a dagger hurtled towards Le Diable. He stepped aside lithely and it buried itself in the hole of a tree at his back, the jeweled handle quivering. Le Diable's men fell upon Zoltan, ready to beat him to death, but their chief commanded them to stop.

"We will settle this in the manner of *die Zigeuner*, and it shall be done in the gypsy camp, not in some dark corner away from the eyes of men. You will face me in combat, before them all—your chieftain there to witness that it is done in fair sight."

There was someone standing near Le Diable who now placed a hand on his sleeve to get his attention. "But, sir, if you go there I cannot accompany you. You know that well, and the reason for it."

Francesca was thunderstruck to realize that this leather-clad, warlike person whom she had taken to be a long-legged stripling, spoke with a woman's voice and, looking more closely, saw waving raven hair beneath a wide-brimmed hat, high cheekbones and slant eyes in a suntanned face.

Le Diable shrugged impatiently. "Do not bother me with your family quarrels, Gilda. Get you off with the raiding party, then."

She flashed him an angry look, her fierce eyes going over Francesca, then she stalked away, swinging into her saddle and disappearing into the forest.

Le Diable's second-in-command, a burly, soldierly-looking man with red hair and mustache, grinned after her; then astounded Francesca by addressing his leader in English with no trace of foreign intonation. "And the lady, sir? What of her?"

He had sharp, laughing eyes which crinkled pleasantly at the corners and he walked across to her with a practiced, nonchalant swagger which marked him as gentry. An Englishman, among gypsy robbers? It was impossible. She was feeling so confused, so stunned by the swift succession of events, that she could not believe in anything so heartening as finding a compatriot. Le Diable scrutinized her, his eyes raking her disheveled beauty. She was poised with the taut look of a wildcat, her face white, the stain of a bruise beginning to purple her right cheek. Her huge eyes sparked up at him in defiance, though her face grew hot as the color flooded it, insulted by the way he was studying her, slowly, speculatively . . .

"She comes with us. She is our prize, after all." He spoke with an accent just strong enough to render the deep cadences of his voice even more intriguing, but his words infuriated her. How dare he treat her like a chattel to be disposed of? And how dare these rogues humiliate her so? She wanted to shout and scream at him and tell him exactly what she thought of him!

Le Diable swung round to receive the moneybag which his lieutenant had just found. He hitched it to his own saddle, while the guards and their prisoners prepared to move off. Mark was hoisted onto his horse, where he sagged across the saddlebow, his smashed, bloody face buried in his arms. Zoltan was permitted to ride, though escorted on either side by men with muskets.

The English aide paused with one foot in the stirrup, his humorous blue eyes switching from Zoltan to Le Diable. "She may be your prize now, sir, but what if he wins?"

"He won't," came the clipped, confident reply. "I've waited a long time for her, Roger, and no one is going to rob me now!"

He turned swiftly, and before Francesca realized his intention, she found herself swooped up in powerful arms, tossed over a shoulder, and carried to his horse. The breath was knocked out of her body by his rough handling. It was a second or so before she could choke out a protest.

"Let me go! Stop it! Put me down at once!" she yelled in fury, hanging head down, hammering on his broad back and shoulders with futile fists.

She began to sob with exhaustion when he did not pause or take any notice, and flopped like a limp rag doll, her hair streaming, her brain whirling with the height. What use to struggle further? She was a captive in the hands of greedy, lustful men, fighting over her like a pack of wolves!

Chapter Two

ONCE FREED from the glade, taking a pathway deep into the woods, Le Diable shifted Francesca's squirming body until she sat sideways across the front of his horse, her heaving breasts pressed to his chest, his arm clamped like a steel band across her back. She held herself rigid, straining away from those hard muscles, but her feeble attempts at withdrawal seemed to amuse him as he leaned back against the cantle slightly to issue an order to his men.

They rode in silence, intent on reaching their destination; there was a matter of no small moment to be settled—that lifelong feud between Le Diable and the gypsy—a contest long overdue. Francesca began to steady now that the wild panic was over. She stopped shaking, though still icy with shock. Her bruises now began to throb, the abrasions on her soft skin felt unbearably tender, every jolt of the horse over the rough ground sent pain jarring through her. She was sickened at Mark's suffering, wondering how he managed to keep his seat, and indignation flared within her. Didn't these damned foreigners realize just who she was? The daughter of an earl, no less! Her spine stiffened, she threw up her head and in a brittle, controlled tone asked, "Where are you taking me, sir?".

A mocking smile curved his lips, but he continued to stare ahead, guiding his stallion along the track, thickly wooded on either side with tall trees and screening bushes. "You'll find out soon enough."

Barbarian! she thought furiously, hating his proximity. Francesca tried to pull the cloak tightly about her, remembering that someone, she wasn't sure who but had the impression it was the Englishman, had flung it over her. She relapsed into sullen silence, her mind busy with gloomy speculations, cursing the folly which had put her in this hazardous situation. She had never felt so low-spirited and disillusioned. Her love for Mark had died like a snuffed candle; she saw him for what he was: a scheming opportunist. Now all that was left was pity.

Her mournful train of thought was interrupted when they jogged into an open space in the middle of the woods. It was the camp of the *tziganes*, those mysterious people who lead their nomadic existence in every part of the globe. Francesca recalled meeting gypsies on her father's estate, intrigued yet scared by their reputation for stealing and for magic; dreaming of their promises of a handsome husband, wealth and happiness, as she rode home to Tallents through hedges thick with summer and the rolling moorlands of Devon. Tears of homesickness prickled her eyes as she thought back, but she was too proud to shed them. This ill-mannered brute holding her captive should not see her cry!

The riders halted on the perimeter, then a cry of greeting shook the glade, ragged children came running, the men following more cautiously, the lean hounds tied under the wagons starting to bark, hackles up, until cuffed into submission. Everyone soon sensed that there

was trouble afoot and fell silent. They recognized their
kindred, but the sight of strangers made them close
ranks. The air was charged with suspicion and an overriding hostility. The sudden silence, the unwinking
stares of this dark-eyed, swarthy folk was most unnerving, and Francesca stayed close to Le Diable's side.

One of his henchmen, a lanky, fearsome scoundrel
with a bushy beard, a turban and primitive jewelry,
went forward, and Francesca waited, gazing at the
scene. The men squatted on their heels by the fire in a
weird sort of immobility, the red-gold flames flickering
over their bronzed countenances. Smoke drifted across
the clearing, carrying a mouthwatering smell from the
iron pots slung on tripods over the glowing embers. The
women kept well in the background, wearing embroidered smocks and rough cloaks, scarves covering
their greasy, braided hair, firelight winking off the rings
in their ears. Wild females, with full lips, thin aquiline
noses and blazing eyes. Some of the younger ones were
beautiful, with babies in folds of their shawls, straddling a hip or clinging to their skirts.

The turbaned warrior, Luca, beckoned, and Le
Diable strode across, followed by his men and a
glowering Zoltan. They gestured widely as they talked,
jabbering away in some strange, incomprehensible
language which Francesca guessed to be Romany, the
universal tongue of these untamed people. Le Diable
was speaking as fluently as the rest and resembled them
in coloring, features and proud bearing. Francesca withdrew into herself, chin lifted, looking down her delicate
nose at such riffraff. She seemed to have been forgotten
so she quickly glanced round to see if she might try to
escape, but she noticed that several of the band were
keeping a watch on her, while apparently leaning non-
chalantly against a tree or tending their mounts.

The voices rose, aggressive, quarrelsome, with Zoltan's loud among the dissension, but the uproar was immediately silenced when a tall, elaborately attired man appeared from the most ornate of the wagons. His loud, commanding voice rang across the glade. The respect accorded to him singled him out as a being of great importance. He walked down the carved steps, hands outstretched to greet Le Diable. She was astonished at the extraordinary sight of them embracing as if old friends, then he turned to upbraid Zoltan whose simmering rage could hardly be contained, his thickly-jowled neck and fleshy face turning an unpleasant shade of puce.

Someone prodded Francesca in the back, urging her forward and she found herself close to the fire, those terrifying nomads perusing her with interest. Close up, they were filthy, with crinky, wooly hair and heavy mustaches beneath which their teeth flashed brilliantly white. A few wore battered hats, the rest gaudily patterned scarves and, like their women, heavy silver earrings which glittered among the unsavory curls.

The *tzigany* chieftain looked her over with the eye of an expert, as well used to quickly assessing the merits of a lovely woman as that of a thoroughbred. She managed to return his bold stare, very much on her dignity. The Duke, known as Mihail Valentin, was older than she had first thought, very dark complexioned, with sable ringlets which fell to his collar. He was showily dressed in purple velvet encircled by a heavy silver belt, fingers aflame with rings, jewels flashing in his ears, and the gleam of gold from the chains which circled his neck and chest was in glaring contrast to his followers, most of whom were clad in rags. His eyes were weird, with queer orange pupils and a light which seemed to come from within. His demeanor increased her nervousness, and she viewed the whole tribe with gravest misgivings, having been taught that gypsies were a race apart, with an unholy reputation for thieving and cheating. Then he disconcerted her even further by addressing her in halting English—the very last thing she had expected.

"So, you are the fine *gorgio* lady on whom Zoltan dared to lay his hands, eh?" His accent was very marked, his sense of authority undisputed. Even Le Diable was respectful, but Zoltan was in a dangerous mood of wounded pride and blind rage, reading insults into every chance remark, head lowered threateningly, mean eyes as red as a boar's in a thicket. "What have you to say for yourself, Zoltan?" continued Mihail in a purringly quiet voice, menacing in its control, his manner faintly sarcastic. "Had you been overindulging in wine, my friend, so that your wits were fuddled?"

Zoltan began to mutter a reply in Romany, but Mihail lifted a finger to silence him. "In deference to our guest, you will use her mother tongue to make amends for your loathsome behavior. There is no excuse. You had your orders, both from Le Diable and myself. You knew that she was to be unharmed. You are well aware that we are to bargain with that old witch, the Duchess Renata, for her safe return."

Francesca found her voice. "Not only did he subject me to a brutal assault, but he badly hurt my companion," she blazed, appalled to learn that she was to be used as a pawn in some strategic game of which she knew nothing. "I wouldn't be surprised if he died from the beating he received at the hands of those cowardly ruffians!"

"The women shall attend to his wounds," Mihail answered at once and gave an order. Mark was raised from where he lay slumped on the earth, and carried to one of the wagons. Mihail turned back to Zoltan. "By gypsy law, I could have you severely punished for this affront."

"My quarrel is with him." Zoltan thrust a stubby finger at Le Diable who was watching him, arms folded across his chest in a kind of cold-blooded detachment. He appeared the embodiment of a wild, savage prince, and the Duke felt a dash of almost paternal pride in the young animal before him, pleased that he had learned their lores, adopted their skills, developed their native cunning, accepted them as kin. Zoltan's hatred was obvious, his face working, brawny hands clenched into fists as if he longed to launch into an attack on this arrogant man who had so often challenged his leadership. Nothing save blood and the death of Le Diable would satisfy him.

Francesca ran her tongue over suddenly dry lips, sickened by those hot waves of antagonism, wanting to run from this terrible place where the men all looked like demons with their wild eyes and vulpine teeth, their women shameless she-devils, their old ones sinister crones. She was repulsed by the shabby wagons, the dirt, the half-naked children and skinny animals. Homeless vagrants, scraping a shoddy existence, the men working as tinkers or trading in horses, the women-folk weaving baskets, begging on doorsteps, reading palms. She felt hysteria rising, hedged in by glances— envy and mockery in the women's, sly lust in the men's. She felt hopelessly alone, and nothing could dispel that feeling of trapped desperation.

Mihail missed little; what his sharp eyes and ears did not report, his intuition did, aware of the ripples in the ether. He observed Francesca keenly, intense eyes reading her face, traveling ever and again to Le Diable's. A strange, knowing smile lifted his lips as he said:"Very well, Zoltan—have your way. It is our custom that when two men dispute over a woman, they must fight until one of them is slain.'' There was nothing more to be said.

A great space was cleared under the trees near where the horses cropped the turf. The sun was low in the west, a flaming ball of fire, shimmering at the ragged-edged tops of the pines. A few moments more, and it would be gone, leaving a cluster of pink and mauve fans of light which would melt and merge into the reddish clouds and the dark blue of the sky, as chill threads of night began to weave a funereal pattern across the heavens. Francesca was seated on a fallen log to which Mihail had conducted her with a curious, old world courtesy, insisting that she take the place of honor at his side. She shrank from watching the ghastly combat, but had crossed that threshold of exhaustion which leaves one strangely detached, sinking down wearily. The tribe had congregated, forming a human circle, the dancing flames lighting the sharp planes and hollows of their faces, the glaring crimson and black reminding her of the pit of hell. An old gypsy, who seemed much revered and was the chief's advisor, stood in the middle of the empty ring. In each gnarled hand, fragile as a bird's claw, he held a dagger.

There was a flurry of movement from one of the wagons, a ripple of interest, and the crowd parted respectfully to allow a slender, stately woman to pass through. Those nearest to her murmured a greeting, and hushed their young, and Mihail introduced her to Francesca. Her name was Elvire and she was high in the tribal hierarchy, his wife and a princess in her own right. She was magnificently arrayed in flamboyant finery, her gathered skirt of green silk, her velvet bodice encrusted with silver threadwork, matching the silver in her ears and the rows of necklaces, some of coins, others of engraved talismans. She nodded to Francesca, her bearing regal, her eyes two luminous pools which seemed to see further and deeper than anyone else's. She showed no flicker of surprise at finding a fair-skinned stranger in their midst.

"So, she has come," she remarked to her husband. "Did I not foresee it? This is she of whom the cards spoke." She fixed Francesca with that alarming gaze. "We will talk together later, English lady. There is much which Elvire can tell you of your future."

Zoltan swaggered up to them, surrounded by his minions led by Arpad, who bowed unctuously before Elvire. The *tzigany* princess looked at him disdainfully down her thin nose, unimpressed by this fawning. Her voice was coldly cutting as she spoke to Zoltan.

"What trouble have you brought on us now? You were always a fool and a braggart. Why did you not heed my warning? Did the cards not tell of strife before the moon waxed? Foolish man, d'you think to cross Le Diable? Fortune smiles on him, for he favors our people. None shall challenge him and live."

Zoltan's eyes blazed and his mouth was ugly. "You've always cared more for him than your own, Elvire. He's not a true Rom, and I am! I spit on your warnings! My mother has the sight too, and she's taken care to protect me from harm."

Elvire's head lifted, her lean face with its broad cheekbones was filled with that pride and fierceness of independence which marked them all. "Your tongue is as false as the serpent's, Zoltan. In temperament, he is more Romany than *gorgio*, and you know it! Our blood is strong, even a small drop of it in the veins is sufficient to color a whole life."

All eyes turned as Le Diable appeared in the circle. Zoltan tossed his ragged shirt to Arpad, his great, fleshy

body bare to the waist, a heavy pelt of shaggy black hair
covering his chest, upper back and shoulders, making
him look even more like some ferocious beast at bay. Le
Diable stared at him, irritation in his dark features,
acknowledging Elvire's greeting with a small, ironic
inclination of the head. Then, as if eager to get the
matter over and done with he shrugged off his coat,
handing it to Roger who was acting as his second. He
was now stripped to the waist, and the leaping firelight
played over his magnificent torso. His skin was sun-
burned, fine and smooth, with a deeply muscled chest
and wide shoulders, his powerful arms covered in curling dark hair. He, like Zoltan, wore full crimson
breeches, girded by a wide leather belt.

The protagonists paced towards the old man and
received their weapons which they examined closely,
balancing them in their hands. Zoltan's eyes glowed
with savage joy, already savoring victory. A deathly
hush descended over the clearing, then Mihail raised his
hand—the signal to begin.

With eyes locked, they circled slowly, each seeking an
opening. Francesca sat rigid, hardly daring to breathe;
her throat was dry and she twisted her skirt in her
fingers. Le Diable must win or she would be prey to that
vile creature. Yet what would be her fate if his haughty,
hard-faced adversary was judged the winner?

A gasp went up from the audience as, with an animal
spring, Le Diable bounded forward, dagger raised.
Zoltan ducked and the long blade sliced off a lock of his
hair. Le Diable lost his balance momentarily and Zoltan
leapt upon him. His dagger flashed, and there was
blood on Le Diable's upper arm. With a lithe twist, he
rolled from under Zoltan's imprisoning bulk, crouching
in a fighter's stance, chest heaving, the blood making
red rivers along his brown skin. Weaving and feinting,

he avoided Zoltan's next savage swing.

"Does that satisfy you?" he ground out. "You have drawn first blood."

With amazing agility for so bulky a man, Zoltan replied by hurling himself on Le Diable again; but he, graceful as a panther, moved aside on light feet, his knife slashing downward and plowing a deep furrow in Zoltan's chest. The gypsy grunted with pain, the sweat running from his coarse locks, dripping smartingly into his eyes. He gnashed his teeth and his broad nostrils flared like an animal's scenting death. They engaged, as closely locked as lovers. Le Diable's muscles bunched with effort as he struggled to find an opening in Zoltan's defense. He had the advantage of speed, but Zoltan relied on his weight. They stumbled and fell to the ground with the gypsy finishing up on top. In a reflex action, Le Diable seized the wrist holding the knife which was inching its way towards his throat. For a long, tense second, they strained, both men pouring sweat. Francesca was caught in the tension, her hands clenched so tightly into fists that the nails cut into her palms. Then, Le Diable forced Zoltan's arm up and back at an unnatural angle, the gypsy yelled and dropped his weapon. Le Diable was on his feet in a single bound, poised over his rival, ready for the death blow. The crowd was in a frenzy, shouting, "Kill him! Kill him!"

But he paused, foot planted firmly on Zoltan's throat, while the latter lay helpless, in agony from his wrenched arm, weakened by loss of blood, staring up into that dark face, waiting for the end.

"Make a clean job of it," he gasped. "Kill me swiftly, in the name of our Romany forebears!"

Le Diable straightened, one hand still clamped round the bloody knife. He looked across at Mihail. "I don't want this dog's death on my conscience! Let him live to writhe with shame because he was beaten by me!''

Pandemonium followed, but through it, Mihail rose, eyes unwavering as they met Le Diable's. He inclined his head. "As you wish, my friend.''

Zoltan moved restlessly as if to escape the pain; there was real desperation in his eyes. "Le Diable, I beg you—kill me! I am dishonored. Kill me . . .''

Le Diable threw the knife down on the grass, eyes hooded, an expression of supreme hauteur on his face. "No! You shall keep your miserable life, but trouble me no more.''

Roger was at his side, binding his wound with a strip of linen while Le Diable stood, hands on his hips and feet spread. His expression was grim, bitter but not triumphant. Elvire spoke to him, her eyes troubled. "This is not wise, my son. I foresee disaster.''

Le Diable shrugged and turned away as if no longer interested, flinging his coat across his shoulders. "The matter is closed as far as I am concerned. He may do as he damned well pleases!''

The huge bonfire flickered and danced in the velvet night, and there were happy smiles on the dark faces as they shouted congratulations to the victor, toasting him in potent red wine. There was such a confusing mass of gypsies around him that Francesca seized the opportunity to make a break for freedom. Her only chance was to run, and she took it, her heart pounding frantically in her breast. She leaped up and, before anyone realized her intention, ran for her life, plunging deeper into the woods, praying desperately that Le Diable would not notice her flight.

Her hopes were quickly dashed, for he moved like lightning, venting an angry oath; she had not gone more than a few yards into the dense bushes when his hands grasped her from behind like iron talons, pinning her arms helplessly to her sides. She was lifted from the ground and held, kicking and twisting, against his chest. Furious, she fought him, heels drumming into his shins, surprising them both by her unexpected strength. Cursing, he swung her round, fingers digging into her shoulders as he set her down on the ground with a force which jarred right through her body.

"I see that fright hasn't robbed you of your spirit, madame!" he snapped, though there was a trace of amusement in his voice. His face was in shadow, but she could see the hard line of his jaw and the brooding curve of his full bottom lip. "But don't try any more tricks, for you'll only serve to make life more difficult for yourself."

Fuming, she longed to hit him, but his touch on her bare skin was scorching like fire, rousing a bewildering jumble of emotions. "How do you expect me to behave after what has happened?" she flashed, her bosom heaving as she stared up at him.

He laughed, his mockery infuriating her. "Precisely as you have, my little hellcat! Such fiery hair and feline eyes usually spell trouble."

An icy calm suddenly swept over her. Unable to register further shocks, exhaustion washed over her in waves, so that his face above her seemed to grow large, then shrink away to a pinpoint. More than anything else, she longed to sleep, to rest her aching limbs and battered mind. Even so, she clung stubbornly to the tattered remnants of her dignity, trying to pull away from him. She staggered, putting out a hand to support herself against a tree and, somehow, Le Diable's arm was about her, drawing her toward him. She felt the roughness of wolfskin beneath her cheek, the heat of his body under it, and breathed in the rich odor of the fur, coupled with the warm, masculine scent of his skin and hair. The combined effect was so overwhelming that she was powerless to struggle, lying helplessly enfolded in his embrace as he slowly bent his head to kiss her. His mouth was unexpectedly gentle and sweet, almost hesitant, as if he was unsure of her acceptance. This moved her strangely, and she stood as though paralyzed, unable to protest. Shocks of lightning shivered down her spine, followed by a thrill of half-fright, half-excitement. An odd, treacherous, melting feeling invaded her whole being as she was held firmly against his muscled length, very aware of his long legs pressed close to hers, his lips moved caressingly over hers, driving away any vestige of sensible thought.

Abruptly, he released her, and she was as stunned as if there had been a violent explosion. "You are very beautiful," he said gruffly, and there was a strange smile about his mouth as he picked up one glossy mahogany curl which lay across her breast. The hair, as if having a will of its own, coiled lovingly around his hand. "But I must remain mindful of my purpose. Come, I'll take you back to the camp."

He put her in Mihail's charge, striding toward the rail where his horse was tethered, saying, "I must go now, Duke. Will you see that the prisoners rest here for the night? I shall leave men to escort them to Balvany at dawn."

Francesca was left gazing at his back, tall, straight, indifferent, as he mounted his stallion, raised his arm in a farewell gesture to the gypsies, and was swallowed up in the darkness. She felt suddenly bereft, a choke of loneliness catching at her throat; then Elvire took her by the arm, kindliness softening her austere face.

"Come to my *vardo*, child, and do not fear. Your friend is being cared for and he will soon recover. You may see him, if you wish, but I feel that you are not over concerned, eh? He has hurt you in some way. I sense the pain in your heart, the anger and disappointment. But you must forgive—he is weak and easily led. Greed and envy promote his actions but, in the end, he will render you a great service.''

The woman spoke in riddles, and it was all Francesca could do to fight back her tears and allow herself to be led, unresisting, to the wagon. It was gaily painted, picked out in yellow, green and black, heavily decorated with carving and ironwork. Inside, it was spotlessly clean, alive with glittering glass, shining brassware, ornaments of the finest china, and highly polished woodwork. The floor was covered by a rug in an elaborate pattern of carefully blended colors.

Elvire insisted that she undress, providing a lawn nightgown trimmed with lace, turning back the vivid patchwork quilt which covered the sheets of the bed area. This occupied the whole width at the far end of the wagon, and Francesca stripped like an obedient child, engulfed in the lavender-scented linen as the simple garment dropped over her head. She climbed over the spindle-rail and sank down into the luxury of the feather mattress.

Her aching body relaxed in the warm comfort, though her eyes followed Elvire's every movement, as she busied herself at the squat, black stove with its pipe which disappeared through the roof. She was stirring liquid in an iron pan, a strange odor rising from it. She carefully poured some into a tankard and brought it across to Francesca who struggled to sit up, in spite of being somewhat suspicious of the potion. She might well be serving her poison! The brew gave off a strong, though not unpleasant, smell of herbs.

Elvire's lips quirked into a smile, her almond-shaped

eyes friendly. In her fringed green dress, with her long smooth plaits and fine jewelry, she looked oddly elegant. " 'Tis a little concoction of my own," she confided, sitting down on the side of the bed and reaching out a gentle hand to rest on the bruise marking Francesca's cheek. "It is quite harmless and will make you sleep. You need the blessing of deep, healing slumber, my poor little one."

Francesca lost her fear, suddenly trusting the stranger—one does not offer poison in that tender tone of voice—and she drank down the contents in a single swallow, feeling warmth surging through her chilled body, bringing back life and hope, and a feeling of drowsy contentment. She nestled back against the frilled pillows, and fantasy began to smother her mind. Elvire kept watch, the golden light of the oil lamp planing her face. Francesca came to her senses once to ask, "Why do they call him 'Le Diable?' Who is he? Is he a gypsy?"

"So many questions, my dear!" That deep, mysterious smile played over the serene features. "Yes, he has Romany blood, though it is far back in his ancestry. He has that nickname because of his temper, his arrogance, his ability to ride like the wind, appearing unexpectedly like some avenging demon. His enemies never know when or where he will attack next! He is a ferocious fighter, an expert swordsman, a crack shot. He has a fearsome reputation and is irresistible to women! As to his identity, ah, that is another thing entirely, one that you shall learn in time."

Le Diable, who had saved her from Zoltan . . . he was kin to this regal woman, who was tending her with as much love as if she was one of her own children. Francesca's small, cat-shaped face wore a worried expression as his harsh, hawk-like features and glittering golden eyes flashed into her mind. Le Diable! It was as if his face and form were seared into her brain. A thrill of fright and something else, as yet unnamed, raced through her veins as she recalled the tall, broad-shouldered body which had fought Zoltan for possession of her, and that aura of recklessness, of controlled male passion, that had seemed to reach out and touch her even before he kissed her. The memory of that kiss made her shake with primitive, animal longing, and she hated herself for her body's betrayal. The drug was working, all the while her mind was wandering off on sidetracks too dreamlike to be called thoughts. Somewhere among the confusion there was another question which was bothering her, eluding her before she could capture it. With an effort, she spoke suddenly, clearly, "How is it that you speak English?" It was quite ridiculous, rationality insisted, to be here in a *tzigane* camp, somewhere in the Carpathian Mountains, and hearing her own tongue mouthed with such eloquence.

Elvire chuckled, rising to place another log among the glowing embers. The smell of woodsmoke coiled through the wagon. "We Roms travel far, child. I spent many moons in your country. Two of my sons were born there. You will find that you are not among strangers, Lady Francesca."

"You know my name?" The words tripped Francesca's tongue; she was finding it increasingly difficult to stay awake.

"I did not know it when I first saw you, but now it has come to me." The understanding smile which lit up Elvire's narrow features made her seem years younger. "I saw it in the smoke just now—'Lady Francesca Ballinger' ".

Once, Francesca would have dismissed this as nonsense, games to frighten children, but not any more.

The situation was entirely beyond her and she did not attempt to make a show of being able to cope with it. The gypsy's face loomed closer, those eyes like inky pools in which she might drown. Her lips moved wordlessly, giving the impression that she was conversing with invisible beings.

"You belong here." Elvire's voice sounded strange, hoarse and hesitant. "This is your destiny . . . this land . . . this joining of your English blood with ours happened before, many years ago. You have come to fulfill a purpose—nothing could have stopped you. It is fate. There will be trials and much heartache before it is accomplished. You will suffer, but like the tempering of the blade in the fire, so that suffering will bring its strength and reward. But you must beware. I shall do what I can to protect you; it is written that I must." She drew her shawl closely around her, face gray, looking weary enough to drop. "The curtain is drawn across my vision. I'll tell you no more tonight. Sleep, child—sleep."

Francesca was aware of a sense of doom. She was possessed of an urge to remain awake and alert, but the herb was producing a drowsiness impossible to resist. Numbness had spread right across her head and shoulders, her limbs were heavy and it was too much effort to move. As she drifted off, one strong impression remained, an image, not on her retina, but on her brain—it was that of Le Diable's face and the dark fire of his glance, terrifying in its intensity.

Morning light filtered through the canopy of leaves, washing like green water through the tiny windows of the wagon. A sunbeam stole across Francesca's sleeping face, touching her curling eyelashes with gold, caressing the dewy sheen on her lids. She woke to lie bemused, unable to remember where she was or how she had got there.

At her first movement, Elvire appeared, bearing a silver salver which supported a porringer and slices of wheat bread. Francesca stared at her groggily, as if she were a figure in some opium dream. Though sleeping long and heavily, she was still stupefied by weariness and nervous strain. Her face throbbed down one side when she tried to speak, memories of the heavy-handed Zoltan flooding back. And where is Le Diable? she thought agitatedly. Off with that common gypsy strumpet, no doubt! That brazen slut who has no shame, dressed like a man! They are welcome to one another! She could not understand why this thought put her in such a rage.

She sat up shakily and found that, once she had made the effort to eat, she felt better. Her situation was no less desperate, but her spirits began to revive. Elvire had not been idle on her account, and her daughters had followed her brisk instructions, bringing in Francesca's baggage and neatly spreading out her riding habit ready for wear. Francesca whipped herself awake, steadied her nerves by dressing in familiar clothing and spending time before her handmirror, which she propped against one of Elvire's vases in the window. She patted a little powder over her face, touched a perfume stopper to her wrists and throat, and smoothed some carmine into her lips. Her hair was snarled and it took some time to work the tangles out of it, but finally it spread over her shoulders like a tawny shawl, a tumbling mass of seductive curls, topped by her dashing tricorn hat. She felt much better; young and resilient, her natural energy and buoyant optimism returned. True, she was in grave danger, but on such a glorious morning it was difficult to believe in yesterday's violent happenings. Elvire was encouragingly friendly, her dark-eyed, shy girls looking at the fair English lady with unconcealed wonder. Even her sons bowed and smiled as she stepped from the wagon.

Captain Roger Willis was waiting for her, offering her his arm. As wary as a captured tigress, she rested her fingers lightly on his sleeve, but his eyes were filled with admiration, his manners most gentlemanly, his tanned face and curling auburn hair hearteningly attractive.

"Sir, are you not English?" Her wide green eyes looked up into his with a disarming clarity. "Why are you here, consorting with gypsies, ruffians and the like?"

He threw back his handsome head and laughed; laughter seemed to come as naturally to him as breathing. "A good question, madonna! And one that would take too long to answer. I would not bore you with my life history. Yes, I'm English, and a mercenary soldier to boot! As such, I go anywhere I'm needed, and serve under he who pays the most."

"Sir, can you tell me why I have been captured?" She stared at him, chin lifted, holding her slender body very erect. "I have done nothing to merit such treatment."

Roger was steadying her horse while she mounted, looking up at her, sandy lashes hedging deep blue eyes. "You will find out when we reach our destination, madame."

"And where, pray, is that?" she snapped tartly, working her fingers into her gloves and wondering if he was to be trusted.

"Castle Balvany," was his maddeningly curt reply, before he turned away to exchange convivialities with Mihail.

His men were saddling their beasts ready for departure, when Mark emerged from one of the wagons. He was in terrible condition, though the women had cleaned up his blooded garments and bathed his face. He was limping badly, walking like a man half drunk, and had to be helped onto his horse's back.

"Mark, how are you?" Francesca nudged her gelding with the heel of her riding boot, edging him nearer to her former lover. He turned his battered face toward her: one eye was black and completely closed, the other puffy and inflamed, his once handsome nose had been broken, and bruising spread across both cheeks. His lips were swollen, and he seemed to be in considerable pain from a cracked rib. He had not been impressed by the gypsy medications.

"They've made a poultice of some stinking herb and packed it round my ribs and back," he complained. "Goddammit, 'tis most uncomfortable, and it itches!"

"It's probably made of comfrey—very efficacious in the healing of broken bones," she said soothingly, delving into a dim recess of memory to recall lessons learned in the stillroom of Tallents. He did not bother to answer, sunk in self-pity, and she could not fail to note that he was so absorbed in his own misfortunes that he had not even bothered to ask how she had fared at the hands of the brigands. The optimism which she had grasped on waking began to evaporate, his depression communicating itself to her. Added to this, she was now surrounded by Le Diable's men, fierce of aspect and bristling with weapons. In the clear light of day, even the gypsy encampment looked sordid, the poverty of the people mercilessly exposed. The finery of the Duke and his family seemed tawdry, but Elvire reached up a brown hand to lay it on Francesca's velvet-covered knee.

"God go with you, child. Have faith and courage and

remember that I shall be thinking of you. We shall meet
again in the not too distant future. Yon weakling is not
the mate for you. There is too much fire in you for such
as he. You are destined for another and, when you
finally recognize him, dream your dreams with him, to
take, to share, to give—follow where he leads you."

Roger rapped out an order and the small cavalcade
left the camp. Throughout the morning they climbed
steadily along a track which curved in a series of hair-
pin bends. The scenery was amazing, each view surpass-
ing the next as they went deeper among the mountains.
That massive arc had the aspect of a natural fortress
from which Francesca was convinced she would never
escape, yet everything dark and wild and reckless in her
responded to the magnificence which stunned both
heart and eye. Great limestone cliffs reared above her,
covered in conifer trees. The rocks were volcanic in
origin and, in the course of time Nature, that superlative
sculptor, had carved out fantastic shapes using winds
and weather, leaving a bizarre landscape. Francesca
shivered at the thought of being stranded there alone at
night, her quick imagination peopling it with the black
denizens of the netherworld.

They passed through several tiny villages clinging to
the mountainside and, in contrast to the appearance of
the Hungarian peasantry, she was immediately struck
by their miserable existence. Their huts were mean, and
they watched their passage with unfriendly, lackluster
eyes. Once, to her horror, they were forced to ride by a
stark gallows set on a small, windy plateau, where six
bodies in various stages of decomposition creaked in
chains.

"Who did this?" she demanded of Roger, white to
the lips.

"The soldiers of Duchess Renata," he replied with

bleak eyes and grim mouth.

Francesca rode on in stunned silence. Why had the mother of her betrothed acted in such a vengeful manner toward the people under her rule? Were they miscreants or thieves? There were so many wearying questions which she wanted to ask about this savage land, and no one to whom she could appeal for answers. All the doubts she had fostered about coming here rose to torment her, her heart thudding with trepidation. The sun was low now, slanting across the mountain moraines, filling them with mysterious purple shadows, turning the limped lakes into pools of fire. The weary horses plodded on.

"Look!" shouted Roger suddenly, reining in and pointing with his crop. "There is Balvany!"

Francesca followed his gaze, shading her eyes with her gloved hand for the fiery sun was shining into her eyes. It loomed on a crag against glowering skies, a grim turreted castle. She gasped in superstitious terror. It was an awesome sight, clinging on to the jutting rocks malevolently, like a grotesque fungus. As if in answer to the dread which paralyzed her, a giant fork of lightning split the heavens and thunder reverberated across the mountains.

The final ascent was through a steep wood where the view was untamed, the trees and boulders intersected by a winding river. The noise of water became almost deafening as they breasted the last rise, coming out on a clearing before the fortress whose walls rose sheer over their heads. It was built above a gorge, and the river foamed and thundered to the bottom of a huge cleft in the rocks.

Hooves drummed on planks, crossing the drawbridge, and the jagged shadow of a portcullis forked across the riders as they passed under the gateway. It was surmounted by larger than lifesize figures of prancing lions holding up a coat of arms, guarded by mailed knights of stone with long curling plumes in their feature-shrouding helmets. Roger called a halt in the courtyard beyond the keep. The evening was growing ever darker and thunder still rumbled overhead. Great drops of rain began to fall and the men dismounted quickly to avoid a soaking, joking and blaspheming, roaring for the grooms, the needs of their mounts of prime importance. Wide of eye, Francesca stared up at the mighty walls which hemmed her in, dwarfed into insignificance by this massive, ancient and unfriendly citadel. Then her fear turned to astonishment as she saw very familiar vehicles parked outside the stables: her father's coach, its crest scratched, its black enamel much the worse for wear, but undeniably belonging to the earl, as well as other vehicles in which they had traveled across Europe.

Roger gave her no time to ask questions, helping her down while she tried not to stagger, her limbs cramped from such hard riding, and escorted her under a highly ornamented entrance attained by two flights of stone steps. It opened out into the Great Hall, a lofty reception room lit by flickering logs and smoky flares set in iron brackets. Men at arms leaned against the gray stone walls, in fact everything seemed gray to Francesca's alarmed sight—the paving of the floor, the pillars rising to the roof where crossed pikes, rusty shields and tattered banners bore silent witness to wars fought years before. Rooms led off through the grayness, dark, like the yawning mouths of caverns, and an enormous staircase twisted upwards into deeper gloom.

She stood with Mark, while Roger went forward, approaching one of the two impressive fireplaces where logs crackled. Each had stone supports and hoods on which was carved the same device which had dominated the gate—those snarling lions, rearing on their hind legs, holding the armorial bearing in their front paws. To one side of the hearth stood a chair of carved wood and stamped Spanish leather, deeply fringed and upholstered with gleaming brass nails, wherein lounged a man, his booted feet resting on the edge of the andirons, his slim, brown hands laced round a goblet.

Roger leaned over the back of the chair with casual intimacy. "Sir, we are here. The journey was without incident."

There was a moment's pause before he rose, and Francesca stiffened for something about him was shockingly familiar. Roger was grinning broadly, coming across to take her by the hand. "Lady Francesca Ballinger. May I present Count Alexis Romanesco, Lord of Castle Balvany?"

She knew a moment of pure panic, followed by a frantic upsurge of bewilderment. Le Diable stood before her, his eyes insolently playing over her astonished face. Le Diable—the savage brigand of the mountains.

Chapter Three

No one spoke for a moment. The only sounds which broke that ominous silence were a crackle as a log collapsed in a shower of sparks and a metallic clank as one of the guards eased his weapon into a more comfortable position. Sheer surprise held Francesca rooted to the spot. Then Alexis' glittering golden eyes met her wide emerald ones with a shock she felt in her bones, and she was not frightened any more, just mortified by her silly emotions, glaring at him with spitfire vehemence. Nearly choking on the angry words that came spilling from her lips, she shouted furiously, "You! A count? I took you to be a common rogue! Will you kindly tell me what in God's name is going on?"

He shook his head in disapproval, eyes filled with lazy mockery, replying primly, "Tut, tut! Such coarse language from the lips of a well-bred young lady! Whatever would the Earl of Marchmont say?"

He spoke with a slight drawl which went with his elegant clothes. Gone were the rough garments of yesterday, a well-cut jacket of maroon wool fitted his shoulders superbly, contrasting vividly with the white lace at his throat and wrists; while buff-colored breeches revealed the hard strength of his long legs, and shining black boots spoke of a valet's application to the polishing cloth. His hair was no longer an unruly mane of black curls, but had been brushed back and tied at the nape of the neck with a knot of satin ribbon. But despite this grandeur, which would have been totally acceptable in any drawing room, his face was the same: intensely masculine with that bold nose and slightly flaring nostrils, the high cheekbones and olive skin. Unable to tear her eyes away, Francesca stared at his mouth, and she had to admit that it was beautiful; the upper lip finely cut with a curl which hinted at contempt for incompetence, while the lower was full, sensual and firm, adding to the strength of his jaw with the shadowed cleft in the chin. She imagined it hard with passion, remembering what it was like to be kissed by such a mouth.

She pulled herself together with an effort, stamping on that traitorous thought, clinging to her invigorating rage like a lifeline to sanity. "My father? The earl? What do you know of him?" she retaliated hotly, very much on her dignity, irritated because Mark was standing there making no comment, shrinking into himself to avoid attracting the attention of this alarming person his way. He's afraid! The snivelling coward! she stormed silently. Was there no one to defend her? Merciful Heaven! Oh, for a knife in her hand so that she might stab her captor, who was looking down at her in a way which caused her heart to thump painfully in her chest!

She could feel Roger shaking with amusement, his laughter running down into her arm through the hand which he still had tucked under her elbow. She shook him off as if his touch burned, treating him to a scathing glare which should have blasted him where he stood.

"Well?" she repeated tartly, hands on her hips, tapping one toe impatiently. "What have you to say, sirrah?"

Alexis relaxed back against one of the pillars, leaning his broad shoulders on the gray stone and crossing one booted foot over the other. "You know, it will be a real pleasure to tame you, madame. Your father must have spoiled you outrageously, and the fops of London finished off the job, I shouldn't wonder. Our relationship will be a stormy one, but I think the entertainment will outweigh your shrewish temper," he announced calmly.

That temper, difficult to leash at the best of times, now snapped at this rudeness. Her eyes sparked dangerously. "We shall never have a relationship! I do not consort with villains who abduct innocent women! Where are my servants? What have you done with them? Murdered them and flung their bodies into some foul crevice in this Godforsaken hell?"

He threw back his head and laughed, shifting easily and switching on the full force of his charm. He came to stand close to her and she was unbearably aware of his nearness, feeling suffocated by it. "Lady Francesca, there is really no call for this unpleasantness. Come, sup with me. You will find that we are not such uncivilized barbarians at that. Will you join me?"

"It seems that I have little option." In spite of her anger, she could not help being conscious of the succulent smells coming from the direction of the kitchen. Her stomach was grinding with hunger, for they had only partaken of a very brief repast during the day. She loathed the idea of accepting any form of hospitality from him, but common sense told her that it might be the only way of finding out his intentions towards her and the servants who were her responsibility.

She was desperately worried on Hetty's account. Supposing she had been seized and ravaged! And dear, faithful Launey whom she had deserted in his sickness. . . . Shame at her selfish action was like a heavy weight in her heart. She had sacrificed her real friends for a man who had been only using her. She saw it clearly and bitterly; very well, now was the time to use strategy, perhaps bargain with him. At all costs, she must keep her head in this dire emergency, thus making retribution for her thoughtlessness.

There was a refectory table to one side of the fireplace, with benches and stools, and an oaken carver at the head. Francesca found herself seated on the count's right hand, with Mark and Roger on the other side. The black-skinned Luca came in to join them, and several other men high in Alexis' favor. Those tough, experienced veterans of many a vicious skirmish, treated their chief with a familiarity tempered with admiration and respect. He lapsed into their language, then back to English, and though not talking a lot, he occasionally made some remark which evoked a burst of laughter.

So far, Francesca had not seen any other women, though she was half-expecting the gypsy wench to appear. They were waited on by a couple of stocky manservants, wearing leather aprons and with sleeves rolled high above brawny elbows. The whole atmosphere was decidedly military and gave the impression of being a castle under siege.

She had thought that the food would be poor and badly cooked, but was surprised to find it was superb and impeccably served on silver platters, while the wineglasses and decanters were of the finest cut glass. Candles in branching holders lit the gloom; it was still pouring torrential rain outside and the thunder continued to roll ominously. Lightning flickered through the narrow, arched windows, high up, where once there had been a walk for bowmen, flashing across the faces of the men, and she thought she had never had such strange dinner companions. The whole thing was fantastic! Unbelievable!

Alexis leaned across, filling her goblet from a squat, dusty bottle which contained a yellowish liquid. "You must try Tokay, the marvelous wine from Hungary. The vineyards are on the hilly slopes above the river Tisza." He lifted his own glass so that he might see the light from the candles glowing through it, and his voice became pensive. "What a color! Have you ever seen the like, madame? It reflects the golden rays of the sun, and breaths of the long, dry autumn weather when the grapes are harvested."

Completely nonplussed, Francesca sipped her drink. There seemed to be no end to the changes of mood of this extraordinary man. He must be educated—certainly, he spoke well—what then had he been doing in the gypsy camp? She could feel herself blushing as she looked at him over the rim of her glass, and saw the slumbering fire in his eyes which were of a similar color to the Tokay. Nervously, she put down her drink and concentrated on the food, while Roger snapped the tension between them, eying her with a lift of one peaked brow.

"Is it not a delightful treat to have a lady grace our humble table, sir?" He asked his leader.

Alexis nodded gravely. "A rare pleasure indeed in the harsh, disciplined life of the mercenary." They exchanged a maddeningly superior male smile, as if they shared some secret. The other men rumbled and grinned at her, giving ribald winks, but they seemed congenial, despite the fact that their swords were close at hand, as if expecting imminent attack. These, supported by broad leather baldricks, swung from the backs of their chairs, and pistols jockeyed for place among the wine bottles and cutlery.

Mark had not yet uttered a word, picking at his food, his eyes darting apprehensively over the company; but Francesca, after a hesitant mouthful or two, found the first course delicious. It was a rich soup with meat balls, and this was followed by roast venison, accompanied by a variety of vegetables cooked in cream.

"My dogs pulled down the deer," Alexis informed her, indicating his hounds with the point of the dagger, with which he was slicing the meat. There were four, and they lay beside his massive chair. Large, lean and leggy, they reminded her of the gypsies' beasts. She glanced askance at them, for they looked ferocious with their deep chests and strong backs, those curious, snake-like heads with light eyes which followed any action, although their chins remained dutifully on the floor between outstretched forepaws.

"Titus is a borzoi," he continued, and the huge dog raised his head at the name, jaws snapping on the morsel flung to him. He lounged gracefully to his feet, his silky black and white coat gleaming as he padded away with his prize. "The others are crossbreeds. The gypsies call them lurchers, and there are no better hunting dogs on earth."

Francesca pushed her plate away and, staring hard at Alexis, decided that she had never met a man who annoyed her more! What the devil was he about, making small talk? She was beginning to feel the effects of the wine, her angry resentment bubbling up. "I have no interest in your dogs, sir! And I only eat with you because I am forced to! You said that you would tell me why you had the audacity to abduct me. Kindly do so without further delay!"

Alexis scowled, settling back in his chair, a glass of

plum brandy between his hands, elbows resting on the arms which rolled over into lions' heads. A silence fell across the board, his men watching them guardedly, alert for storm signals.

"Don't use that tone to me, madame," he growled out. "You are in no position to make demands."

Roger was smoothing his scrubby mustache thoughtfully. "In all fairness, sir, I think you should explain," he suggested tactfully, knowing his commander's erratic temper and recognizing that hers was equally combustible. The situation was fraught and sparks were bound to fly.

The wide shoulders under the dark red coat moved in a shrug. "Very well, Roger. I would not have Lady Francesca continue to think me an ungallant boor." His sarcasm came out almost in a purr. He sat upright, eyes coldly considering her. "I have known for a long time that you were on your way to marry the margrave. It was in my interests to apprehend you. I have a score to settle with Duchess Renata, and you will be an excellent hostage."

It was like a hard blow in the stomach. She gave an involuntary gasp and rose to her feet. "A hostage? I don't understand. What harm have I ever done you?"

His insolent, heavy-lidded gaze met her furious eyes. There was an unpleasant twist to his mouth. "A woman who even considers marrying into the Pascaly family deserves everything she gets."

Each word he uttered, each moment spent in the hostile atmosphere of Balvany, seemed to weigh on her spirits like lead. She was caught in the not-too-sane, aerial feeling of being trapped in a sticky web of intrigue which folded round her, the innocent victim of some ancient feud.

"That is unjust," she protested, trying to keep the

quaver from her voice. "It was arranged by my father, years ago. I was merely doing as he bade me."

"No doubt you were not averse to acquiring a large slice of land and a grand title," he said coldly, standing and moving to the fire, staring moodily down to watch two small flames fighting across a log.

Francesca's lip curled scornfully. "I had no need of that. I already have a title, and am heir to one of the largest estates in England."

"*Touché!*" murmured Roger, lounging lazily in his chair and listening to their ill-natured exchange with thinly concealed amusement. Luca and the rest had shifted positions to the far end of the table, and he pulled out a pack of cards, spreading them into fans with his blunt fingers. Yet, while appearing to be engrossed in the coins and the turn of the cards, they also kept a wary eye on their leader, ready to spring to his defense. The smoke from their clay pipes spiraled upwards, their low voices murmuring in a curious mixture of Rumanian and native patois, intermingled with French and German. Francesca could comprehend some of it, but the rest was a weird babble in her ears, emphasizing her loneliness.

It was hard to fight back her weak, womanish tears before this stern, uncompromising man who now held her captive in his ruthless hands. But, with a whisper of petticoats, she paced slowly over to him, wanting to break through his stubborn pride, hating him and longing to hurt him, to scratch, bite and kick him into setting her free. He lifted his somber eyes to her and she had to admit that she had felt much bolder when there had been a distance between them. The whole area seemed to be filled with his dominating presence. She had never seen so large a man, his tallness accentuated by the fact that she wore flat shoes while he had on heeled cavalry boots, which added a good two inches to his already impressive height.

Flinging her head up proudly, she defied his hugeness, his masculinity, his position as victor. "Are you going to release me?"

He gave a hard bark of laughter at her presumption. "Certainly not! I've not gone to the trouble and expense of having you trailed halfway round Europe to have you slip through my fingers!"

She swallowed the sick lump which seemed to have lodged somewhere in the region of her throat. "You mean to say, I have been spied on . . . followed?" She could not finish the sentence.

Alexis leaned on the carved pilaster of the chimney. The expression in his eyes had altered, and she felt that he had come close, suffocatingly close. She was mesmerized, gazing up into that darkly handsome face. He was mocking her again. "Your so-called guards were singularly lacking in vigilance, my dear. Perhaps they did not expect such ungentlemanly behavior. Yes, my men have kept you in sight for weeks, reporting back to me. Then, by an incredible stroke of luck, you chose to separate yourself from your escort, making the task of catching you much simpler. What were you doing with that young spark? Running off for a night of love?"

Francesca's face crimsoned at this barbed teasing, picturing herself swimming nude in the forest. Had Zoltan seen her? And that horrible creature, Arpad? She bit her full lower lip, forcing herself not to drop her eyes. "That is none of your business!" she returned with gusto.

Alexis' laughter rolled round the hall, then his eyes flashed across to where Mark sat huddled on the bench.

"So he *is* your lover!" he announced triumphantly, standing with his legs apart, thumbs hooked in his belt. "Well, madame, I don't think much of your choice!"

Francesca was trembling with anger and a confused feeling which she could not explain. Alexis was having the most strange effect on her. Bluster and argue she might, but she had to admit that he had read Mark's character in a single glance. "Would I be taking a lover, sir, when I am already betrothed?" she countered, revealing nothing.

The teasing light had died from his eyes, replaced by something akin to that which had raged there in his quarrel with Zoltan. It was like a flame in his black pupils, a look which sucked out all her strength. "Ah, yes, I think you could," he said softly, moving nearer. Francesca barely controlled the urge to step backwards away from him, but she stood her ground.

"It must be impossible for a man such as you to understand honor and decency," she hissed with venom.

His eyes hardened, his smile went cold, and he deliberately reached out and touched her cheek. Francesca flinched as if he had slapped her and struck his hand away. The air was so tense that it seemed to crackle about them, then he considered her slowly, contemptuously, through slitted eyes. "Lady you may be, but I've never yet met a wench so ripe for coupling, or so eager!"

Sheer astonishment robbed her of words. She was painfully conscious of the effect of his touch—her cheek burned from it. Finally, she rapped out, "Will you let me go, so that I may continue my journey?"

"No!" his reply was like a pistol shot. "You will remain here for just as long as it suits me. Duchess

Renata will pay highly to have you and your dowry delivered safely to Govora."

Francesca became an ice maiden all of a sudden, very cold, very regal, her slim body held stiffly, her face a mask of hauteur. "Then have me conducted to whatever dungeon you will, be it never so base! I would prefer it to spending a moment more in your vile company!"

His smile thinned ever so slightly at her scornful words, and for a moment the frightening expression she had seen earlier flashed in his eyes. He gave a small, ironic bow, and snapped his fingers at one of the servants who leaped to do his bidding.

"Conduct madame to the room prepared for her, Dinu. See that a guard remains constantly on duty at her door. I would ask for your word that you will not try to escape, but I have no confidence that you would not break parole," he added, with his hard gaze and enigmatic smile.

With a baffled cry of rage, she spun round and stalked off, determinedly resisting the urge to slap his mocking face. He was a conceited, highhanded, illmannered blackguard! She longed to tell him exactly what she thought of him! And with relish rolled the insults off her tongue as she followed the lean, spare Dinu up the staircase.

She was still listing Alexis' faults as they traversed the passages which connected the upper rooms. There was dim light either from the arrow slits or smoky flares in rings set in the walls. Castle Balvany was very old and large, filled with meandering corridors. Yet, for all its imposing structure, its damp walls spoke of neglect, its whole appearance one of decayed magnificence, as if its present owner could not afford its upkeep. Francesca's eyes slid to Dinu, poker-faced and gangling, striding along purposefully. He caught her glance and smiled at her wryly, a grin which softened his cadaverous features and made less alarming his black mustache which was twirled up at the ends into ferocious points.

"Do not fear, madame," he ventured in broken English. "I am his valet and I know him. His bark is much worse than his bite. You will see."

They stopped outside a heavily studded oaken door where a guard with a musket leaned, smoking a pipe of tobacco. Dinu spoke to him, and he turned the massive iron key in the brass lock. The valet flung it open and stood aside for her to enter. She crossed the threshold, and heard the door thud behind her and the rasp of a bolt slamming home. Then Hetty was in her arms, and Lavinia waddling across, homely face quivering with anguish, wig aslant, bosom heaving.

"Oh, my dear lady! Thank God you are safe! Such a dreadful ordeal. Lord, I think I'm about to faint again! Where's my *sal volatile*, girl?"

She staggered to a stool and slumped on it dramatically. Most of Lavinia's gestures were dramatic. She was one of those people who act rather than live their lives. Francesca suspected that she was rather enjoying the whole thing; nothing so exciting could possibly have happened to her before. Hetty, sniffing and wiping her tears on the back of her hand, produced the smelling salts bottle, waving it under the nostrils of the chaperone. She leaned back, an arm pressed to her forehead, eyes closed. Francesca felt a spasm of annoyance and very little sympathy; no constructive help would be forthcoming from Lavinia for a while!

Hetty's freckled face was filled with concern. "Ma'am, what happened to you? I thought you safely away with Sir Mark."

Francesca told her the whole story, while alarm and consternation crossed Hetty's mobile countenance. When Francesca paused for breath, her maid blew out her cheeks in comic amazement. "Well, here's a story!"

"And how did they capture you?" Francesca wanted to know. While they talked, she prowled the room restlessly, a vivid figure against the gray walls, her ceaseless tread reminding Hetty of a caged lioness. Somehow, the chamber had sprung to life as soon as she entered, for she was such a vibrant person, always busy with something, and her devoted maid wondered how imprisonment would affect her.

"That peasant couple was in his pay," she told her.

"His men had been following us for weeks, so he said," Francesca added, going over to one of the windows set in the thickness of the walls, and pressing her small, straight nose to the thick, dimpled glass. As she had surmised by the distant sound of rushing water, her room was in one of the towers overlooking the gorge with its frothing avalanche of water. She stared down a sheer drop onto white spume and the ragged teeth of rocks. The clouds chased wildly across the black sky, but it had stopped raining and the storm had died away.

"We can't escape in that direction, ma'am," breathed Hetty, at her shoulder. "And there's the court of guard and the keep on the other side."

"Where are Dr. Ranby and Colonel Launey?" Francesca was wringing her pale hands together in frustration, needing their support.

Lavinia heaved to her feet, lumbering along to Francesca's side, the harbinger of bad tidings. "The colonel died, poor man." She was watery-eyed, using a singsong, disaster voice. "We left the villagers to bury him."

Francesca pressed her hands at the stab of pain and pity which wrenched her heart. Launey, that good old man, laid to rest in a foreign land, far from his native shore. It was all Le Diable's fault, she reflected sourly, conveniently forgetting her own wilful part in it, spitting out the name to Hetty.

"Count Alexis, d'you mean?" Hetty perked up at this, rolling her eyes to indicate vast admiration. But then, Hetty was easily impressed by men. "Oh, what a splendid person! You say you mistook him for a gypsy? I'm not surprised, he has those dark, fascinating looks. Have you discovered anything about him?"

Crossly, Francesca shook her head, not wishing to discuss that despicable robber! She stalked the room, which was furnished with the same faded splendor as the rest of his lair. The walls were hung with tapestries which softened their bleakness, and threadbare rugs were strewn on the small stone tiles of the floor. There were coffers for clothing, high-backed chairs of unrelenting hardness, the linen woven and spun by peasants, in narrow stripes of vivid red and black. The bed was huge, a massive fourposter, its tester supported by stout oak, intricately carved, a wooden panel at its head and drapes of faded bottle green damask. Everything wore a shabby, dusty air, as if no woman had set foot in here for a decade.

"They didn't harm us, ma'am . . ." began Hetty, but Lavinia broke in, eyes bulging with outraged indignation.

"How can you say that, foolish chit? I have never been so insulted! There we were, struggling to find a decent nurse to lay out the poor colonel, and a priest to perform the rites, when those ruffians burst in upon us! Armed with swords and guns—a terrible gang of brutes! Bundled us into the coaches without as much as a word, and carried us here! La, how my delicate constitution stood the shock I shall never know. What are their intentions? Are we to be slaughtered? They can't hold us here—we're English citizens! As for that person . . . Count Alexis . . . well, never have I met such an arrogant, overbearing man!"

"He's mighty handsome," put in Hetty dreamily.

"Ha! So he may be, if you like those black, glowering looks, but, my dears, no woman would be safe with him! I tell you, I feared for my virtue! We must band together and die rather than yield up that most precious gift of chastity." Lavinia heaved a great, theatrical sigh, clicked her tongue, and regarded them with an expression of martyrdom.

Hetty suppressed a giggle, and Francesca felt her own lips twitch in response at the absurd picture of Alexis making an assault on the honor of the fat, blowzy chaperone. It was just too preposterous. But laughter could not overwhelm her for long, worried anger surging up to quench it. Hetty and Lavinia were looking to her for help and she was powerless. Resuming her restless pacing, driving her fists into the palm of her hand, she explained as well as she could, in spite of feeling almost as bewildered as they.

"It appears that he has some personal vendetta with Duchess Renata, and I am to be used as a pawn in their political games. There is nothing we can do save bide our time and seek the first opportunity to escape." Her mind was already active, plotting and scheming. She swirled round to face Hetty. "I'll do all I can to persuade Captain Willis to help me, and you get to know the valet, Dinu. He is a trusted servant, and from him you can get information. Use your womanly wiles, Hetty."

Hetty was not averse to intrigue, in fact it was the breath of life to her, quick-witted and shrewd, well able to twist even the most obdurate fellow round her dainty fingers. She nodded eagerly, eyes sparkling with mischief.

"Come, we'll let it appear that we're compliant." Francesca was already putting her plan into operation, urging her maid to begin unpacking, and soon the room was strewn with feminine garments. Hetty rummaged in boxes and trunks containing Francesca's luggage, always more enthusiastic than methodical. Petticoats and filmy shifts draped the chairs, silk stockings swung from the stools, dresses were spread out on the bed, and the two younger women chattered, their spirits rising, a sense of adventure sweeping them along. I'll show him! Francesca assured herself. He'll find it mighty difficult to hold me captive! His own friend and most trusted lieutenant will betray him for me! I'll teach him to pretend to save me from Zoltan just because I'm useful to him!

She fed her anger, stamping on the memory of his hard arms and tender mouth, working herself up into a frenzy of hatred. At that moment she would have allied herself with an enemy who sought to destroy him. She must meet Ranby and the others as soon as possible, discuss with that sober-sided doctor exactly what she must do.

The night was too far advanced for further specula-tions, so they prepared for bed. Lavinia had been given a room with a connecting door, and she retired, all the while swearing that she had no intention of removing a single stitch of clothing, and would not be able to snatch

a wink of sleep for thinking of those black-hearted
scoundrels who wanted to rape her! Francesca was glad
to have Hetty to attend her, for her nerves were strung
as taut as bowstrings, and the firm stroke of the hair-
brush across her scalp was soothing. Cold waves of
tiredness swept her from crown to toe—the fear, the
rage and those bewildering emotions which any thought
of Alexis aroused in her making her head swim. She sat
down at the dressing table, where a mirror hanging on
the wall threw back out of its dark void a small white
mask of hopelessness. It was her own face with huge,
staring eyes. Hetty impinged for a moment, tentative,
though encouraging; withdrew with a birdlike uncertainty, then came behind her shoulder, bringing color
and movement back to the reflection.

"Don't fret, my dear lady," her voice was consoling,
gentle, as she skilfully hid her own dread. "All will be
well."

When her mistress was prepared for rest, Hetty
undressed and, with a tired sigh and a yawn wide
enough to crack her jaw, occupied the trundle bed
which she had wheeled out from under the fourposter.
Her breathing became deep and regular, but sleep
evaded Francesca. She lay awake wide-eyed, staring at
the single candle flame, flat on her back, trying hard to
grasp the elusive edges of slumber, while her wayward
thoughts kept slipping away down pathways of their
own. A strange heaviness possessed her. She could hear
the sentry's measured tread outside her door. He
ground his musket on the flags every time he turned, an
infuriating reminder that she was a prisoner. Le
Diable's captive, to do with as he willed. Nothing, not
even harsh thoughts, would banish him from her mind
as she tossed restlessly in the bed, bedeviled by alien
emotions which disturbed and infuriated her. Angrily,

she thumped the unoffending pillow as she unwillingly remembered his kiss, warmth and sensual longing coiling like a spring in her loins. She could not stop thinking about it, comparing it with the feeling she had once had for Mark.

It was as if the flickering flames which danced in the wide hearth and filled the room with moving shadows reached out a long tongue and intimately licked at her. What was happening to her? She clung to her hatred with desperation, though it now seemed a pale, feeble thing compared to that other, tumultuous feeling. With a small moan of defeat, she burrowed into the welcoming softness of the mattress, alarming herself just before falling asleep by dreamily wondering what it would be like to have him make love to her.

Chapter Four

THE IDEA of escape became an obsession with Francesca; she could think and talk of nothing else. It was true that they were being well treated, but on meeting Ranby next day, she was annoyed to find that he was on parole, having given his word not to leave the castle and its vicinity. At first, she stayed within the confines of her room; there was no need for her to leave its shelter and risk a disrupting encounter with Alexis. Food was served there, and she could exercise by pacing its length. In addition, it had its own secluded toilet area, relic of the middle ages, tucked away in the thickness of a buttress, with a shaft going down into the river. It had a clean, though chilly, stone seat and lid to be replaced after use, and Francesca thought it an excellent arrangement after the hedges and ditches of their journey and the dubious middens of the inns.

She had contemplated refusing to partake of food, but after a day of this felt so weak with hunger that she relented. Munching angrily, hating herself for her lack of willpower, she determined on another tactic, putting into effect the ploy of luring Alexis' officers away from their duty. Hetty had already flung herself wholeheartedly into this campaign, hobnobbing with Dinu on every possible occasion. On the pretext of fetching a drink for her mistress or desiring to wash their linen, she wheedled her way past the guard, whisking deftly about the castle, spying and listening, spending time in the enormous, subterranean kitchens. Language was a difficult barrier to overcome, and it was mostly from Dinu that she obtained information.

"They've sent Luca with a message to the duchess," she confided, as she helped Francesca to dress one morning. "Dinu says that Alexis was outlawed by her years ago, and that she is a tyrant, greedy and cruel, crushing the peasants beneath her heel."

"I cannot believe that my father would have given me in marriage to a family who were not the soul of honor and integrity," Francesca answered reprovingly, though unable to shake off the ghastly memory of the bodies swinging on the gibbet, and the starved-looking, downtrodden appearance of the villagers.

She backed up to Hetty so that the maid might lace her boned bodice, her small waist nipped in to doll size, her breasts swelling above the curved neckline. The gown was of a soft, old-gold taffeta, with narrow sleeves trimmed with a froth of lace at the elbows, matching the fichu which swathed her bosom. The skirt, long and full, puffed out on either side, showing the panel embroidered with silver thread and seed pearls which ornamented the center of the dark green underskirt. It was a relatively simple costume, in which she felt confident and business-like—ready for anything! Hetty had already dressed her hair in ringlets, and she had subtly painted her heart-shaped face, and now gathered up her cloak and fan. She had been given permission to take a stroll on the battlements, accompanied by Roger Willis.

He tapped on the door, happy to be her escort, bowing over her hand, raising it gallantly to his lips with a ravishing smile from his fine eyes. "I am delighted that you have decided to leave your cloister, madonna," he said, as they walked toward the flight of stone steps which wound aloft. "You are too lovely to lead the existence of a nun."

She made suitable answer to his compliments, but her ears were alert, her eyes watchful in case they might bump into Alexis. Her heart bounded as she imagined him, the dark fire of his golden eyes, his moods which changed like ripples passing over the surface of somber water.

The storms had passed and the day was serene, though touched with autumnal melancholy. The breeze lifted Francesca's hair as she rested her hands on the parapet, while Roger pressed his shoulder against hers, joining her in admiring the view. The height and grandeur of it took her breath away. The road by which they had entered the castle disappeared beyond the escarpment, and the scene was one of rugged magnificence. Here and there were deep rifts left by Ice Age glaciers, almost entirely covered by forest, the limestones taking on the most spectacular shapes. The sinuous chain of mountains faded into the misty distance, obscured by low-lying clouds.

" 'Tis such an unfriendly landscape," Francesca shuddered.

Roger gave a grunt of laughter. "You should see it in winter! Blizzards, avalanches, snowstorms, howling winds—the passes become completely blocked and we are marooned up here."

"Why do you remain?" Francesca gave him a searching look which he answered with his lopsided grin. She placed a hand on his arm, sensing a chink in his armor. "Don't you long to see England once more?"

"My dear, I'd not dare set foot in London! I prefer to stay here and face the wolves!" There was a wicked twinkle in his eyes which spoke volumes. She did not ask what villainy had made him an outcast, afraid to go home. A smile curved her red lips, for Roger was good company, full of fun and jokes, a most lovesome man. What did it matter that he was a rogue, living on his wits and his sword? Intuitively, she knew that she had found a friend and, overconfident, she began to congratulate herself, feeling the heady wind of freedom already blowing in her face.

She turned to him impulsively, her lovely features alight with eager life, strands of her fragrant hair touching his cheek, whipped by the breeze. "Will you help me? I must get away from here."

The slow, lazy smile widened his mouth, the sunlight slanting off the bridge of his nose, touching his red hair with fire as he considered her. Indeed, she was a tempting enchantress, a study in contrasts that caught the eye and held the attention. That rich, russet hair, almost shocking against the gardenia whiteness of her skin, and that narrow, feline face with the intriguing, slanted emerald eyes that sparkled with laughter, flashes of indignation or anger, back to fun again. The perfume of her body pervaded his senses, breathing out warmly from between her breasts, seducing him, and his gaze roved those inviting curves, then her lips, pouting with provocative invitation.

"You are asking me to help you escape?" He shifted his elbow on the battlements, cocking a questioning eyebrow at her. "Believe me, my dear, I'd be more than happy to oblige, if I thought it right. But I cannot betray Alexis' trust, even for you."

"Damn Alexis!" She flared at him, pulling away, eyes stormy. "Why do you support that man? What power has he over you?"

Roger leaned back against a wall projection, shirt undone over a brown, hairy chest, soaking up the sun like a big tomcat and watching her with humorous eyes which, like the corners of his mouth, were crinkled with laughter and vigilance.

"In truth, I admire him more than any man alive. I've been in his service for years, and know his cause to be just. He'll not stand by and watch brutality and injustice, no matter the cost to himself. If he has seen fit to hold you hostage to forward his ambitions to free the people, then I'll not aid you to give him the slip, even though you are the prettiest little minx that ever I saw."

Tears of exasperation stung Francesca's eyes. She gave a toss of her head, and began to pace the lofty battlements. "I don't believe him to be so noble! Can you deny that he is proud and domineering?"

He matched his long-legged stride to hers, glancing sideways at her furious face. "He is but human, my dear, made up of many facets. His life has not been easy, believe me. In his thirty years, he has seen much sorrow and trouble, more than you, with your sheltered upbringing, can comprehend."

She refused to be placated, or to give Alexis any credit, thinking that Roger was bedazzled by his commander's charisma, that personal magnetism which hung over him like a wicked aura. "He's related to the gypsies, is he not? And everyone knows that they are not to be trusted."

"Yes, he has Romany blood. One of his grandmothers was a *tzigany* princess," he conceded. Then he added: "Reserve judgment until you have spent time with them, for they are very loyal in friendship, and will gladly die for those they love. Alexis is the same. I'faith, I'd rather have him as a friend than an enemy!"

Francesca twisted her fan between nervous fingers, eyes rebellious, lower lip rolled out. "Then you'll not assist me?"

"I'm your devoted slave for life, sweetest Lady Francesca," he vowed, slipping an arm casually around her waist. "And will do anything else you command, but I must refuse you this."

Further argument was useless, but defeat stuck in her craw, and she was in a violent mood when he conducted her back to her room. "Sup with us tonight," he urged as they parted. "Put on your finest garb and talk with Alexis. It will not be time wasted, for he can teach you much. After all, if you intend to marry the margrave, it will be as well to know the country and its people."

"Will he ever allow me to attain that position?" she asked, framed against the doorway, her amber gown like a candle flame in the dusk of the corridor, her face flushed with annoyance, though he could see the fear that lurked there too.

He patted her shoulder, resisting the temptation to pull her into his arms and taste that sensuous mouth. "Of course he will. He has no quarrel with you, sweetheart, you are just an unfortunate dupe. It could have been anyone else in the same snare."

Small comfort indeed, when her whole life had been disrupted. There was nothing to be gained from seclusion, and she was heartily bored with the company of the doom-ridden Lavinia, so she changed into an elegant gown of shot silk green which emphasized the color of her eyes, and joined her captor in the Great Hall. Oddly enough, she enjoyed herself, for his men swarmed round her, schooling their roughness, complimenting her effusively in a variety of languages, though keeping a wary eye on Alexis.

He, brooding in his throne-like chair, paid her scant attention, abstracted and thoughtful, idly playing with the long, silken ears of Titus. Francesca had the distinct impression that he was, on the whole, much easier in the company of his animals than humans, though he did enter into conversation with Ranby. She was astonished to see him warm to that scholarly man, leaning forward eagerly, lucidly discussing some erudite point of philosophy. The university of Vienna was mentioned, and it appeared that Alexis had been a student there.

"Feel free to explore my library, doctor," he urged. "It contains many old and rare books which may interest you."

Francesca, trying to listen without showing that she was doing so, was irritated when Mark persisted in talking to her. His bruises were fading, though his good looks would be marred for a long time to come. It was the first time she had seen him since the night of their arrival. Seated by her side at the table, he was determined to make peace with her and, almost foppishly attired in brown velvet, he once more resembled the man of fashion whom she had once loved.

"I'm sorry for what happened, Francesca." He adopted his lost little boy look which she had originally found so appealing. "I did not make much of a show in your defense. Truth to tell, I have an almighty fear of being hurt. Can you understand and forgive me?"

Francesca was hardly attending to him, watching Alexis who was slouched in his chair at the head of the table, painfully aware of his extraordinary attraction, something in his personality so dazzling that wherever he went he would draw all eyes to him. She had never seen a handsomer man. She pulled herself together in horror. Most women would be wild with desire for him—but not Francesca, she told herself firmly. He was her enemy and she hated him!

She turned the full blaze of her unusual eyes on Mark, seeing the self-loathing and unhappiness in his face. Yes, she could forgive him, but she would never love him again. She said something to this effect and he sat dejectedly beside her, very crestfallen. It was impossible not to draw comparisons between his cowardly performance and that of Alexis when he had faced the mighty Zoltan—and he had done it for her! Fool! whispered her newfound cynicism. You know that he only fought for you because you are a valuable piece of property!

The author of her misfortunes had her in his field of vision across the table, his eyes smoldering darkly. She was so conscious of him, so aware of those eyes filled with the quick flame of desire, his full mouth so frankly sensual, that the meal was a blur in her memory. She did not know what she ate or drank, but his intense and unrelenting face was burned into her mind for all time. His sinewy, suntanned fingers were curled round a crystal goblet, and she was unable to prevent a shiver of excitement from sliding over her body, raising the fine down on her limbs.

When he spoke, she jumped with shock—it was so unexpected. "So, Lady Francesca, you have deigned to associate with us, have you?" His voice was hard, sarcastic, his lips curling mockingly.

Instant anger swept away softer emotions. Damn him! Why was it that every time he spoke it riled her so? "I was dying of boredom, sir," she retorted, and the room hushed, as if their antagonism was a threat to all present. She flicked open her delicate painted fan, peering at him over its lace edge, eyes guarded.

"Ah, I do apologize most deeply," his sardonic smile deepened the grooves each side of his mouth. "It was most unthinking of me not to arrange fetes or a ball or two for your entertainment. No doubt, you spend your life engrossed in such frivolities in London. But this is a poor country, the peasants cannot find the wherewithal to feed their starving children, let alone take time from their toil to do other than attend Mass."

He spoke as if it was her fault that the poor could not eat, and she hotly resented the unspoken implication that she was an empty-headed dilettante, and none too bright at that! "I ask nothing from you, sir, save my freedom." Alarm, anger, and the desire to cry at his unfairness warred within her. "You wrong me, if you think me a lightminded butterfly. I'll wager that I could surprise you with some of my accomplishments."

"Such as?" he yawned behind his hand, as if Francesca and her vapid existence filled him with ennui.

Thoughts were buzzing in her head like gnats. Could she trick him or was he too subtle for her? She plunged on, risking everything in one wild throw. "I can outride and outhunt most men," she declared, remembering hours in the saddle at Tallents, following the hounds, outdistancing the local gentry.

Roger was eying her with amused suspicion, already one jump ahead, but Alexis skeptically accepted her challenge. "I think you'd be hard pressed to best me, madame." He was goading her on, and his men issued friendly warnings about his formidable reputation as a horseman.

"Try me!" She dared him.

"You are bold. I'll grant you that," he conceded, his lordly air grating on her taut nerves. "I have an Arab in my stables which you would find well nigh impossible to control."

"Say you so?" she queried loftily, chin held up in that familiar mulish way which Ranby recognized with a sigh. It always meant trouble. She turned to him swiftly, wanting his corroboration. "Am I not a competent horsewoman, doctor?"

Ranby dabbed at his lips with a damask napkin and gave a nervous cough, unwilling to encourage her in some further mad escapade. "I understand that you are a perfect Diana of the chase," he prevaricated, "superb on mounts that you know and on familiar terrain, but here—I think not."

Francesca frowned at this tepid recommendation, determined not to be thwarted. "I think the count hesitates because he'll not risk being beaten by a woman." She stabbed him a caustic glare, glad to see by the darkening of his expression that the barb had gone home.

Alexis, gazing into that adorable, maddening face which had been haunting him since the very first moment that he had come upon her struggling with Zoltan, was furious with himself because he could not get her out of his mind. He was not a whit deceived; her motives were as transparent as glass. He knew full well that she intended to try and give him the slip once he took her outside the castle, but he thought it high time the haughty little bitch was taught a sharp lesson! One that she would not forget in a hurry! How dare she torment and bedevil him with her beauty, those red lips which he had crushed beneath his own once only, feeling the urgent response which she so vehemently denied? Every movement she made was alluring, each practiced, provocative sway of her rounded hips, calculated to make desire rise hard in a man. And she was selling herself into that nest of vipers, the Pascaly family! He refused to believe her assertion that she knew nothing about them. She was a cold, calculating society woman, bred to sell her charms to the highest bidder in the marriage market. He had met her type before, in Vienna and Budapest, their one object to get their greedy little hands on as much wealth as possible, with no consideration for the feelings of others, no heed for how that money was obtained, so long as they could squander it!

Not all the nobility were heartless, of course, there still remained a few masters who treated their serfs with humanity. But the Pascalys were notoriously cruel despots, bleeding the peasants dry, demanding unfair rents and taxes and taking the best of the crops—and Francesca was about to ally herself to them in the same way that Maria had done. Maria! At the thought of his former wife, his jaw clamped tight, and his anger against Francesca doubled because she had made him think of her, that woman who had betrayed him so many weary years ago. He had been little more than a boy, callow, idealistic, brought up in the mountains by his godfather, that venerable nobleman Ciprian Sahia. He had met Maria in Vienna during his student days, and had loved her madly, marrying her and bringing her back to Balvany. A son had been born, and he thought himself the happiest man in the world, despite his troubles. Unfortunately Maria was too young to settle in the remote castle, very lovely, but fickle. Life with him was not exciting enough for her and one day, when Alexis was away on a hunting trip, she had run off to Castle Costin where Duchess Renata held court. There she had died, and the child too, inflicted by smallpox. The old hurt still throbbed within Alexis, his burning hatred of the Pascalys flaring up, focusing on the man who had lured Maria away—Baron Cezar, Renata's chief minister and adviser. And now this chit of a girl was bringing a resurgence of agonizing memories. For the first time in years a woman had got under his skin! Grimly, he determined that she should pay for it!

His eyes were flint-like as he rose to his feet, looming over her, his men waiting with baited breath, knowing his dirty, evil temper. "I will order the grooms to saddle the Arab. We'll ride out now."

Francesca trembled, both with fear and in triumph because her ruse had worked. She almost despised him, for he was proving to be but a man after all, and she had ever found it easy to bend them to her will. She did not bother to reply, just gave him a searing, scornful stare and swept up to change.

Hetty was worried, clucking like an anxious mother hen as Francesca stripped off her dress and donned her riding habit. "Lord, ma'am, what are you about now?"

Francesca outlined her plan, thrusting her feet into her red leather boots and snatching up her crop. As an afterthought, she rummaged in the bottom of her valise and produced a slender, deadly-sharp stiletto. She had never used it, keeping it as a paperknife, but her mouth took on a hard line as she tucked it into her waistband, concealed beneath her jacket.

"But where will you go, my lady, if you succeed in outwitting him?" Hetty's face betrayed genuine alarm. Her mistress's headstrong actions caused her much concern, for she loved her deeply.

"I shall ride for Govora, and there raise an army to punish that damned villain!" Francesca vowed, storming toward the door.

Dusk crept over the forests, the trees rustling with secretive, furry creatures of the night. The mountain tops were touched with crimson, and in the distance they could hear the ever-present roar of water, and the musical sounds of cowbells as the herdsmen drove their goats back to the homesteads to protect them from wolves during the hours of darkness.

The Arab was certainly a high-mettled creature, but recognized Francesca's firm hand on the rein, the knowledgeable pressure of her heel against his ribs, the mastery in her voice. She had known a moment's trepidation when he had been led into the courtyard with flaring scarlet nostrils and rolling eyes, jerking up his proud head on the beautiful arched neck, snorting as his small hooves pawed the ground. She had gentled him, calm and reassuring, making no protest as she was lifted up into his saddle, while the apprehensive stable-boys goggled in amazement. Knowing that Alexis was watching her, she had sat stiffbacked, following the strict training of equestrian school, knee hitched over the pommel, skirt flowing over the Arab's black flank. The Lord of Balvany was in for a shock! He would find her no bungling amateur. Untamed Arab be damned! The earl had expected his daughter to master spirited thoroughbreds of a much more cussed nature than this one!

In silence, they clopped over the drawbridge, taking the pathway which wound along the edge of the ravine. She shot Alexis a sideways glance, sure that he had selected that route to unnerve her, for the view was dizzying, but his dark profile was shuttered and he did not meet her eyes. The track took a sharp, downward turn and they came out on the short, springy turf of a corrie, a semicircular mountain recess which formed a natural amphitheater. The great deep hollow was lit by the glare of the sinking sun.

"We'll race across it," Alexis said curtly.

Francesca nodded and they reined in, side by side. Then, at his shouted signal, they were off. The Arab shot away like a bolt from a crossbow, and Francesca leaned low across his withers, wild exhilaration pounding through her with each light touch of his flying hooves on the spongy soil. Her hair streamed behind her, mingling with his black mane, and she yelled encouragement, urging him on. She had no intention of stopping for she had seen a break in the trees away on the far side and was making for it, certain that she could outstrip pursuit, gallop into the forest, and shake off Alexis.

Aware of nothing but this desperate bid for freedom and the sleek, powerful body under hers, she did not realize that he was fast overtaking her. Suddenly, he was thundering alongside. She was nearly there, the blanket-

ing trees seemed to stretch out welcomingly—one more
effort, a single burst of speed and she would be lost in
the woods. Then she felt the brush of Alexis' thigh as
his horse closed the gap between them, and an arm with
muscles like steel snaked out and fastened round her
waist, effortlessly lifting her from the Arab's back. She
was thrown like a meal sack over the neck of his own
steed. She struggled and swore, but was hanging face
down, feeling the blood rushing into her head. The saddle bumped and bruised her, its hard edges sticking into
her breasts and belly. Alexis had gripped the Arab's
bridle and led him along, slowing his pace and riding
into the woods where a small stream flowed. He dismounted swiftly, hauling her down and settling her on
her feet with a jar. One hand remained clamped round
her wrist, an iron manacle.

They faced one another like two warring cats, both
disheveled and furious. Francesca was breathing heavily,
her breasts rising and falling. His face was a mask of
anger, and the very air seemed to quiver with the
violence of their emotions.

"You treacherous little bitch! You tried to break your
word." He snarled, giving her arm a savage jerk.

"I never gave it!" She flashed, livid with rage at being
thwarted, and her free hand swung up and slapped him
across the mouth with all the force she could muster.
His head snapped back, and his eyes narrowed dangerously, an ugly, tight look crossing his hard features. His
hand shot out, grabbing her tangled hair, yanking her
head backward with such strength that a scream of
mingled fury and pain escaped her. Then his lips came
down on hers with a bruising violence which brought
blood to her mouth as he crushed it beneath his in a
deep, brutal kiss.

For a moment, Francesca hung heavily in his arms, all
the breath knocked out of her, then she reacted to his

touch, her small fists beating against the muscles which scarcely felt her blows. With a muttered grunt, he ignored her frantic efforts, taking her mouth again, forcing her lips apart, exploring her with his tongue. She could do nothing to still the fiery sensations which were racing through her body, though she still squirmed and struggled. Her convulsive movements to escape only added to the flame of lust which was sweeping him as her thighs strained against him, her twisting softness pressing into his groin. She was a faithless, wanton witch, like Maria! This time she was not going to escape him.

She raked at his face with her nails, her claws marking him, the stinging pain adding to his anger and excitement. He caught that punishing hand, and struck the other aside before he ripped open her jacket, tearing at the neck of her shirt, baring her full rounded breasts to his insolent gaze. Outraged and thoroughly frightened by the raw, unleashed desire flaring in his eyes, and by her own unchaste response to his mouth, she suddenly sank her teeth into his hand. Snarling a curse, he dumped her on to the hard ground. As she fell in a sprawled heap, her velvet skirt rode up around her slim hips and her long legs gleamed in the twilight. She was motionless for a second, then she bounded to her feet. His face was hard with hungry passion as she faced him, her lips bruised and scarlet from his avenging mouth, her eyes wide with frightened awareness.

He lunged for her, and she leaped sideways with a cry of terror, prey to conflicting emotions, hating him and his very touch which destroyed her reason. "You're no better than that animal, Zoltan!" she panted.

He spoke with bitter contempt. "And you are making a great show of defending your honor! A highborn whore who has probably been bedded by every debauched rake in London! Don't try to make me believe that you are a virgin saving her maidenhead for the margrave!"

Francesca's heart was beating like a drum, and she was appalled by the imperious, primitive longing which his very presence roused, hating herself for wanting to taste his mouth again, to feel his powerful arms holding her. His anger, his savagery, drove her to fever pitch, but when he reached out for her again, his hand encountered naked steel. With an oath, he pulled back sharply, staring in astonishment at the blood welling from the gash across his palm, glaring at Francesca, who gripped the stiletto firmly as if she knew how to use it.

"Hellcat!" he muttered angrily. "My God, I really believe you would kill me with that pretty bauble, if you got the chance!"

"Oh, I would, sir! I assure you!" she blazed, alert for his every movement, limbs coiled like springs, ready to run.

They were playing a dangerous game and both knew it. Alexis, his golden eyes slits of baffled fury, raked her slender body for a weakness. He was much stronger, but that razor-edged blade gave her an advantage. He felt a grudging admiration for her, so small, so ferocious, spitting venom at him. Then he pounced, twisting her arm behind her back with cruel ease. The knife went spinning off into the bushes. His blood was smearing them both as he grimly held on to her struggling form. "You'll pay for that, slut!" he grated, and flung her to the earth, pinning her down with his heavy body.

Francesca, in a state bordering on shock, lay watching him, her thoughts in a ferment. Uppermost was a curious feeling of terror tinged with an excited desire to finally discover what it would be like to surrender to this man. She was powerless and knew it. One of his long legs was thrown across her thighs, stilling her weak attempts to wriggle free and avoid his hands as they explored her naked breasts, his touch sliding over her warm skin like engulfing fire. His mouth followed his fingers, leaving a tingling trail as he lowered his head, kissing the soft hollow at the base of her throat, nuzzling her breasts, his tongue burning her nipples as they leaped to his lips. Waves of sweet sensation were rolling through her as his mouth left her throbbing breasts and fastened on her lips in a demanding kiss.

She tried to cry out and twist her head to one side, but his mouth captured hers, silencing protest, and he ran a hand over her body. He gently kneaded her flat belly, pushing up her skirts, his invading fingers slipping between her legs. Francesca pressed her thighs together, trying to prevent this outrage, but the tingling, searing flame which exploded within her as he caressed her there made her thrust up her hips to press against that exploring hand. An intent, urgent look changed the expression on his face above her—it was frighteningly bright and animalistic—the unconsciously sensual movement of her pelvis was driving him beyond control, she could feel the naked hardness of his manhood hot against her flesh. She struggled frantically. This had to stop!

Suddenly, he moved so that his body lay over hers. She could feel the sweat soaking through the back of his shirt as her fists pounded him, and the pungent male smell was in her nostrils, his black hair tousled, falling forward across his brow. He was heavy, and though she fought in deadly earnest, mortally afraid of how it would end, his fingers dug brutally into her thrashing thighs as he held her prone on the grass. With one knee he spread wide her legs, undeterred by her frenzied hands as they clawed at his face and throat, her wild attempts to escape only serving to enflame him further. He was muttering, cursing as her nails struck home, any notion of mercy ruthlessly crushed.

Her scratches were smarting on his skin, and he slapped her around the head, shouting, "Stop fighting me! You know you want it as much as I! I can see it in your eyes, taste it on your lips, and feel it in your breasts under my hands!"

"No! You lie!" she yelled, fierce tears of pain and wounded pride sparkling like diamonds on her cheeks in the dim light, her white face a pale blur. The imprint of his open palm was like a brand burning into her flesh, making her his own. For answer, he pinioned her wrists, holding her spread-eagled, then he poised above her trapped body and, with a savage thrust, penetrated her, his size and hardness seeming to split her asunder.

Francesca screamed in agony, but he was deaf to everything except the sweeping demands of his body, moving more and more rapidly until he reached fulfillment, oblivious to the sobbing woman beneath him. He slumped heavily on her for a moment afterward, then supported himself on his elbow, looking down at her. His breathing grew quieter, though she was still shaken by the thudding of his heart. He stroked her hair with an unlooked for gentleness, a hint of apology in his eyes, a wry twist to his lips. "I'm sorry I hurt you, darling, but I had no idea that you were still a virgin."

The assault inflicted on her unwilling body was as nothing to the agony of mind Francesca suffered, and she lay unmoving, speechless, as he stood up and arranged his clothing. Her loins were flooded with pain, but it was humiliation which sent the tears streaming from her eyes. She sprawled there like a dead thing, making no attempt to smooth down her torn skirt or cover her nakedness, and anger and remorse tormented Alexis as he realized that, once again, he had allowed this selfish lust to get the upper hand, blinding him to the stark fact that she had not been playing the tease, was no harlot, and had *really* been fighting for her honor. Self-loathing and bitter disgust sent him to his knees beside her. It was not in his nature to apologize or retract, but he attempted to pull her tattered garments over her nudity.

His touch instilled immediate panic. She rolled away from his reach, eyes wild, her face a twisted mask of terror. "Leave me be! Don't touch me!"

Like a deer cornered by baying hounds, her eyes darted around frantically, seeking escape. Before he could stop her, she was on her feet and away, borne on the wings of an almost insane fear. She plunged through the bushes, running over stony, uneven ground, pushing her way against brambles which tore at her skirt and grass which whipped her legs with wet, stinging lashes. She lost all grip on reality. Pain welled in her, sending bile into her mouth; she bent double, groaning, and was violently sick. But terror that he was after her sent her rushing on again, her head spinning, black spots rising dazzlingly before her eyes, the whole forest heaving. She was scratched and bloody from the thorns and branches which caught at her cruelly in her frenzied flight, and she could feel moisture creeping down the insides of her thighs, certain that he had damaged her so badly that she was bleeding to death from an internal injury.

The undergrowth thinned, and she found herself in a clearing. She gasped, lifting her eyes and looking upward. Above the black regiment of sentinel trees a bank of dense cloud had split to reveal part of the moon's crescent—it was blood-red and startled her. She had not expected it: so sinister, so lovely, so much a part of that insane night. She froze, hearing a weird howling nearby which made her scalp crawl . . . wolves . . . those denizens of this terrible, unfriendly land! It was a scene of brooding desolation. A black stretch of water glistened almost at her feet, a deep, secret mountain lake barring her way. Flanked by treacherous weeds, it lay in a hollow between hills and woodland, darkly foreboding, and she was gripped by fierce, elemental terror, seeing no way round it. Then she thought she heard the bushes rustling behind her. Alexis!

With a cry, she plunged into the icy water. Death would be infinitely preferable to being captured by him. She must escape this gnawing mental torment, this feeling of being torn in pieces, riven by her own weakness which would make her his plaything, his slave! Dark oblivion was what she craved, a cessation of thought, of feeling, just velvet blackness.

The wind freshened, sighing in the reeds, stirring the surface. Her feet sank in the mud, cold crept up her legs, the water sucking at her skirts. Glancing back over her shoulder, she was certain that she saw him, his tall figure outlined against the trees. She lost her footing, sliding into green darkness. Instinct urged her to swim, to fight her way up and fill her lungs with air, but her soggy clothing tangled her legs, dragging her down into the depths. Her nostrils seemed filled with slime; she could taste it, brackish and foul, as if she had swallowed a mouthful of fetid mud. Panic set her heart pumping madly; she felt a touch, like clinging hands on her ankles, tugging her towards destruction. Was it the weeds or the spirits of others who had drowned there? Her chest was bursting, flashes of light stabbing behind her eyelids. Her limbs were weighted, every agonizing movement unnaturally slow; an eon had passed since she entered the water, yet it was only a matter of seconds. The blood was beating in her eye sockets—the thundering in her head rising to a crescendo on which, she knew, she would go spinning off into the void.

Chapter Five

SUDDENLY FRANCESCA felt herself gripped firmly and hauled above the waterline, her face upturned to that strange moon which swung crazily overhead. Her body responded automatically and she gulped in great mouthfuls of air, dimly aware of strong arms about her, thrashing feebly, too weak and winded to protest, then giving up, sliding into a deep, merciful well of unconsciousness.

Alexis, soaked and furious, dragged her to the bank, laying her on the mushy earth while she retched up water. He could see that she had fainted and rolled her over on her stomach so that she did not choke. The water was running in rivulets down his angry, bewildered face. The earlier remorse he had felt was uncomfortable, and he was annoyed and bothered by the feelings of compassion which she aroused. Angry women he could understand and handle, but he had been alarmed by the insane look of desperation on her white face as she had fled into the woods, following her quickly, knowing only too well the dangers lurking there—the wild beasts, the unexpected lakes and crevasses. He had chased her to the clearing, horrified when she plunged into the water, and angry too—the silly wench was trying to drown herself!

He stared down at her inert form in perplexity, then went to his saddle and unbuckled the cloak packed behind it, his boots squelching as he walked. He cradled her limp body gently, murmuring soothing, meaningless words as he carefully wrapped her in its warm folds, then lifted her and laid her across his saddlebrow. With one foot in the stirrup, he swung up easily behind her and, holding the Arab on the leading rein, turned his horse's head toward Balvany, setting off at breakneck speed.

Lights sprang up at the lower windows as he hurtled into the courtyard, stirring everything into flame. He dismounted and carried Francesca into the Great Hall, the servants and guards scurrying to do his bidding. She hung limp as a rag doll, shoulders supported by one of his arms, knees by the other, as he ran lightly up the broad, curving staircase, barking brusque orders, taking her to his own chamber and dumping her down on the bed.

She moaned and stirred as he chaffed her frozen hands; she began to shiver violently and her teeth were chattering. He called to Dinu to prepare a bath then, seizing the decanter which stood on the bedside table, he poured a stiff measure into a glass and forced the brandy into her mouth. She choked and spluttered, coughing up a good deal of it, but some of the fiery liquid crawled down her throat into the pit of her stomach, its warmth fanning out, flooding her veins with life—life, the very thing she had been trying to destroy. Slowly, her wits began to return, though she was still very confused, knowing only that she had stared death in the face and found his countenance not so hideous after all.

Servants were in the room, touching tapers to candles, drawing the thick cloth curtains at the arched windows and setting to work igniting the small twigs and kindling which lay at the base of the logs in the wide hearth. Soon the chamber began to glow, firelight dancing over polished wood and beamed ceiling. Dinu and his minions came bustling in, carrying a huge copper bathtub and placing it before the blaze. White, fluffy towels were spread on the backs of chairs to warm, while bucket after bucket of steaming water was tipped into the tub. While these preparations were in progress, Alexis stripped rapidly, pausing only to take swigs from the decanter, dumping his sodden clothing in a heap for his valet's attention. He stood there naked, unconcerned, his powerful, muscular body red as a demon's in the light of the flaming logs. Then he shrugged his shoulders into a purple East India robe, embroidered with gold thread and generously finished with sable at the neck and cuffs. He fastened a jeweled girdle round his waist.

It was a strange, exotic costume which accentuated his distinctly foreign looks. He stood by the bed looking down at the half-conscious girl, hands on his hips, the huge fur collar making his shoulders seem even wider, the long, sweeping robe with its wide sleeves adding to his height. Under his heavy, hawklike brows, his amber eyes stared at her, narrowing slightly as he gazed into that beautiful face, feeling the stirrings of desire in his loins again. There was a ruthless slant to his mouth as he fought mawkishly sentimental emotions which such lovely helplessness evoked. She was troubling his conscience and he did not like it at all.

Francesca's lids quivered and she opened her eyes on this awesome spectacle in his bizarre attire. A scream rose in her throat as full awareness returned on a painful flood. In an involuntary movement, she shrank back on the bed, fires of defiance beginning to blaze in the depths of her emerald eyes. Alexis relaxed, seeing that hatred and resentment. She was still a spitfire, and he was relieved. Had she wept, he would have found it well nigh impossible to resist soothing and petting her, giving way to abominable weakness! This was much better. The blind, unseeing stare which she had worn after he had raped her was gone, but there was still a pinched look about her mouth which disturbed him.

The servants had left and they were alone. He gave a mocking bow and said, "Your bath is ready, madame."

Francesca stared at him uncomprehendingly, still paralyzed by the fear he instilled. The room was unfamiliar, though fine; its walls hung with oriental tapestries, a couch piled with cushions near the fire, curious statues and ornaments on shelves and court cupboards. The enormous bed where she lay had damask draperies embroidered with lilies, and took up a lot of space in the chamber, large though it was. For light, there were the leaping flames in the carved chimney and the soft glimmer of tall yellow candles standing in a huge bronze tripod. Her wide eyes alighted on the gleaming tub, wisps of steam rising from its interior.

She glared at him angrily, realizing that he had her trapped in the master chamber, his own room. "Why am I here? I want my maid, Hetty. You surely do not expect me to expose myself to you?"

Alexis rocked on his heels with laughter, flinging up his wild head and subjecting her to a bold stare. "You're mighty shy! Don't forget that I have done more than look at you! And from now on, you will reside here, where I can keep an eye on you. I have no intention of affording you another chance to give me the slip!"

"But that is monstroud. I need my women about me," she spluttered, almost speechless at his effrontery. His robe was open to his waist, revealing a tanned chest with its mat of curling hair, and she experienced a stab of fear as she remembered the feel of that strong body. It was like some vivid nightmare. Perhaps she was dreaming at that very moment—if so, she decided, she would dream herself back in her own bed in England and pray the rest of the night away. She closed her eyes in sudden anguish. If only she had been more sensible, followed the wise advice of those who knew better, instead of running off with that philanderer, Mark! But it was too late for futile wishes now and, opening her eyes under the fringe of sooty lashes, she saw that he was still regarding her closely.

Unable to control herself, she begged, "Let me go! You've had your selfish pleasure, now send me to Count Carl!" It cost her a great effort to plead, but she was willing to do almost anything if only her life could continue as before—though she knew despairingly that, since meeting Alexis, it would never be the same again. Her eyes swam with unshed tears, and she bit her lip to still its betraying tremble.

His black brows drew down in a scowl above his aquiline nose. "Don't be a fool!" he snapped, and threw himself down beside her, drawing her struggling body close to his own. She was pushed into the feather mattress and he lay with one leg half covering hers, with a mercurial change of mood, smiling down into her furious face. He gently smoothed back the tangle of wet tresses from her forehead and surprised her by saying seriously, "You must get out of those wet things and into a hot bath immediately, or you'll start a fever." He cupped her chin in one hand, holding her firmly and staring into her alarmed eyes. The look he gave her was almost blinding in its intensity. "Listen, stop fighting me. I am sorry for the way I took you. If I had known you were a virgin, I should have treated you more gently."

Astonishment held her still. The lordly and arrogant Alexis was actually apologizing to her! Was there no end to the perplexing moods of this quixotic individual?

Then he added, with a laugh, "And incidentally, you are making my bed wet, and I intend that you shall share it with me tonight."

Francesca's mouth dropped open in outrage, but he did not seem to notice for the cloak had fallen apart, displaying her nearly naked body. Instinctively, she attempted to gather the folds together but he stopped her, moving his hands caressingly over her cold flesh, saying, musingly: "God, you're so beautiful. It would be sacrilege to send you to Carl."

Her hopes plummeted. Though she had little inclination to join her unknown betrothed, the alternative of staying in this den of savages horrified her. She was bitterly disappointed at her failure to escape, and now found herself in a far worse position than before. She cursed herself for a fool. Had she only been content to wait patiently until Luca returned from Govora, she might soon have been peaceably on her way; but no— ever rash and impetuous, she had given Alexis the opportunity to deflower her. Whatever the outcome now, the indisputable, damning fact remained, that she was soiled, certainly no fit bride for a margrave.

She could not deny the sense of Alexis' advice about her health; she was chilled to the bone, and the thought of a long, leisurely soak was most appealing. If only he would go away and leave her in blissful solitude. It was obvious that he had no intention of doing so. And yet, very curiously, it seemed so right to be lying next to him—it was like going home—a dark recognition, unlike anything she had ever experienced with other men. He was so familiar, just as if she had known him before in another lifetime—but this was impossible. The feeling left her breathless, as if she had been flung into a mysterious whirlpool, fighting the spinning emotions which held her in thrall. Stubbornly, she reminded herself of his callous disregard for her opinions or desires, fighting to quell the warm, throbbing ache that flared at his disturbing touch.

He began to undress her slowly, peeling off the garments which clung damply to her unresisting form, made a little clumsy by the bandage which Dinu had bound round his hand, referring to it jokingly, teasing her for being as quick as a gypsy to draw her sharp poniard. Francesca allowed herself to relax, too weak to resist the tide which was sweeping her remorselessly on. When she was naked, he scooped her up in his arms and carried her to the waiting bath.

Seconds later, she was luxuriating in the scented water and nothing, not even his shattering presence, could spoil her enjoyment as the warmth flowed round her abused body. Alexis took his ease, lounging on the bed watching her, for all the world like some Eastern potentate contemplating the favorite of his harem. She intrigued and infuriated him by turns. Was she really a sultry temptress or a half-awakened maiden? And she was the margrave's future wife. An ugly emotion coiled round his gut at the thought. Why should his hated enemy possess this exasperating mixture of high-spirited girlhood which contrasted bewilderingly with her obviously well-educated background? This bewitching creature with her softly yielding body which could suddenly change into freezing dignity, making him feel like a debased ravisher! She was undeniably lovely, seated in the tub, knees drawn up, red-brown hair in a damp, waving mass which changed her whole character, making her features take on a magical, ethereal look, as if he had indeed snatched a naiad from the deeps, bringing her home to enchant him. There was no knowing what went on inside that pretty head; her changing moods were as elusive as quicksilver. He was experienced with women. There had been many since Maria, but he had never loved again. Now his knowledge recognized her eager response to his kisses, yet he was never sure if she was going to turn on him, rending and tearing. But with it all, she was never boring! Her anger against him rankled, though. Oddly, he wanted her to think well of him, but was cynically impatient with himself for such a mawkish idea!

Francesca, soaping herself vigorously, as if to erase his touch, refused to look at him, her lashes lowered modestly even though she was tinglingly aware of him. When she was ready, he padded over on bare feet, holding out one of the warm towels, and she had no choice but to rise from the bath and allow him to enfold her in its softness. They stood by the fire and he kept one arm about her, rubbing her back dry with the other hand.

"That's better," he said quietly. "I don't want you to be ill. The water of that lake comes straight down from the mountains and is mostly composed of melted snow. There's nothing quite so chilling." He seated himself in one of the big, padded armchairs with its festoons of fringing, drawing her down beside him. "And now, let us do something about that hair."

She crouched at his feet, staring into the peaks and caverns of the embers, while he took another towel and dried her tresses, soothing her as if she was a highstrung filly. Francesca, though tense at first, gradually leaned back against his knees, a feeling of well-being bubbling inside her. The only sounds in the room were the soft hiss and crackle of the logs; it was as if everyone else in the castle slept, held under some spell, and they alone inhabited it. Time had stopped and they were bewitched, drowning in each other's eyes, afraid to speak lest the enchantment be broken.

He found her a black velvet robe, almost as exotic as his own, and she slipped it on, her back turned coyly to him so that she missed the smile which crossed his face at this reticence. Shortly afterward, Dinu appeared, staggering under the weight of a tray filled with dishes. Tempting smells rose when he lifted the covers with a flourish, setting a small table before the fire within easy reach of their chairs, before bowing himself out, a knowing look in his eyes which made a hot blush flood Francesca's cheeks.

It was a strangely peaceful meal after so much violence. Alexis was at his most charming, and they circled warily, two cautious protagonists who intended to know each other better. She found herself telling him about London, the words tumbling from her lips as she talked of her father, tongue loosened by the Tokay with which he plied her. She stopped with a jerk, finding it all too easy to be disarmed by his apparent interest, his leading questions.

He pulled the cork from a dusty green bottle which Dinu had placed near the fire to warm. "You must taste this, it is Chardonnay, a fine wine."

She wanted to protest, to place her hand over her glass, saying that she had already drunk enough, but he filled another, misunderstanding, nodding and agreeing that she was quite right not to taint it with the dregs of Tokay. She sipped the rich red liquid, full-bodied and warm in her throat, saying rather tartly, "You keep a good table and an excellent cellar. How does a brigand find the money for this?"

A frown creased his brow, the good feeling evaporating. "As a 'brigand,' as you so succinctly put it, you should realize that you are sharing my spoils. But can you honestly say that it is less palatable through being roughly appropriated?"

She had to concede defeat on this point, unable to

resist smiling at him, but the sharp reminder of his profession jarred the atmosphere. "In England, highwaymen are hanged if they are caught," she informed him, "and I suppose that you are their equivalent."

"My death would be much more painful than mere hanging." That somber, brooding look had returned to his face. One of his long, strong hands was resting on the table, and in the other he twirled the stem of his goblet thoughtfully. The light gleamed on the heavy gold ring on his little finger. Set with a garnet, it sent out sullen, reddish sparks. "Duchess Renata cannot wait for the opportunity."

"Why is there this emnity between you?" Eager to know heart and mind, she was snatching up each crumb of information.

His heavy-lidded gaze returned to her face, and one dark, curved eyebrow shot up. "It is a long story, darling, and one which I'll not waste time discussing now. Maybe, one day you will understand. Take my word for it, the duchess does not like 'brigands,' particularly those who aid the peasants."

The wine was taking its toll, and she lay back in her chair sleepily, unable to tear her eyes from that handsome face, dwelling on his mouth, so beautifully molded, which could bark order, wound her with harsh words, threaten to seduce her with deep kisses. "This is a barbaric country," she ventured, her tongue tripping on the words. "So unlike England where everything is soft, green and moist. These savage mountains, the great chasms, the forests filled with wolves and other wild beasts . . ." She gave a little shudder. "It is like nothing I have ever known."

"It's the most beautiful place in the world," he avowed, and his eyes glittered with a passionate enthusiasm as he told her some of the history of Balvany. She was seeing an entirely new aspect of his character: the responsibility he felt with regard to his men, his concern for the villagers, his feeling for the gypsies camping in his domain. It gave her a sense of awe and heightened her growing respect. "You've seen so little of it yet," he continued as they conversed, each probing the other, and he was surprised at the intelligence she displayed. He leaned forward, topping up their glasses, and it was as if she spoke with a liege lord, not a common robber. "Soon it will be the harvest festival and, if you are still with us, you must attend this great occasion. Custom and tradition are strong here, and superstition too. The gypsies are wise in their ways, and even the peasants encourage them to perform magic dances to insure a good crop next year."

She wanted to ask him about the duke and Elvire, and his own kinship with them, but was still shy of him, half-expecting a rebuff. There were so many confusing contradictions here. If he loved the land so much, was so well-versed in command and so clever, why was he not high in the duchess's favor, helping her to run the domain?

Alexis had been diverted by her artless questions, but now his eyes rested on her face, her eyelids drooping languidly, her red lips glistening. She was curled up like a kitten in the chair, and his glance slid over the exquisitely formed body barely hidden by the robe. She saw his face change and harden, very aware of how easily her covering could be discarded. Her breath shortened, heart pumping in anticipation and fear. Francesca was warm and well-fed, dizzy with the sweetish, heavy, aromatic wine, and it was as much as she could do to move at all, her limbs leaden. It must be very late, she decided, for the fire was burning low as she gazed owlishly at it. Alexis lounged up from his seat, stretching and yawning, pushing aside the table and coming across to rest an arm on either side of her, leaning down, brushing his lips over her waiting mouth. The wine fumes stunned her, the room whirling and dipping, and she clung to him to steady herself.

"You've had a little too much to drink, my dear, coupled with the exhaustions of the day," he murmured. There was no passion in the arms that held her so securely; his eyes showed only mocking amusement as they gazed down into her puzzled ones. His unexpected change of manner completely bewildered her, and she was intensely aware of a desire that he remain in this charmingly soothing mood. A shy smile appeared at the corner of her mouth and he was sharply conscious of a queer jump in the region of his heart, for she looked so very vulnerable and childlike. And, much to her alarm, Francesca found that she did not want to move —she wanted to stay there in the haven of his arms.

Alexis released her, straightening his back, leaving her with an aching, unfulfilled emptiness. He smiled down at her flushed face, seeing the softly parted lips, the look in her eyes, and fought his own instincts, surprising her even more by leading her to the bed with an arm slung carelessly over her shoulders. He flung back the covers and she was glad to creep beneath them, giving a deep, tired sigh, lying back among the pillows as he determinedly tucked her in.

"Sleep, little one," he said softly, and she felt a light kiss on her forehead as she drifted on a cloud of numbness. She noted the movement of the bed as he lay beside her but, in her hazy state, felt no start of fear as his arm rested across her. It was almost the comforting touch of a friend. Then nothing could hold her back from slumber, and she slipped into oblivion as if it were a deep, soft, feather mattress.

Francesca woke suddenly. The room was in darkness, save for a faint dull glow from the ashes in the hearth, but a slight, almost imperceptible lightness at the edges of the window drapes told her that dawn was not far away. For a moment, she lay there, the faint smell of burned candlewax pervaded the air, then recollection came flooding back, filling her with burning shame. She groaned and buried her face in her hands, all too aware of Alexis still sleeping at her side. She had never before shared a bed with a man and, all night, her dreams had been vaguely disturbed by his alien presence; though she had been too deeply enmeshed in sleep to think it more than part of a dream.

The light grew stronger. Somewhere outside the confines of the castle, a cock began to crow, his strident call stirring the birds in the crowding pines. Balvany began to wake. She could hear sounds from the mess hall: the barking of one of the hounds, the squeak and rattle of the pulley as a bucket was lowered into the well in the courtyard, the thump and rumble of logs being rolled into the Great Hall. As memory returned, disgust racked her; she wanted to leap from the couch and take another bath in an attempt to cleanse her flesh. The only thing she craved was a cup of fresh water. It was as if defilement had settled on her skin, under her nails and in her hair and, catching sight of her torn, muddied garments lying on the floor by the bed, she thought: I shall never be able to wear them again without remembering him.

Alexis felt her sudden movement and rolled over beneath the sheet, throwing one heavy thigh over her legs, trapping her. His hand came to rest possessively on her hip. She lay stiffly, legs clamped together, arms held rigid at her sides; his head was against her shoulder and she felt his lips begin to traverse her skin sleepily. He kissed the side of her averted cheek, then her ear, rubbing his chin over her bare arm, making her shudder. She realized that she was naked, wondering anxiously just at what point during the night he had removed the black dressing robe. She unsuccessfully battled with a queer flash of pleasure that washed over her, seducing her from her purpose. There was something wickedly decadent about lying in bed with a good-looking rogue. It made her feel deliciously wanton, worldly and sinful! Their union had not been sanctified by either church or man, and everything dark and dangerous in her nature responded to this forbidden situation. It had been firmly under control until he awakened. She had been feeling saintly, very martyred and full of noble resolve, but now she had to will her body not to respond to him, straining away to the far side of the tumbled bed to avoid giving in to the wild urge to meet his hunger with demands of her own. He would not free her, chuckling deep in his throat, fully awake now, mocking her in the dawn light.

"I want to get up!" she hissed through her teeth. "Release me at once!"

She was struggling in earnest now, filled with unhappy, mixed emotions. What was happening to her? She hated him! He had captured her, dishonored her, treated her nearly as badly as Zoltan, and yet she had felt the beginnings of friendship with him last night, and now wanted to melt into his arms, for all her pride. Alexis' good humor had fled and he became furiously aware that she was deliberately holding herself aloof. It would have been so easy to have his way with her, but he hankered after a willingness which she was steadfastly denying.

"What the hell's the matter?" He muttered savagely. "All right, pretend that you don't enjoy my caresses, but I've a notion that you resist yourself more than me. I'd lay a wager that the time will shortly come when you'll be begging me to take you!"

"Never!" she retorted hotly, throwing him a sullen look.

"You'd best resign yourself to the fact that, until you leave here, I can have you whenever I fancy," he stated unpleasantly, on his feet in one lithe movement, while she sat up painfully, glaring at him through the tears which smarted in her eyes.

"I hate you, Le Diable!" she spat. "I'll be revenged on you, I swear it—though it take me a lifetime!"

"Rot!" he snapped contemptuously and stalked naked to the window, jerking back the curtains. Undaunted by the chill air, he threw open the casement, leaning on the stone sill, gazing out at the rugged landscape. "You like it, but you're such a damned hypocrite that you won't admit it!"

He was an arresting figure and Francesca stared hard at his indifferent back, trying not to admire him. The daylight filtering in glittered on his ruffled black curls, the gold of his eyes was hidden beneath his brooding lids, the high cheekbones and sensitive, tormented mouth were bathed in the first rays of the sun, his chin and the hollows of his cheeks shadowed in contrast. His body was magnificent—with a splendid breadth through chest and shoulders, sleek narrow hips with tight buttocks, and handsome, muscular legs. His flesh was hard-surfaced, the skin of his torso browned by exposure to the sun. Every movement he made had the easy gracefulness of an animal, seemingly unhurried, but lithe and quick.

Devastatingly handsome he might be, but he was also an exasperating boor she decided, still outraged because he had taken advantage of her and subdued her by force. Her lips curled, she narrowed her eyes to green slits, and rose to her feet, gathering the sheet about her as if it were an imperial robe, haughtily reminding herself of her station in life. Stony-faced, she asked, "May I leave now? I would like to go to my room. I have need of the ministrations of my maid after your treatment!"

He turned, padding lightly across the floor and picking up his clothes. There was an amused twitch at the corners of his mouth. "I told you last night that you are to remain here. I'll ring for Dinu to fetch Hetty, my dear."

He tugged at the bellpull near the chimney, while Francesca stood guardedly in the center of the room with only the sheet covering her nakedness. "How soon are you expecting an answer from the duchess?" she demanded icily, inferring that the quicker she left the castle and his loathsome company the better.

"A few days, perhaps," he shrugged, and began to dress, tucking his shirt into the high-waisted dark red breeches, stamping his feet down into his black leather boots until they fitted, skintight, round his slim, shapely legs. His smile deepened as he put on his jacket with the wide-cuffed sleeves, adjusting the frills at his wrists. "Time aplenty to give you lessons in the art of making love. I shall send you to the margrave, a most accomplished mistress. Not that he will appreciate it."

"What do you mean?" A puzzled frown knit her wing-shaped brows.

He gave a mysterious, maddening wink, and tapped his nose significantly. "Did they not tell you what kind of a fellow to expect in your prospective bridegroom? No? Then you'll have to wait and find out, won't you?"

He turned to face the mirror, fastening the neckband of the lace-edged cravat which fell across his chest. He wore his finery with a kind of careless arrogance; it served to emphasize his almost overwhelming masculinity. Francesca gave a small, weary shake of her head. His abrupt changes of mood were baffling and his words alarmed her. What further unexpected horrors lay in store? What was wrong with Carl? Why had her father not been honest with her? The more she heard of the Pascaly family, the more her apprehension deepened. Alexis did nothing to still her confusion and she wished that he would remain the hard-faced, terrifying stranger; instead of sometimes appearing beguiling, even fascinating—the sort of man one might love, not hate.

Now he was smiling crookedly at her, his hair neatly brushed back, though one lock strayed carelessly across his brow, and she fell prey to a treacherous, trembling feeling of anticipation, like a child on Christmas Eve, as if at any moment something wonderfully exciting was going to happen. Dear God! she thought in despair. He twists my emotions into such knots that I can't think rationally any more!

Dinu knocked and then entered, the borzoi loping at his heels. He made for his master, his long feathery tail swishing, and Alexis reached down to fondle his ears and pointed muzzle with a kindness which Francesca had never seen him display to humans, certainly not to her! She felt almost jealous of Titus.

The valet grinned at her while he listened to Alexis' instructions and, a short time later, Hetty arrived with a gaggle of servants hefting Francesca's luggage. Lavinia still lay abed, for which Francesca was thankful. The very last thing she felt able to cope with was being cross-questioned by her chaperone. Hetty, with her womanly intuition, guessed what had happened, annoying Francesca, when they were alone, by being enthusiastically pleased.

"He's a fine man," she kept repeating, while she unpacked her mistress's belongings in her usual slapdash manner. "Lord love you, ma'am, I'd not say him nay! Dinu says he's a real gentleman."

"Then why is he living like this? Answer me that!" Francesca retorted, in a very belligerent frame of mind. She was lost in a sea of uncertainty, fostering a burning sense of injustice to uphold and sustain her, vowing to

bring him to his knees. It gave her a sour satisfaction to
see her frilly, feminine garments making the austere,
bachelor atmosphere of his room untidy, and she swept
the top of the dressing table clean of his shaving equip-
ment, setting her cosmetic pots and perfume bottles
there instead. He wanted her in his room, and by God
he would have her, and all that it entailed!

To calm her jangling nerves, she dressed with more
than usual care, painting her face and having Hetty
arrange her hair. It was like putting on a masquerade
costume, something to hide behind, and gave her a feeling of stability, making it easier to forget last night and
her own shocking part in the affair. She had selected a
dress of flowered muslin, girlishly trimmed with arti-
ficial rosebuds, not realizing that she was making a
desperate bid to retain some symbol of virginity. In it
she looked quite charmingly fresh and untainted, but
her face gave her away, for there were blue smudges
beneath her eyes, and she was suddenly convinced that
she was haggard, as if that lurid night had imprinted
itself on her countenance for all time.

Her ruffled ego was soothed when she went out later
with Mark. They had been allowed to stroll on that
stretch of smooth sward beyond the drawbridge, well
within sight of the guards, and he was recovering from
his injuries, dandified as ever, breathing of comfortingly civilized behavior.

"They are saying in the castle that you lay with Alexis
last night," he said as they paused where a rough stone
wall girded the ravine. He reached across to cover one
of her hands with his, noting the hardness in her eyes.
"Is this true?"

Since hearing the gossip early that morning, he had
amazed himself by experiencing spasms of jealousy.
Until then, he had believed that he cared little for
Francesca now that her dowry was denied him, and yet

he felt admiration for her courage, watching as she defied Alexis, a veritable Amazon! Today, she looked more than lovely: there was an ambience about her which had told him even before he asked that Alexis had established her in womanhood—every male in the vicinity was aware of it.

She nodded, sighing deeply. "He took me by force, Mark, and insists that I sleep in his room, but I'll not share his bed again. I swear it! I'd rather lie on the floor!"

His face was stoical, eyes staring into the distance, a little muscle quivering at the side of his jaw. "I feared that it would happen when you rode off with him. Were I capable of heroics, I suppose that I should challenge him to a duel, but I am a poet, not a warrior. All I can offer is my sympathy." She gave a start of surprise, looking at him with questioning eyes, remembering his heartless behavior in the forest. He stopped her words by placing a fingertip on her lips. "I know that you doubt me, and admit that I am a blackguard and far from honorable; but I have this confounded weakness for the gaming tables. I hope that, in time, you will forgive me."

Her heart warmed to him, reading in his face an echo of her own deep misgivings. She was glad that she could communicate with him again, for she had loved him once—or imagined she did—and now needed friends desperately. So she gave him her most dazzling smile and tucked her hand into the crook of his arm as they continued their walk, heads together, deep in conversation. She was totally unaware that Alexis stood on the battlements watching them through slitted eyes, his hands knuckled into hard fists on his hips, his expression suspicious and wrathful.

Chapter Six

FRANCESCA DID not see Alexis again until evening and spent the afternoon playing whist with Lavinia, Mark and Ranby in the solar. Her old tutor did not reproach her in any way, but she did catch him watching her oddly once or twice, a question in his eyes which sent the crimson into her cheeks. Lavinia had been itching to find out if there was any truth in the rumors circulating around the castle, but Francesca put her in her place, coldly reminding her that she was a mere servant in the earl's pay, and had no right to cross-examine her. As it grew darker, she experienced a sinking sensation in the stomach, remembering Alexis' hard eyes, and knowing that she dared not disobey him. Soon her servants would have their curiosity satisfied, for he had given orders to the guards that she could no longer occupy her room and must use his.

Roger came, at Alexis' instructions, to conduct Francesca to the Great Hall for supper. They feasted by torchlight, and she was on edge, only too conscious of the man seated at the head of the table in his carver, staring at her unwinkingly. His face was moodily pensive, perturbing gaze somber under the black brows, taking little heed of his roistering companions. She gave up the pretense of eating, a blush staining her cheeks at their sidelong glances, their winks and bawdy comments, anger surging up against him for putting her in this shameful situation. With her tawny head held high, she glared across at him, only to be infuriated still further when he raised his glass to her in mocking salute. She sat like a statue, enduring the embarrassment for what seemed a dragging eternity, terrified of the night ahead. At last he rose, bidding his men adieu, turning and crossing to the stairs. He glanced toward Francesca, who still sat in dumb confusion, and paused to wait for her. With as much hauteur as she could muster, she stood up on trembling legs, ignoring the jests and raillery, passing him and leading the way to his chamber, burning with fury under his amused stare.

He closed the door behind them and moved about the room, perfectly at home in its firelit warmth, shedding his jacket and hanging it on the back of a chair. Francesca, seething, stood watching him, her bosom rising and falling with the quickness of her agitated breathing.

"I suppose you realize that you have made me a laughing stock," she challenged coldly. "The whole community of Balvany thinks I am your whore!"

He stood, legs apart, on the hearth, warming his back at the fire, and she could not see the expression on his face clearly, but heard a note of laughter in his voice. "Tush! For so dainty a damsel you can be incredibly foulmouthed, Francesca. In point of fact, were you my light-o'-love, I'd expect far more warmth and less whining."

"What?" She yelled, longing to hit him. "I don't whine!"

"Ha!" he barked derisively, flinging himself onto the couch and commencing to tug off his boots. "You've done naught but complain since you came here. Screeching like a fishwife!"

Deeply mortified, she retorted, "Well, sir, if you are

to descend to name-calling, I'll state that you are a lecher and a swaggerer!''

His brow darkened, and she felt a quake of fear as he continued to undress, chuckling unpleasantly. ''Hoity-toity! Madame objects to being classed as having the temperament of one of the lower orders, eh?''

''You are insufferable!'' she countered, her eyes, like frozen emeralds, staring at him, at first his hose, then waistcoat and shirt, came off. She was almost painfully aware of how the firelight played over his bronze skin and the way the firm muscles of his back and shoulders rippled with every movement. Hurriedly, she averted her gaze when he started to unfasten his breeches, letting them drop to the rug unconcernedly, while she stood there indecisively, discomforted by her lack of privacy, offended by his offhand manner.

She heard him pad across the floor and the creak of the ornate fourposter as he took possession of it. Damn him! she thought angrily. I suppose he's waiting for me to join him. Well, he'll wait until doomsday. I'd rather sleep in the stables!

Yet, beneath the bravado, she was close to tears in this humiliating situation, bone weary and needing to rest. The couch by the side of the fire looked inviting, but she was accustomed to having a maid in attendance and needed Hetty. Fierce pride would not allow her to stoop and ask this favor, so she stalked regally to the armoire where Hetty had pushed aside some of Alexis' clothes to make room for her mistress's. Francesca took one of her pretty nightgowns from a hanger; a pink silk affair, cut like a chemise but longer, with a great deal of ribbon trimming and big, ballooning sleeves. With it went a matching peignoir, and she carried these purposefully back to the hearth, though her heart thumped at the thought of having to undress with that barbarian eying her the while! She would have much preferred to

remain fully clad, but her boned bodice was too uncomfortable to sleep in. There was nothing else to be done
—somehow, she had to change while preserving as
much maidenly modesty as was humanly possible. How
she hated Alexis at that moment! Without a doubt, he
was thoroughly enjoying this spectacle and had deliberately engineered it to make life as difficult as possible
for her!

Keeping her back turned to the bed and its insolent
occupant, she struggled with the lacing which closed the
front of the bodice, cursing beneath her breath as she
broke a fingernail in the attempt.

"D'you need any help?" inquired a lazy voice from
the depths of the comfortable, canopied mattress which
she had shared with him the night before.

"No, thank you!" she ground out, dashed in her
hopes that he might have dropped off, thus missing her
muttered exclamations of irritation. With flushed
cheeks, she completed her toilet, thankful that the room
was in darkness except for the leaping flames. She
warmed herself by them for a while, trying to get her
thoughts into some sort of order.

Alexis was far from asleep, sharply aware of her
slightest move, though he lay there casually relaxed, his
narrowed eyes revealing the only sign of tenseness. His
self-control had been sorely tested as he watched Francesca removing her garments, and now his quick passions were goading him almost beyond the limits of his
iron will, for Francesca was unaware of the transparency of her gown as she lingered uncertainly near the
glowing logs. Her body was clearly outlined, bathed in a
rose hue, her full, coral-tipped breasts temptingly
defined, as was the dark, shadowy triangle between her
legs, and her unbound hair gleamed like copper, flowing
nearly to her waist. God damn the wench! Why did she
shrink from him so, when he remembered only too well

their first kiss in the forest on the day they met, when he had tasted the warmth and passion of which he knew she was capable?

She sighed, and glided toward the couch, her diaphanous robe undulating about her slender limbs in a manner which almost made him groan with the desire to relieve the surging of his loins. He gritted his teeth against this wild spasm of longing. He had as much, if not more, excessive pride as she. He'd neither force himself on her nor beg. She must make the first move. He angrily swore that he would roast in hellfire before he let the little bitch know how much he wanted her!

She curled on the couch, pulling a cushion under her head and trying to cover herself with the peignoir. Alexis sat up abruptly, swinging his legs over the side of the bed. Francesca's breath caught in her throat with the fear that the sight of his male nudity aroused. She clasped her arms across her breasts, and he read the terror in the green eyes lifted to his. There was a cold, implacable look on his face as he angrily jerked one of the fur covers from the bed, throwing it over her.

"Take it!" he ordered brusquely, his big hands almost forcing it round her body. "I don't want to listen to you moaning about my brutality tomorrow, saying that I compelled you to freeze to death!"

"If you are so concerned, why don't you let me occupy the bed?" she asked flatly, feeling weak and unsure at his nearness.

He bowed ironically, gesturing toward it with a sweep of one arm. "You are welcome to your half. I'm not stopping you. It's wide enough for two."

"You know full well what I mean," she stammered, finding it difficult to hold a coherent conversation with him, for he had a disconcerting habit of looking straight into her eyes, unblinking and compelling, until she forgot what she was about to say and trailed off into bemused silence. She gathered her wits with an effort, adding "Your behavior is most ungallant."

"I am not renowned for my gallantry, particularly to ladies," he answered with a grim twist to his mouth. "I've always found them perverse, willful jades and you do nothing to alter my opinion. I bid you goodnight, madame, and trust that the discomforts brought about by your own deuced stubbornness do not prevent you from slumbering."

There was stunned bewilderment as well as relief in her widely spaced eyes as she stared at him for a moment. He swung away from her and flung himself into the middle of the tester bed, wrapping the covers about him, and soon his deep, even breathing filled the room. Francesca eased the pelt round her, though it kept slipping, making her prey to drafts, while sleep evaded her. She was too aware of his presence so close to her, stirred by some strange, pleasurable spark that flickered along her taut nerves.

Though convinced that she would never be able to rest, the first rosy hues of dawn were creeping through the drapes when she was roused by noises in the room. She was awake and on guard in an instant. Dinu was moving about, there was a breakfast tray on the table, an earthenware pitcher of water on the dressing table, and Alexis stood before the mirror, shaving.

He cocked an eyebrow at her, one side of his face covered with lather. "Good morning. Did you sleep well?"

What a question! She was stiff all down one side from being too long in an awkward position, her head ached and her feet were frozen. The rug had slipped off during the night. She sat up crossly, sipping at the strong, sweet coffee which Dinu solemnly offered her. "Well enough," she muttered ungraciously.

"You will become accustomed to the fact that I rise

early." Alexis was using the cutthroat razor with sure, practiced swipes. "Today, I hunt. There are many mouths to feed."

He was naked to the waist and she could not help noticing that several small scars marked his body and the muscles beneath his tanned skin spoke of a hard, rigorous life, much of which was spent wielding a sword or in the saddle. A man of courage and tenacity, unused to taking his ease, scorning leisure—he was a complete antithesis to the men she had known in the past, and presented an intriguing challenge. Would it be possible to break that iron reserve? Not that she was interested, of course! The fellow was a bad-mannered oaf! She couldn't wait for him to get out of the room, so that she might rise under the calming influence of Hetty.

She huddled beneath the pelt, smoothing a hand over her disordered hair, and threw him a sullen look. "Must I still remain here?"

Alexis washed off the razor, dabbed his smooth cheeks dry and came over to stand by the couch, one hand on the carved overmantle, staring down at her, his expression a mixture of concern, amusement and impatience. "You may roam the castle at will and take short walks outside, under guard," he repeated slowly, as if dealing with an obdurate child.

Dinu was going about his business, making up the fire, laying out his master's clothing, his face inscrutable; but she knew he must be listening and, most probably laughing at her. Stung to rage, she almost leaped up, then remembered her flimsy nightwear. Blushing hotly, for Alexis' eyes were running over her half-exposed breasts with unconcealed interest, she stormed at him.

"I hope you realize what you have done to me! My life was planned before you abducted me! I was to marry Mark . . ."

"I thought you were intended for the margrave," he interrupted with a cynical twist to his lips.

She brushed this aside, swept on by her indignation, her wounded pride, and that disturbing emotion which she could not yet name. "No matter . . . I was happy . . . looking forward to the future . . . then you came along . . . capturing me . . . violating me! You had no right to do it! The callous action of a greedy mercenary out for gain. Totally uncivilized!"

"You judge harshly, madame, without knowing the truth," he said sternly, eyes and mouth hard as he dressed rapidly, finally swinging his cloak about his shoulders and reaching for his hat.

"Can you deny that you are a vagabond?" she shouted, wanting to prevent him from striding away from her with so much still unexplained between them. "What are your plans? Or do you just live from day to day, appeasing your lusts where you will?"

Alexis paused with his hand on the door handle, looking back over his shoulder, his face dark and tormented. "If I told you my hopes and aspirations, you'd not believe me."

"Why don't you try?" She was sitting bolt upright, her hands slim and white against the darkness of the fur clasped to her bosom, her great green eyes wide, almost pleading.

"Lady, you are difficult to understand," he barked and slammed out.

Alarming, unhappy thoughts nibbled and snapped in her mind as she automatically bathed and allowed Hetty to dress her, and it was in this delicate, wavering mood that she passed the day, pleading a headache so that she did not have to face Alexis at supper. This was no lie, for her temples had been throbbing relentlessly for hours, her scalp sore with tension and worry. She sought her makeshift bed early, snuggling down among the furs, going to sleep at once. Later she woke, half-opening her eyes and seeking the source of the candle-light which roused her when Alexis came dropping into bed in the small hours. She snapped them tight shut again to avoid having to talk to him, turning deeper into the warm pelt, listening to his quiet movements, drowsily content.

Next morning while they breakfasted, she remarked on his lateness, wanting to break the oppressive silence. He seemed exhausted, moody and preoccupied, but looked up, giving her a piercing glance.

"Were you worried, my dear? Such charming concern." The sarcasm rolled out from between his contemptuous lips. "I was not lying in the arms of another woman, if that's what is bothering you!" He stabbed his dagger into the rapidly cooling chop on his plate, and Francesca bit her lip, immediately regretting her impulse to start a conversation.

"It is of complete indifference to me in whose bed you lie," she answered steadily, denying the wild lift of relief which sent her soaring, refusing to admit that this thought had been plaguing her.

"Good!" he bit the word off savagely, slamming his napkin down on the table and pushing back his chair with an impatient force which set the china rattling and slopped the water in the fingerbowls. "What I do or where I go is none of your damned business!"

With a final, wrathful glare, he stamped out of the room, leaving Francesca staring after him, resentment sending scarlet shafts of anger bolting through her. "Oh, that pigheaded bastard!" she hissed into the sudden silence of the chamber, a chamber which rang with emptiness after his explosive departure. "To dare presume that I care about him!"

That evening, Alexis was absent from the supper table. "He's tending Titus," Roger explained with a smile at her inquiry. "He was impaled by a boar's tusk when hunting yesterday, and Alexis spent most of last night with him. I doubt that he'll recover."

So that's where he was! Why could he not have told me? Francesca thought agitatedly, remembering Titus with his flowing, elegance, his devotion to Alexis. Compassion stirred her. He would take it badly if his favorite hound were to die. She said little during the meal, though Roger was his usual entertaining self, but not even his amusing quips could lighten this feeling of desolation. She found her eyes returning constantly to the empty seat at the head of the board and excused herself early, leaving them to their drinking and dicing.

Hetty did not fail to notice her silence, trying out one or two conversational gambits which fell flat, and contenting herself with preparing her mistress for the night, though shaking her head disapprovingly at her adamant refusal to use the bed. Francesca dismissed her, slipping her arms into the sleeves of her fur-trimmed, brocade robe and fastening it over her nightgown. She curled up in the armchair, trying to read a book which she had borrowed from Alexis' well-stocked library, holding it to the single candleflame; but it was no use, her mind was playing tricks and she could not stop thinking about him. She even contemplated waking Hetty to keep her company but rejected the idea, so instead gave up the struggle, lying back and letting her thoughts run riot, dwelling on his features, the feel of his hard muscles and strong arms. Grimly, she reminded herself that she was going to take revenge, unable to understand why the prospect did not delight her. The harder she sought an explanation, the more confused she became, a sense of injustice nagging at her, hating all men and Alexis in particular.

It was late, and still that longed-for feeling of drowsiness would not come. She went to the window, looking out on the starry night, and felt an uncontrollable restlessness, imagining him out there somewhere in the darkness, nursing his sick animal. Without giving herself time to hesitate, she came to a sudden decision, opening the door and stepping into the passage beyond. She traversed the dark, chilly corridors lit by the occasional flares, quelling any objections from guards with a haughty, "I seek Le Diable. Direct me to the stables."

She shivered as a breeze rushed across the courtyard; above her, stars twinkled frostily. She groped her way along, guided by a faint, glowworm glimmer from the latticed windows of the stables. Once used for housing cattle during sieges, the lower floor was now used for storing wagons, harness and coaches. The tethered horses of the garrison stirred restlessly as she entered, rustling the straw. In the dim light she spoke to them softly, reassuringly, and a single ray from the lantern hanging on a hook from a beam touched a glint from one of the coach's brass fittings. The place was deserted but, following her instinct, Francesca ducked her head beneath a low doorway leading into the tackroom, accustoming her eyes to the gloom, relieved only by the banked-up logs in the small fireplace. She was instantly aware that Alexis was there, crouched on his heels by the hearth. The firelight bathed him in crimson as he tended his hound. He was in his shirtsleeves, jacket thrown aside, bare, sinewy forearms resting on his knees, and he gave her a searching glance from under frowning black brows.

"What do you here?"

Her heart gave a sickening lurch in her breast, then she steadied, reading weariness in his haggard face. As she looked at him, she was possessed of an extraordinary emotion. To her alarm, she found that she wanted to take his head in her arms and smooth away that hurt, worried expression. Never in her life had she felt such tenderness sweeping her and she was appalled by her weakness. This man was her enemy! What madness was this?

"I heard that Titus was sick. I know about herbs for wounds, and came to offer my assistance." Her voice sounded stiff, unnatural, not like her own at all.

"D'you mean to tell me that you can do something useful?" he snapped offensively.

Francesca chose to ignore his rudeness, moving closer. "It was considered a vital part of my education to know about such things. I spent a good deal of my time in the stillroom at Tallents, making herbal lotions, salves and medicine."

He shrugged his wide shoulders, muttering ungraciously, "The great lady, stooping to soil her dainty hands . . ."

"It was a practical move!" She flashed, furious with him. "My father is no fool and deemed it necessary, expecting me to have a sound knowledge of how to run a large household. Albeit, I might not have been called upon to exercise these skills, but at least I should have known if my servants were cheating me!"

He did not bother to reply, preoccupied with the dog who lay on a heap of sacking, no longer his usual alert self, panting and feverish, eyes half-closed. Francesca could see the wide gash in his back where the knife-like tusk of the enraged boar had slashed him. The wound was infected, its edges raw and inflamed. Alexis dipped a cloth in the bowl of water at his side and, speaking quietly, began to bathe it.

"I think it should have been stitched," he remarked.

"Not at all." Francesca was quite firm about this, remedies for such cases dropping automatically into her mind. "Best let the poison escape unhindered. I'll make a poultice to draw it."

Alexis nodded towards a cupboard set against the

wall. "The grooms keep medications in there for the horses. You may find what you need."

The shelves were in disorder, and she clicked her tongue in annoyance, going through pot after pot, sniffing, examining, wishing that they had been labeled. Having made her selection, she went to the table, pushing back her sleeves, measuring out amounts. She took a skillet of boiling water from the fire and added a little to the herbs in the crock. A strong aroma arose, reminding her of the garden at Tallents, lying lazy under the heat of the summer sun. She dropped in a lump of goose grease to make it bind, stirring until the ingredients had dissolved into a thick paste. It had to be used at once, and they both worked silently, absorbed in the task, applying the unguent to the wound, covering it with a heated pad of flannel and binding the whole with strips of linen.

When they had finished, Alexis sat back on the floor, stretching out his legs. "You have much healing skill, madame," he said with grudging admiration. "I think that he has a chance to live now."

Francesca was having difficulty in concentrating with his golden eyes looking at her like that, and her fingers shook as she busied herself clearing away the mess, neat and orderly. She was astonished by the change in him, deeply moved by his concern for Titus, unable to believe that this was the same harsh brigand who had captured and ravished her. Alexis' mood shifted like ripples passing over the surface of dark water. He stood up, resting his shoulders against the wall by the chimney breast, arms folded across his chest, never taking his eyes from her as she worked. All too aware of him, she kept her head bent over the table, wiping the surface clean with a wet rag, her hair falling forward, hiding her flushed cheeks. As his eyes raked her slender form adorned in the loose-fitting, fern green robe, and lingered where her curls fell away from her neck, baring a soft, tender nape, he knew a deep hunger, a longing for such beauty to house a loyal, trustworthy soul, a helpmate and partner, as she had been that night. He felt cheated—doubting this to be true. She was a woman, changeable as the wind! A man would be a fool to put faith in her.

Francesca peeked at him through her thick lashes as she passed him on her way to replace the jars. There was no gainsaying his powerful attraction and the flagrant virility betrayed by his every movement and the slumbering fire in the depths of his eyes. She was shocked to the core by the carnal longing which scorched her at his nearness. Her stern resolve had been badly shaken by their mutual care for the hound, which had thrown them into an achingly sweet rapport. These conflicting emotions were utterly depleting and, work finished, she was consumed by weariness, shivering as she stretched her cold fingers to the fire. Alexis noticed this at once, taking up his jacket and laying it about her shoulders, his arm lingering there. "You are cold, my dear. Let us hasten back to my quarters."

Standing before him, she felt weak and helpless; her head did not reach his collarbone yet, for all his size, she met his gaze boldly, no longer afraid. That simple, friendly action had given her a sense of pleasure and contentment. She was in his charge, dependent on him, and he seemed to welcome the role. It gave her a warm feeling of belonging to him.

In that mellow room which was his chamber, all warm paneling, tapestries and firelight, neither spoke, as if fearing to break that delicate web of understanding which was building between them. Alexis pushed her into a chair near the blazing logs and filled two glasses with brandy. He sat on the rug at her feet, arms clasped about his knees, staring into the glowing logs. She waited breathlessly, for it seemed that there was something on his mind which he wanted to voice. The dancing light etched his profile, the heavy brows, the thin, hawk nose, the determined jaw. As they had entered the castle, the sky had been obscured by clouds, and now she could hear rain beating against the window panes, emphasizing the shelter she enjoyed within. The warmth of the fire, the taste of the brandy glowing in her throat and the sight of this handsome man closeted with her for the night made her pulse race.

She heard him sigh deeply then, with a swift change of mood, he leapt lithely to his feet, saying with a grin, "Would you like another drink?" She nodded, though knowing for certain that this was not what she had been waiting to hear. Sadly, the moment had passed when there might have been significant conversation. But both were hedging, playing for time, the tension mounting unbearably between them. Alexis took her glass, setting it down with the decanter on the table, startling her by suddenly bending low and carefully lifting a loose curl from her cheek, brushing it across his lips, inhaling the fragrance. She felt a tingling rising from the base of her spine, as one long finger gently traced the line of her chin, her throat, and finally, the peak of her breast.

Francesca could not move, her heart was racing madly. Looking up into the lean face above her, she discovered that his smile had gone, replaced by that dark intensity which caused a shiver to run through her. Feeling her tremble, Alexis lowered his head and captured her softly parted lips with his. Her mind reeled from the intoxication of his kiss which invaded, demanded, with a sensual thoroughness. He raised his head slightly and his tongue passed along her mouth, then penetrated to softly search, slowly, almost languidly, possess. Compulsively, her arms crept up around his neck, her fingers caressing his thick black curls, and that dissolving feeling invaded her entire being as she returned the kiss, mind emptied and whirling.

He chuckled deep in his throat and, not breaking that kiss, pulled her up against him, his hands moving down her back, cupping her taut buttocks, pressing her unresisting hips to his strong thighs. She could feel him hard with desire, and could do nothing to still the fiery sensations which were racing through her own veins. He lifted her slim body in his arms and carried her to the waiting bed. Laying her gently down, he pushed aside the robe to release her breasts to his caressing hands. He kissed and fondled her nipples and as his mouth found hers again, she was lost in a swirling sea of desire. Her robe lay in a discarded heap on the floor, his knowing hands roamed with increasing demands over her flesh, and she was drifting on billowing clouds of delight which numbed thought. She stared up dazedly at the golden eyes and full mouth which hovered over her, and accepted her fate. It did not matter how hard she struggled, Alexis would win in the end, bending her to his will as he did everyone else with whom he came in contact. What did it matter now? She was ruined. He had seen to that.

Alexis was determined that this time she should enjoy the encounter, wooing her very gently, rousing her body with skilful hands, bringing his considerable experience into play. Francesca relaxed, allowing pleasure to rise in her, wave after wave, arching her back so that his lips and hands tortured her nipples, curving her body into his, seeking closer and closer contact. There was too much clothing between them, and she deftly unfastened the row of small rhinestone buttons which closed the front of his silk waistcoat, opening it wide, sliding her arms round him under it, feeling the soft linen of his shirt, the hard muscles beneath. Alexis smiled into her eyes and released himself just long enough from her clinging arms to divest himself of garments, returning to hug her to him eagerly, magnificently naked. She was astonished by her sudden, overwhelming desire to touch him. Hesitant at first, her hand moved over his wide chest, finding old scars and running a finger round the new one on his upper arm where Zoltan's knife had cut him. Then, finally, she moved lightly over his belly, where the dark line of hair curved down from his navel. She felt him stiffen and catch his breath, then his hand closed over hers, guiding her lower.

Her touch inflamed him, and the feel of his arousal, the knowledge that she, so unschooled, was pleasing him so much, was like a heady wine. She was shaking with excitement and he kissed her hungrily, his tongue roving her mouth, while her own replied with small, darting movements. His hands were moving with increasing urgency down her hips, pushing between her thighs, stroking the soft inner flesh, moving upward. She could not help the involuntary impulse to tighten her legs, but he took no notice and his touch was like a flame shooting through her.

"Don't pull away, don't close your legs," he insisted, his breath against her ear, running his tongue round the velvet rim so that the skin on her neck and shoulders rose in delightful anticipation. His fingers moved deeper, parting the curling triangle of hair, sliding across that tiny, swollen peak which glistened like a pink pearl, throbbing in response. And she was lost, her thighs falling apart to let him explore the very core of her being, aching for something she did not yet understand or recognize, only aware of the mounting feeling which made her sob for release.

Mark had disappointed her—she had been ignorant of the needs of her own flesh, totally unprepared for the sheer physical bliss which now swept her. A moan broke from her lips as his fingers had their way, moving in rhythm with her writhing body. He was so expert, so consummate a lover. Sometimes his touch was delicate, as if she was being brushed by a butterfly's wing, then he would change pressure, making it hard, almost painful but, before it became too much to bear, returning to lightness again, while the ache gathered into a great knot, spreading between her legs and through her loins. The blood was drumming in her ears and she twisted wildly, crying out incoherently, running her hands up and down his back, digging in her nails in frenzy, until a huge bubble of sensation exploded within her. Only then did he enter her and this time there was no pain, just joy. Floating somewhere on a blissful cloud of pure ecstasy, she felt him thrust into her, making her complete—his wildness, his roughness and his need driving him on until his big body shuddered with the intensity of his climax.

She drifted back to sanity to find herself cradled in his arms, his lips brushing her forehead and nose, traveling lazily down to her mouth, kissing her deeply. Francesca was stunned by the abandonment of her response. In spite of everything, he had roused her to passion, giving her a first taste of sensual, satisfying pleasure, making her understand the enjoyment a man can give a woman, as well as an inkling of her own power.

"I never realized, never knew it would be like that," she gasped, and pressed her lips against his throat, all other emotions swamped by gratitude to this man who had shown her how to attain such frenzied, breathtaking heights.

He held her face between his hands and looked into her eyes. "Ah, darling, this is but the beginning. Later—a little later, sweet one, I shall eat you," he promised, his voice husky, with dark undertones which thrilled her. He smiled, inordinately pleased at having initiated her and caressed her tenderly, curiously reluctant to let her go. Such virginity and innocence was a rare commodity. Then a hard note crept into his voice and his grip tightened. "What of that fopling friend of yours? Did he not try to seduce you?" Somehow, the idea of Mark even touching her made a red haze of rage cover his vision. His hands moved over her, re-establishing possession.

It was humiliating to have to admit it. "He wanted to, but something always seemed to interrupt us," she whispered.

Alexis laughed with the arrogance of the conquering male animal. "He is but half a man, darling. Believe me, there are so many ways of love which I shall teach you."

Francesca shook her head, a trifle puzzled. There was more to come? Further delights as yet untasted? She felt the first stirrings of passion rising in her again, and Alexis stopped talking, teasing her lips with his mouth until they parted eagerly and her arms welcomed him, holding him closer, her body straining against his. He shuddered and took her fiercely, carrying her with him to the topmost peaks of joy. She heard her own wild sobbing, begging him for release, and when it came it left her shaking, completely helpless, filled to her very soul with contentment.

Finally, regretfully, he slid from her and gathered her close to his warm body. Francesca, her eyes heavy with sleep, her brain dizzy with this multitude of new sensations, snuggled deeper into his embrace. She was worn out and needed to rest. Tomorrow would come with its nagging worries, its shame and resentments, but that was much later—now there was only Alexis.

Chapter Seven

As SHE had half-expected, the cold, sane light of morning brought burning shame and self-disgust. When Francesca awoke, the place beside her was empty. Alexis had risen early and gone out. She must have slept very soundly for Dinu had already been there, tidying the room and putting fresh logs on the fire, and it was Hetty's knock at the door which had roused her.

Francesca sat up and called to her to enter, uncertain whether to be pleased or sorry that Alexis was not there. She dragged her robe about her bare shoulders, tossing the tangled hair back from her eyes, meeting Hetty's shrewd smile as she saw her mistress in Alexis' bed, taking in the situation at a glance. Francesca's face flamed at that knowing look which brought home remorselessly the reminder that she had weakened, allowed him to know the deepest intimacy by going into his bed like a whore! How could she have done it? What madness had possessed her? Nevertheless, she knew that were he to stride through the door, it would be fatally easy to succumb again.

It had been all very well, though inexcusable, to fall beneath his spell by romantic firelight, lulled by brandy and the softening illusion of a budding friendship, but

Hetty represented all that she had held dear in England. She should be setting her a good example, not behaving like a shameless wanton! Hetty was amused and pleased, agog to hear details, but Francesca refused to be drawn at first, very much on her dignity, rising, sipping her morning coffee, already partly dressed before a sudden, awful thought ripped through her mind, setting her gripping the edge of the dressing table, her face white. "My God! Supposing he has got me with child!"

Hetty fluttered around her, soothing and reassuring. "Oh, ma'am, I don't suppose it would happen so soon."

"But it sometimes does, Hetty. I've heard of brides conceiving on their wedding night!" By now, she was nearly hysterical with fright, her quick imagination picturing herself swollen with a baby—his baby! That abominable man whom she hated! "I'll kill myself if I miss my next flux!" she declared dramatically.

Hetty had much experience of such matters and they fell into a deep debate; but Francesca knew that she had at least two weeks of worry ahead before she could be sure that it had not happened. And with a man who had not even said that he loved her! Not once during that bewitched night had he said it, even when their passion was at its height. Oh, he had told her that she possessed the most beautiful breasts, the loveliest legs, the most perfect face he had ever seen; but never, in those mad moments when lust heats up the blood and so closely resembles love, had he pretended that he wanted anything but a responding body in his arms. Thinking back on it, she was deeply offended, chalking up another mental mark in his disfavor.

And where was he? Disgruntled, she felt his absence to be in the nature of a slight, as if she was some drab whom he had bought for sixpence and then discarded. "I'll not do it again!" she vowed inwardly as she

finished dressing, flinging on her cloak and making for
the stables, telling herself that she was going to attend
the sick dog—certainly not seeking Alexis! He was not
there, but Roger was, squatting by Titus, looking up at
her with knowing eyes.

"Your patient is doing well, my dear. Alexis tells me
that you were of great help last night."

So he had spoken of her to his friend. Francesca
could not prevent the little flush of pleasure which
deepened the peach bloom of her cheeks. "He's here
now?"

Roger stood up, helping himself to a mugful of ale
from the leather blackjack on the table. He shook his
auburn head, eyes full of amusement and admiration as
she sank gracefully down beside the hound, her skirts
spread around her. "Nay, fear not, madonna. He left at
sunrise. There is a gathering of peasants in the next
village, and they seek his advice."

She flashed him a glance, green eyes rebellious.
"What advice can a robber give to honest country-
folk?"

Roger considered her slowly, remembering his commander's strange manner that morning. He had been
gruff, disinclined to talk, stamping about giving totally
unnecessary orders before swinging into his saddle and
galloping away. Roger, who knew him well, shrewdly
guessed that something was disturbing him deeply. He
did not act like a callous brute who had taken a woman
only to forget her. No, the burly captain mused, he was
more like a bewildered lover who did not know if he was
on his head or his heels! His grin broadened.

"You are too quick to condemn, my lady. The people
hereabouts swear by him."

But Francesca refused to listen, wrapping herself in
ice once more. That night she chose the couch by the fire
as her sleeping place, deliberately avoiding looking at

the bed with its fiery memories of the way his hands had
teased, tormented and roused her to passion. It lay, vast
and empty, too big for one person alone. Alexis was
also struck by this thought when he finally came in, very
late, having ridden through the stormy darkness after a
wearying day holding council with the rebel leaders. His
eyes lingered on her nubile form curled beneath the furs,
and that perfect, sleeping face, his mouth setting in a
hard line to see her there, instead of waiting for him in
the bed. So the minx was up to her tricks again, was
she? He was furiously angry for, as he rode through the
stinging rain, he had been looking forward to repeating
their love-making, burning to teach her everything he
knew, only to be met by this chilling reception.

He loomed over her, his strong hands raised to seize
her, shake her awake and force her to receive him. As if
aware of him, even in her sleep, she stirred slightly,
sighed, and then burrowed deeper into the softness of
the pelts. Alexis froze, her childlike vulnerability tugging at his heart. In the firelight, her hair was like
molten copper, her complexion flawless, her full lips
slightly parted as she breathed, her cheeks flushed, her
body relaxed in repose. He stood gazing at this slumbering vision for a long while, and he could no more have
hurt her than he could have taken the injured Titus and
left him to die of exposure on the bleak mountainside.
Presently, he moved quietly away and, without bothering to undress, rolled himself in his cloak and occupied
the bed. When she awoke in the morning, he had
already departed, determined to give him no opportunity for recriminations. Her action of choosing the seclusion of the couch had spoken plainer than words.

Francesca kept very busy, almost desperately so, refusing to admit that she was nettled by his neglect and
apparent lack of interest. She knew that he had used the
bed, standing forlornly by it, reaching out to smooth

the pillow where his dark head had rested, breathing in the wholly personal scent of his hair which still clung to it. She tossed up her head, little chin setting stubbornly. Very well, let him shun her! See if she cared! It was a blessing—at least she no longer had to put up with his odious company, or allow him to practice outrageously intimate actions!

Whenever they chanced to meet there was a kind of strained formality between them. They still supped together in the Great Hall but, when he had finished, he would disappear without a word, leaving her with a horrible, aching, choking feeling of loneliness, no matter how many other people were with her. She was finding it difficult to sleep, tossing and turning on the couch, every sense alert, waiting for him to come. Yet, when he did arrive, she would pretend to be asleep, though watching him from beneath her screening lashes, seeing the easy movements of his long, muscular body with something akin to admiration. Once the candle had been blown out, she would listen to his breathing, wondering if he also lay awake. She began to take special care with her appearance, rubbing her skin with rose-scented lotion, sitting long before the mirror, powdering her face with pink-tinted orrisroot, deftly touching a hare's foot dipped in rouge to her high cheekbones, smoothing brows and long lashes with a tiny brush dipped in kohl, driving Hetty mad with her complaints.

The weather was capricious. One day of beautiful autumnal glory was promptly followed by rain squalls which made the mountains disappear in gray mist. It matched Francesca's chaotic state of mind: wild bouts of gaiety which plunged into extreme sadness seemed to be her lot now. She wearied Hetty almost beyond endurance with her seesaw moods, restless and jumpy, irked by confinement, longing for something, anything, to happen to pass the leaden-footed hours. To her chagrin

she found that she had developed extreme sensitivity
with regard to Alexis' whereabouts and was unfailingly
correct in ascertaining if he was in the castle or had
ridden off on some warlike mission. There was increasing activity at Balvany. People constantly came and
went and, from her nook on the battlements, Francesca
would watch the rich pageantry in the courtyard below.
Sometimes it was a crowd of horsemen, led by a stocky,
black mustachioed man, full of fire and eloquence—one
of the revolutionary hotheads, or it might be a collection of Turkish merchants, bargaining shrewdly, selling
ammunitions and weapons. If she happened to be in the
Great Hall, they usually forgot her presence, secure in
the knowledge that she understood little of their conversation.

Once, with great vexation, she glimpsed from a distance that tall, hoydenish gypsy girl, bristling to see her
striding at Alexis' side, engaged in earnest discussion. It
seemed as if they were arguing—she could tell by the
way the girl glared and waved her arms in a gesture of
annoyance, while Alexis' face grew hard and dark. She
did not stay long, swift-moving, impatient, leaping into
her saddle and galloping away.

Early one morning, he rode out, leading his men on a
sortie against a neighboring estate. Francesca saw him
go from high on the top of a tower, straining her eyes
until he was out of sight and she could see nothing more
than the distant glimmer of steel, the flash of scarlet
from sash or scarf. Curiously, instead of happy elation,
she was left feeling bereft and uneasy, wondering if the
mission was dangerous. Bolstering her flagging spirits,
she told herself coldly that it would solve her problems
if he was killed. Even this thought did not cheer her and
she dragged back to her room, pacing nervously, fret-
ting until she heard the clop of hooves and the triumphant shouts which heralded his return. Now, she sup-

posed heatedly, he would celebrate in the company of the gypsy, who was obviously much more to his taste. No doubt, they had a great deal in common . . . killing . . . plundering—her angry thoughts were cut off in full spate by the sound of his voice approaching her door.

He flung it open wide and stalked in, his sword hitting the jamb, an almost recovered Titus padding behind him. She rose and faced him, Hetty goggling at her shoulder, while Lavinia gave an alarmed squeak and backed into a corner, her round embroidery-frame held before her like a shield.

"Fie, sir!" she protested, her rouged cheeks shaking with indignation. "What is the meaning of this intrusion? Where are your manners?"

Francesca had to admire her pluck, for Alexis was a knee-weakening spectacle, wearing his fighting gear— the rough wolfskin coat, the glittering baldrick—hot from a skirmish with the light of battle still glowing in his eyes. In the distance they could hear his men, exhausted but victorious, elated by the brisk fight and the hard ride home.

Alexis coolly surveyed the defensive women who had drawn closer together when he exploded into the room. There was something insolent in his swagger and slight, ironic bow. His lips formed into a wry smile as he addressed Lavinia. "I fear that my upbringing was not adapted to learning the courtly graces, madam. I am a very busy man, and have little time to waste exchanging banalities."

His lawless aspect and his spread-legged stance accentuated his clipped words. The late afternoon sun stabbed through the window in a narrow shaft where dust motes danced, bathing him in crimson, flickering over his face, cheekbones gouged with shadows, so swarthy, so sinister, with his untamed eyes and beaked nose, every inch of him a swashbuckling freebooter. He was as much a part of this remote, alien land as the icy peaks, the chasms, the marauding wolves.

The sun disappeared again behind a mass of great rushing clouds fleeing before the winds from the mountain tops. The fortress room was shrouded in gloom, even the cheery fire did little to dispel its prison-like atmosphere. Francesca and Alexis exchanged a hard, wary stare, then his eyes dropped disturbingly to the pulse that pounded madly at the base of her throat.

"Dismiss your women, Lady Francesca," he said, almost casually. "I wish to have a word with you in private."

"I don't want them to leave!" she returned hotly, eyes snapping with temper. Who the devil did he think he was? Ignoring her for days, and then stamping in and ordering her about!

His eyebrows swooped down in an alarming curve which made her tremble though she stood her ground, a flaming-haired shrew. "You are bold, madame. Do you not realize that the fate of yourself and of your servants depends on my will. I could have all of you shot!"

Francesca could feel the palms of her hands beginning to sweat, fear making a dry taste in her mouth as she sensed his mood of savagery. He must have had a fine day's sport, rousing his bloodlust, murdering! Pillaging! Perhaps ravishing some poor, helpless woman! "Even you dare not do that!" she challenged.

"Dare not! To me!" His eyes flashed dangerously.

Lavinia was already scrambling for the door, while Hetty looked from one furious face to the other. The air fairly crackled with unspoken, fiery emotions and she was sensitive to it. Francesca was clinging desperately to her rage as a buttress against this other overpowering feeling which was squeezing her heart. It was as if she was breaking into pieces, mesmerized by his glittering eyes and the sight of that arrogant mouth that had the power to reduce her to sobbing acquiescence. A shiver of remembered passion ran through her body.

Forcing herself to appear cool and unruffled, she nodded dismissal to Hetty who took herself off with a scared, backward glance over her shoulder. As the door closed behind her, Alexis flung himself into one of the chairs by the fire and poured a glass of wine. His face was smeared with sweat and gunpowder; there was dried blood on his hands and mud on his boots. A fine, dainty suitor! she thought scornfully, a look of unmutterable disgust on her face. She watched him warily as he pushed his long legs out in front of him and lifted the goblet to his lips. Titus lay on the rug, his thick wet coat beginning to steam, soulful brown eyes resting on his master's face. How dare that conceited bully come striding in, smelling of horses and fighting and death? Very well, he owned the place and everything in it, but she had some rights—hadn't she?

"What is it you want?" Her contempt should have withered him, but he just sat there, staring at her, totally relaxed on the surface, but vexed with himself within. Even the tension of carefully planning the raid with military thoroughness, followed by the nerve-tingling excitement of falling upon the manor house of a particularly tyrannical landlord, had not obliterated the disturbing remembrance of those tantalizing green eyes. She haunted him, no matter how much he tried to immerse himself in his work, that white-hot ambition to break the stranglehold of the despotic duchess. How dare that impudent chit trouble his mind?

"I want you!" he stated flatly, the smoldering fire in his eyes almost sending her whirling from the room.

"That you will never have!" Her lips tightened obstinately. "My body can be taken, but you shall not conquer my spirit!" She meant to sweep regally past him on the way to the door, but his hand shot out, and he jerked her down onto his lap. Every fiber of her body tingling, only too aware of the hard thighs beneath her, she glared at him. "That's right, savage! Live up to your reputation!"

Amused rather than angered by her reaction, which was so true to form, he tightened his hold round her waist, pulling her hard against him and kissing her on her protesting mouth. "I missed you in my bed," he murmured into her soft throat, ignoring her now token struggles.

Pressed close to his chest, feeling the shaggy fur of his coat beneath her cheek, Francesca battled with the ache of unshed tears rising like a great bubble of misery in the region of her breast. She was weary beyond utterance with their continual conflict, tossed in a vortex of bewildering passions.

She gave a sad little shake of her head, her eyes very large and appealing. "Oh, Alexis, why did we have to meet like this?"

It was the first time she had called him by his name and he felt a queer tautness in his chest. She was so lovely, her pliant body in his arms, her perfumed hair tickling his nostrils. But even as familiar desire spread through him, his mouth twisted bitterly. She was probably every bit as treacherous and deceitful as Maria—his beloved bride who had tricked and misled him and, with wanton carelessness, made his life a living hell! Since then he had used women mercilessly, taking their bodies, never betraying the smallest weakness. Francesca had the power to shred his hard-won control to pieces and he rebelled against it.

"Don't try to tell me that you are feeling sentimental, my dear," he said with an edge to his voice, though still holding her. "I am far more accustomed to insults from you."

"Oh, stop it!" she cried, becoming angry again.

"Why must you turn every meeting into a battlefield? I believe you hate the female sex."

His voice hardened. "On the contrary, I have spent many enjoyable hours between their thighs!" His eyes glinted with sneering mockery.

"That's all you think about!" Jealousy knifed her and she was flabbergasted. Why should she give a damn how many women he had bedded? "There are no sensitive feelings in you, no warm affection—only lust!"

Although his arms were still round her, that invisible gulf was widening, deepening between them again. "Women cannot be relied on," he said at last. "I would not trust you an inch. You may have been a virgin when I took you, but you were certainly no innocent. Were you not eloping, betraying your vow to the margrave? And are you not still fostering that young jackass's passion for you? I have seen you talking with him recently. Are you still hoping to fool him into helping you escape?"

Francesca was dumbfounded. He seemed so unreasonably disappointed and angry and she did not know why. She twisted in his grasp so that she might see the expression on his sardonic features. "That is unjust!" she pouted.

"D'you still fancy that dandy?" he demanded, bewildering her by his intensity, fingers digging into her back like talons, ready to rip and tear. "Such an idiot, with his pretty manners, his smooth lies! Do you love him?" The question was hurled at her.

"No." She shook her head, the heavy mahogany curls tumbling about her bare shoulders. "I thought that I did once, but . . ."

She could not find words to express the tumult of emotions which tormented her—memories of Mark and their old bittersweet affair now seemed so very far away, filling her with painful nostalgia. In vain she fought back the scalding tears which had been threatening to engulf her. The sob gathered, and then broke, and she was overwhelmed by the torrent of grief, agonizingly held in check for days. She lay heavily against Alexis, crying her heart out, dimly aware that his lips were softly caressing her hair. He was disturbed and distrustful of this sudden wave of tenderness which rocked him. She was like a forlorn child, dabbing at her cheeks with a minute lace kerchief which soon became a crumpled, soggy ball. Misty-eyed, she stared at him, her long lashes spiky, her soft lips trembling.

His unexpected kindness was her undoing. His lips touched hers and something fused between them, her mouth warm and eager for his. She was very much afraid that she was falling in love with this hard-faced scoundrel who taunted and mocked her. But it was ridiculous—her heart pumped madly like the frantic beat of a trapped bird's wing—she could not love a man who acted as he did!

Alexis gave her not time to think further, kissing her with such savage hunger that the room spun, before swinging her up in his arms and throwing her down into the silken softness of the bed. He leaned over her and very gently began to undress her, his fingers as agile with hooks and laces as Hetty's.

Her eyes were heavy, with a drugged look in them, her mouth moist and parted, her marvelously rich hair spread out over the pillow. Soon her body was naked to his gaze and he feasted on the alabaster skin, the ripe breasts with the tempting pink nipples, taking in the slender waist, curving hips, those long, smooth legs and delicately formed feet. Silently, she returned his searching gaze; the gentleness had gone, replaced by urgency, as they lingered on the darkness between her white thighs. He flung himself down beside her, turning to pull her roughly to him, and then her senses were swimming with delight at the feel of his hands on her. She did not want to fight him any more; she wanted him —but not in anger.

Her slim fingers spread out and slowly caressed his warm skin through the opening of his shirt, her hands sliding beneath it to his smooth shoulders. His mouth sought hers and she gave a deep purr of satisfaction against his lips, unable to control her violent response to his love-making. His hands and mouth moved her as no other's had, and she strained against him, grinding her body into his, making whimpering sounds of pleasure as he entered her. It drove Francesca crazy and she beat on his back with her fists, clawing at him with her nails, wild with the hot desire which consumed her, pleading with him to go faster and take her over the edge of satisfaction.

They lay in silence in the warm afterglow of loving. As the tumultous furor of sensation subsided, Francesca gave a soft cry of torment, her mind on shameful fire at her own actions. She didn't want to love him, to be prey to that dreadful tenderness and need which would destroy her. She opened her eyes and the room swung back into perspective. It was growing darker as the evening clouds rushed in and the sun died, a crimson ball on the rim of the horizon. The fire burned between the andirons, its sound dominating the shadowed chamber. On the rug in front of it, Titus stirred and began scratching at the troublesome flea.

"Oh, Alexis, Alexis . . ." she wept, sickened with anguish, tears running scaldingly from the corners of her eyes. In the stillness, he could hear them fall upon the pillow, and compassion made him long to comfort her. But he was afraid to show weakness and stayed motionless while she cried. With a sob she turned over away from him, whereupon he slipped a hand up onto her shoulder and drew her back in spite of her resistance.

"Much better to talk of it," he said gruffly, in a self-protectively hard voice. She shook her head dumbly, long tresses falling forward to cover her face. Firmly, Alexis pulled her body back to curve against his, slowly caressing her arms while his lips traveled lightly over her hair and brushed the sensitive spot at the nape of her neck. When her sobs had stilled to an occasional sniff, he turned her gently to face him, and her heart leaped with joy at the expression in his eyes.

"I don't know what ails me," she lied, knowing full well the state of her emotions—she was his slave forever, and could do nothing to prevent it. She hid her face in his moist shoulder and missed the brooding melancholy which shadowed his features as he dropped a kiss on the top of her head where the white parting showed.

"Don't worry, little love," his voice was deep, husky. He gave her a small shake, rousing her from her misery. "Most wenches cry because I *don't* make love to them —not because I have!"

He was laughing at her, and she stopped wallowing in self-pity. He was insufferably conceited! Other wenches, indeed! But God, he had every reason for confidence. He was such a handsome devil! It was unfair that one man should possess such charm, *and* be so good-looking. With his tousled black hair, his eyes gleaming between astonishingly long lashes, and a smile that would turn the most sane woman's heart right over, Francesca was forced to admit that most women would want him, and few ever forget him.

He released himself from her clinging arms and swung his long legs over the side of the bed, saying lightly, "Get up, my sweet, and don your finest gown. Tonight there is a feast in the Great Hall, for it is harvest time. That's really the reason why I came here—to tell you," he lied, with a wicked grin. He insisted on remaining while she dressed. A hastily summoned, flushed and embarrassed Hetty helped her get ready.

Alexis sprawled in a chair, drinking deeply, his eyes roving over Francesca as if he owned her, and she trembled, terribly afraid that he did! Having given herself to him so eagerly and wantonly, she was forced to acknowledge, in her deepest heart, that she was hopelessly in love with him. It was terrible and wounding, filling her with bleak despair, for she was convinced that though he desired her, he still viewed her as a useful hostage, a source of considerable bargaining power with his enemies. He had called her a slut and almost seemed to hate her; or at the very least considered her a damned nuisance and a thorn in his side!

He left before she had completed her toilet, bored with all this feminine dressing up, though making a farewell promise to see her at the feast. Francesca took her time. Let him wait or, more accurately, let *her* wait—cooling that trembling eagerness which filled her with unrest if not constantly in his company.

Lavinia appeared, very overdressed in sapphire silk, wearing enormously wide side-hoops, with a greased, powdered and curled wig dressed high and surmounted by imitation fruit. She had taken it upon herself to represent her country among those lowborn bandits, her face painted brightly so that she resembled a wax doll, her shapeless body forced into the restrictions of a tight corset, the whole outfit sparkling with paste diamonds and frothing with lace.

"Ye Gods! She looks like a galleon under full sail," giggled Hetty into Francesca's ear. Unfortunately, Lavinia overheard. She was guaranteed to eavesdrop, though often feigning deafness when it suited her.

"One must keep up appearances, my girl," she reproved sternly. "Something that it would do well for us all to remember." She pursed her lips, a look of holiness directed meaningfully at her charge.

Francesca ignored her, busy with selecting the final little touches to complete her own ensemble, knowing this to be an important occasion. The celebrations were well under way when the three women rustled along the chill corridors toward the Great Hall. Music swelled up to greet them, reminiscent of the country dance rhythms of England, but with strangely oriental overtones. Roger was at the head of the staircase ready to escort them and, peering down from the height of the carved railing, Francesca gasped in delighted astonishment at the scene below. The hall resembled a colorful kaleidoscope in constant motion, made vivid by the costumes of the farmers and their womenfolk.

The strangers came in for a good deal of attention as they passed through. Francesca felt vaguely uneasy, guessing that the peasants were making remarks about her in a language which she could not understand, though their dark faces were not unfriendly. Roger led her to one of the fireplaces wherein blazed logs the length of a man. Alexis was seated in his carver, receiving his guests, and he too was wearing Rumanian traditional costume, a full-sleeved linen shirt open at the neck under a short, black waistcoat enlivened with scarlet stitching, his legs encased in long, narrow pantaloons of coarse handmade wool and baggy boots of supple leather. A cap of red cloth was set at a jaunty angle on his untamed curls. People were filing past to wish him well, and he was at ease with them, legs thrust out before him, a couple of his favorite hounds at his feet. He talked animatedly with even the most humble herdsman, then listened and nodded, sifting through their problems, keeping a nice balance between condescension and familiarity. Sometimes he leaned forward, taking up his tankard of ale from the tall stand at the end of the firedog, where he had placed it to warm.

Francesca could see Ranby and Mark standing near-by, joining in the merrymaking. Everyone was laughing and talking, the wine and home-brewed beer flowing freely, food piled high on trestles ranged along the walls under the arched windows. The room was brilliantly lit, candles blazing in circular holders suspended on iron chains from the ceiling. Alexis greeted her with his most charming smile, pulling up a chair for her next to his own, pouring out a glass of Chardonnay. The warm blood of recollection flowed through her as she savored its taste—she had drunk it on her first night in his bed-chamber. Happiness laved her as the wine infused itself into her veins, and her gloom vanished. She stole a glance at Alexis' dark profile, unable to believe that this tough, very masculine leader was really her lover; it gave her the edge on every other woman present, a primor-dial satisfaction which she indulged to the full.

It was a very good wine. The room swayed and each face seemed to be swimming in a shimmering circle of gold, and out of that gilded ring loomed two whom she recognized. The Duke of Little Egypt had brought his followers to Balvany.

The wise, deep eyes of the gypsy princess rested on Francesca. "Ah," Elvire said, satisfied that events were taking place in accordance with the great celestial plan. "So it has happened, my dear. You have found your man."

Francesca blinked at her, mystified. Did it show in her face? Was there some luminous aura about her which proclaimed her guilty secret? With slightly drunken solemnity she pondered on this, then came up with a logical explanation. Elvire must have noticed the visible tokens of Alexis' passion, the purple bruises of his love bites on her throat. She had worn a necklace for concealment, but the gypsy's eyes were keen.

Elvire rested her brown hand on Francesca's arm, her

black eyes boring into the shining emerald ones. The stones of her rings gleamed dully on her hovering fingers. "You are happy now, my dear? Do not deny him. I knew this was to be, but you had to find out for yourself."

"I am betrothed to Carl," Francesca stammered, only half-believing, clinging to her conviction that fortunetelling was nothing more than a hoax to wheedle money from the gullible.

Elvire lifted expressive hands and shoulders in a fatalistic shrug. "It is ordained and cannot be altered, written in the stars long before you were born."

"What do you see for me, Elvire?" Alexis had joined them, and Francesca was surprised to see that he was serious.

"Why do you ask me again?" the gypsy muttered. "I have already told you what I see there, and nothing will be altered. There is trouble afoot, starting very soon. This woman is a part of it, yet your meeting was inevitable. There are three men about to cross your path—they are friends, but beware of what they offer. Do you understand?"

It sounded too ambiguous for Francesca to be convinced, yet Alexis appeared to accept it, frowning a little in worried concern. "I am expecting a visit from Horia, Gloska and Grisan Giorg. We have weighty matters to discuss. I think them trustworthy men."

He stood before the fire, legs spread, his hands clasped behind his back. Francesca stabbed a quick glance at his face; the flicker of a smile beside his mouth showed that he was aware of her. Elvire was running her amulets through her fingers like a rosary, eyes abstracted, her dark brow scalloped with hair greased into little flat hooks under her green silk scarf with its silver coins. Mihail's ears pricked at the mention of those names.

"The leaders of the dreaded Kuruzen, eh? That band of armed peasants who fight the tyranny of the masters. Are you enlisting their aid?"

"I'd ask help from Satan himself, if I could topple Renata!" The grim expression on Alexis' face was echoed on those of his men, never far from his side, and Francesca shivered, trying to recapture the lightheartedness she had experienced before the arrival of the gypsies. She turned to watch the country folk at their revels, thrilling to the color, the sounds, and began to build castles in the air. Just supposing, she might stay with Alexis for ever and refuse to go to Govora. If he wanted her, no one would prevent him from keeping her by his side. If only he had said that he loved her—if only he *did* love her! As his lady, she would look to the welfare of the peasants, they would be her responsibility too. There would be children to carry on his line; she would give him fine sons! She glowed at the thought, longing to get him alone, to work her magic so that he might be persuaded.

The celebrations had reached a climax, everyone stamping and cheering, downing their glasses in a gulp, when there was a commotion at the far end of the hall where the massive door stood open. A group of mercenaries came in, newly dismounted, their finery muddied. Cries of greeting welcomed them, with much hearty backslapping and the thrusting of pots of ale into their hands as they shouldered their way through, seeking Alexis. They clustered around the fire while he spoke to them with quick intentness as they spread chilled hands to the blaze, shaking the rain from their cloaks, beating their hats against their sides to dry the bedraggled plumes.

A collection of scarred warriors, scruffy, stubbly-jawed, with manes of unkempt hair, armed with heavy sabers, guns and axes—these were the members of his ragged army who had been away on a mission. They were bluff, rowdy and alarming, glaring around with truculent eyes, ready to punch the head of anyone who annoyed them. Francesca shrank nearer to the comfortingly protective bulk of their commander, whom they treated with much respect. At that moment, a figure detached itself from among them. With a sickening shock, she registered a blurred impression of long legs and a cloud of blue-black hair—someone tall and strongly built, clad in a leather jacket worn over crimson breeches and high boots. It was the wild girl of the forest. Instantaneous antipathy flashed between them as they recognized one another.

"It's Gilda!" exclaimed Roger with a wide grin. "We thought she'd run into trouble, but she's back in time for the feast."

A sense of sinking apprehension shook Francesca, for the girl had flung herself upon Alexis and he was smiling down into that reckless face. "Who is she?" she faltered, grabbing Roger's arm.

"Gilda?" he answered promptly, and though he was smiling puckishly, his eyes were those of a concerned friend. "She was Alexis' mistress—until you came."

Chapter Eight

THE CRIMSON mist of pain faded, replaced by a burst of fury. Francesca tightened her grip on Roger's arm, the long nails biting deep. Smitten with raging despair, her eyes were riveted on Gilda. Hers was a glittering, barbaric beauty with bold dark eyes and a superb figure which she displayed brazenly, striding confidently among the men who treated her in a joking, comradely manner. On closer inspection, there was nothing truly masculine about her, in spite of the breeches molding her slim hips. Though her shirt was patterned on those worn by men, her cravat was loosely knotted, the neck wide open to the waist, the deep valley between her magnificent breasts bare for all to see. She was like a caged animal, full of nervous energy, a handsome, haughty wench, her brazen lack of modesty causing an uproar among the gypsies who were staring at her, aghast.

Mihail treated her to a severe look of castigation and his voice cut like a lash as he upbraided her, "Gilda! What do you here? You flout our laws. An unwedded girl, with her hair unbraided for all to see, living with the soldiers, immodestly strutting about in breeches!

You are *mochardi*! Unclean!"

A hush fell across the hall. The *tzigany* were notorious for their treatment of their women, keeping them in line with brutal fists and rigid taboos. Their vengeance was swift and merciless if these were transgressed, and Gilda, who would have not dared face him in the camp, now stood bold as brass, arms akimbo.

"You cannot touch me, uncle. I passed beyond your laws long ago. Le Diable is my man, and he alone do I obey!"

"He is *not* your man." Elvire eyed her frostily. "You've not pledged yourself to him or he to you, either in the Romany way or with the blessing of the church. You are his whore!"

A gasp arose from the spectators, but Gilda gave a toss of her head, a sneer curling her red lips. "What will you do about it? Bury me alive as you did Esmeralda when she was caught selling herself to a *gorgio*? Shave my head, crop my ears, slice off my nose, lay my cheeks open to the bone? But no, I was forgetting, that is the punishment for infidelity, is it not? There is naught you can do to me!"

"You should be tied naked to a cartwheel and thrashed with a horsewhip!" shouted the offended Duke. "Unnatural wench! Our girls are chaste, modest in bearing, preserving their maidenheads for their husbands!"

The situation was highly combustible, the fiery, volatile Gilda supremely confident of her position with Alexis, defying Mihail to take one step towards her. "I'd not force a daughter of mine to accept such tyranny!" she flared.

"You will never have daughters," Elvire's tone was ominous, the voice of doom. "No child shall spring from your womb." She spat on the floor at Gilda's feet.

Their eyes locked, and Gilda's face paled at this bitter denunciation, believing in Elvire's powers of divination. Then, with a filthy oath, she spun round on the high heels of her splendid boots, snatching up a goblet of wine and downing it in a single swallow.

Muttering, the gypsies withdrew to a far corner of the hall, putting as much space between themselves and their rebellious kinswoman as was humanly possible, as if the very air she breathed was tainted. Gilda made some scathing comment about them to the mercenaries, invoking a shout of laughter, then turned to face Alexis who had stood silent and thoughtful during the disturbing scene. Francesca bristled at the way in which the girl pressed against his side, laughing up into his face, her every action distinctly proprietorial. Then, across his shoulder, she stabbed a stare at Francesca, demanding rudely, "Why is she here? I thought you were going to keep her locked up. Have you started entertaining her during my absence?"

Alexis was watching the two women with a smile of lazy indifference about his lips, but his eyes had hardened. "Lady Francesca is my invited and very welcome guest," he replied provokingly.

Gilda took a pace nearer to Francesca, staring at her with murderous, spiteful eyes. "I suppose you've slept with her!"

He was suddenly annoyed, and there was that dangerous glow in his eyes which Francesca had learned to recognize and dread. "I do as I damned well please!" he said in a sort of snarl. "Don't nag me, woman! Control your shrewish tongue! By God, do I have to beg your permission every time I fancy a wench?"

Gilda did not drop her gaze and tremble before his wrath; she returned glare for glare. "So, while I was away, bearing messages to Grisan Giorg, you tumbling this high-flown madam, with her milkwhite skin and haughty ways! How could you be so base? You know that I've offended my people by living with you. Didn't those times you made love to me mean anything?''

Alexis scowled, leaning against one of the carved figures supporting the overmantle. He kicked at a log with the toe of his boot. "We've been over this before, Gilda. I don't love you—I never have. Why can't you accept it? I enjoyed your body, a man would be crazy not to, but I love no woman!''

His voice was cold, and Francesca stood as if turned to stone. Her dream of changing him, of making him love her, shattered into fragments.

Gilda started to shriek, a stream of highly colored invective pouring from her lips. She was transformed into a violent harpy, stamping her foot and screaming with thwarted passion. Alexis lost his temper, roaring back at her, infuriated by her recriminations, ordering her to curb her rancorous tongue. Francesca listened bleakly as they argued. It was useless to try and convince herself that there was nothing between them. They had obviously been together a long time, even their heated quarreling indicated strong emotions; they had past memories to share, common bonds of country and custom. She felt an outsider, numbed by what she was hearing, her thoughts in a shambles.

Gilda swung round on her, giving vent to the full blast of her frustrations. "You stupid ninny!" she yelled. "D'you really believe that he could care for such as you? If you can't see what he's like, then you must be blind, stockblind! He laughs at women like you when he's done with 'em! I am his mistress, soon to be his wife and the mother of his sons!''

Her English was near perfect; she must have spent many hours learning it from Alexis. The thought of him sharing intimate moments with this vixen, as he had done with herself a short while since, made Francesca feel physically sick. She drew in her breath, then hissed it out through her teeth. "I think not . . ." her voice was level, chilling, every syllable a measured insult, "You are a common, ill-mannered strumpet, and I'm sure that Count Alexis would not wed you in a million years. He will want to be quite certain that his offspring are really sired by him, not by the last man to whom you opened your legs!"

There was an outraged gasp. "You dirty little whore!" Gilda spat violently.

"How dare you call me names?" Francesca landed her a savage box on the ears, and while she staggered under the blow, grabbed a fistful of curls, barbarous, unbridled exaltation tearing through her as she felt her nails lacerate Gilda's scalp. With a violent jerk, the gypsy pulled Francesca to the floor where she fought like a wildcat, screaming abuse, hampered by her silk skirts. Gilda promptly knelt on her, fingers at her windpipe, but blind, insane rage gave Francesca unexpected strength and she brought up her knee and rammed it into Gilda's groin. Heedless of her stockinged legs exposed to view, she lashed out with her feet, aiming vicious kicks at the gypsy as she bent double in agony. Gilda roared, her features twisted into a diabolic mask which made her hideous to behold. She launched herself on her rival who bit, clawed and kicked like a mad thing, giving Gilda the battle of her life, though she was well-used to fights and toughened by soldiering. Bloody scratches appeared on cheeks and arms and breasts as they rolled on the ground, pounding at each other.

The men were too stunned by the speed of it to move. Then Alexis waded in, narrowly avoiding being hit himself, hauling Francesca off Gilda, whom she had pinned down in an attempt to gouge out her eyes. He grasped both her arms, yanking her up and holding her with difficulty, while her kicking heels damaged his shins.

"Hellcat!" he barked, his voice harsh, but with a thread of amusement in it. "Your temper will be the end of you!"

"Damn you! Release me! Attend to your precious trollop!" Francesca shook with a violent paroxysm of rage and hatred.

Roger was struggling to control Gilda, swearing when she sank her teeth into his hand, dealing her a backhanded swipe which stopped her in her tracks. She hung in Roger's grasp, cursing Alexis in a variety of languages, and including Francesca in this vindictive tirade. He set Francesca on her feet, her small wrist still encircled by his big hand. He was a formidable giant who could have snapped her brittle bones like matchsticks, but he held her with gentle firmness.

"Shut your mouth, Gilda! Unless you want my fist to close it for you!" He warned ominously.

Francesca stood silent, her breasts heaving, skirt ripped to the thigh, her bodice half torn off. Her legs felt like jelly and she was trembling violently, body smarting all over with bruises, teeth and claw marks. She had never felt more humiliated, disgusted because she had allowed herself to sink to Gilda's level. The love which had been blossoming in her heart for Alexis now seemed the grossest betrayal of her high-souled ideals. It must be rooted out!

She was vaguely conscious of Lavinia clucking at her side, and felt a friendly hand on her arm. It was Mark. Ranby hovered uncertainly nearby, giving support to the near-swooning chaperone. Francesca had an overwhelming desire to be alone—waves of sickness sweep-

ing her as she headed for the stairs. She was encased in
granite. The fierce light had gone out of her eyes,
replaced by lead. This was not sullenness or petulance—
it was paralysis of all feeling.

Her chamber was deserted and, helped by Mark, she
entered it gratefully, flinging herself across the bed and
giving vent to the storm which throbbed into life again,
raging inside her. Of course Alexis would have a
mistress! A man like that would not have lived without
women! She hated herself for caring so much, disgusted
by her abysmal weakness. The bed sagged on one side,
then Mark was there, speaking consolingly, handing her
his scented lawn kerchief. She blew her sorely damaged
nose, her sobs subsiding to an occasional hiccup. An invigorating indignation swept through her. They were
more than welcome to each other—Gilda and Alexis! A
pair of heartless gypsies, as common as dirt! Mark
agreed spreading placating hands, his arms going round
her, holding her close. She put her head on his shoulder,
a wan look on her bloody face, eyes dull.

"You love him, don't you?" Mark's voice was muffled, sad. "Despite everything, he has captured your
heart."

She shook her head in futile denial. "Oh, Mark, I
don't know. How can I love such a dreadful man?"

Mark's eyes were bleak as he answered philosophi-
cally, "Love is not negotiable. One may not want it,
may fight against it, but its power is supreme, and it can
drive the most balanced person to extremes."

He raised her hand to his lips, and she felt a sudden,
inexplicable desire for the situation to have been different. Had he been less of a gambler, more a man of
honor, then they might have been married long since
for, had it not been for his avarice, they could have
eloped in Paris or Vienna. But at least he had been

honest with her, impulsively, she lifted her mouth to his, receiving a soft, almost brotherly kiss. At that moment the door crashed open and Alexis came in like a tornado, his face setting into hard lines when he saw them on the bed.

"So, madame. It has not taken you long to seek consolation elsewhere!" He thundered, striding towards them. Mark shrank into the bed curtains, sure that he was about to hit him; but Francesca sprang to her feet, furious at his boorish intrusion.

"He offers me friendship," she fenced, eyes stormy. "Something which I doubt that you would understand between a man and a woman, for it is pure, platonic and rather fine."

He gave a snort of unpleasant laughter. "So that is what he would have you believe, is it?" He jeered. "My dear, you are so naïve."

Her lips were so stiff with anger that she could hardly speak. "Did you come here to insult me further? Go back to your vulgar whore."

The gratuitous thrust went home and he stiffened, then one eyebrow shot up, a mirthless smile distorting his lips. "Don't tell me that you are jealous."

"You have a mighty high opinion of yourself, Le Diable." She mouthed his nickname like an obscenity. "I fought her because she was insolent to me." It was difficult to stand erect and lie to him. She thought she had succeeded until she caught the gleam in his eye.

"That, and something else, I think," his mood had changed and he answered her quietly, smiling and making to take her hand, but she drew away as if burned. She was not to be cajoled. Fear, almost terror, forced her to cling to the one safe emotion—hatred. Ever since he strode into the chamber, she had been drawing on all her strength to combat him and the sapping menace of her love. She longed to surrender, to run into his arms and feel the fine curves of his shoulders underneath her hands, to nestle her cheek against his chest. His spread fingers would play up and down her spine and he would pat her waist with the same loving carelessness he used to fondle his hounds so that they made short, jealous rushes and were tumbled over by his outstretched boot. Then he might murmur little endearments into her hair, and she would put up her lips and kiss the flesh under his firm chin in the way that pleased him. Her yearning for this almost made her feel ill.

A slight frown marred his forehead as he stabbed a suspicious glance at Mark, so silent and wary, seated on Francesca's bed. Was the little bitch playing him false? A selfish strumpet willing to use any man to get her own way? Women! A man never knew what went on in their devious minds.

It had been an ugly scene with Gilda and he had been shocked by her behavior. What a shrew! What a firebrand! She had been his mistress, true. They had known each other on and off for years, but there had never been any question of matrimony, at least not on his part. She should have known better than to descend on him like an avenging angel. No one in their right mind dared to question his actions, least of all to upbraid him for his affairs with women. Gilda was no saint, anyway. Many men had enjoyed her favors.

Francesca looked so beautiful standing there, blooded and disheveled, as defensive as a frightened kitten, claws out, eyes flashing, mouth set willfully. He was seized with the powerful desire to snatch her up, take a horse and flee with her to some remote cave high in the mountains, away from the complications of other loves—the demanding Gilda, the weak, vacillating Mark. Damn the duchess and her minions! He'd a good mind to call off the negotiations with her and keep Francesca with him always.

Softened by this idea, he stretched out conciliating hands once more, but again she backed away, refusing to be mollified. He had a deal of explaining to do before she allowed him anywhere near her. "I want you to return to the feast with me," he began, with his most disarming smile. "There has been a grave misunderstanding, and I would like to talk to you about Gilda."

"I don't want to hear, and I'm certainly going nowhere with you!" The very mention of that name was enough to block any headway he might have been making.

He flinched beneath her slant-eyed fury then, moving like summer lightning, he seized her and swung her up over his shoulder, ignoring her incensed yells. "I'm not prepared to argue. You'll do as I say! I want you down there with my guests."

Somewhere behind his back she saw Mark move as if to come to her assistance; but then Alexis was off along the passageway and she found herself shifted down so that her face was pressed into the hollow of his throat. She breathed in the heady smell of him, that combination of sweat, leather and the wine he had been drinking. With senses swimming, she sighed, "Alexis, why are we forever at loggerheads? Could you not have told me about Gilda before?"

They had reached the top of the staircase and, seeing that she was not about to run away, he let her slide to her feet, keeping an arm about her. "There was nothing much to tell," he frowned, perplexed by the things which bother women. "She and I have always been free—there was no commitment."

"She thinks there is." With her feminine intuition, Francesca knew that Gilda was in love with him and

grimly determined to keep him, come hell or high water!
Then gloom swamped her again, feeling the strong
pressure of his arm, his hand fondling her waist,
knowing just how Gilda must feel about losing him.
"What is the use of us discussing anything? I am
promised to another, and must continue my journey
when you set me free."

His mouth set in a grim line, a fearsome light in the
amber eyes which blazed down into hers. "We'll see
about that!"

Question and answer flashed between them in the
white heat of silence and Francesca caught her breath,
unable to believe the sudden tenderness which momentarily softened his face before he regained his iron control.

The peasants shouted with pleasure as they saw them,
broad Slavic faces wreathed in smiles, glasses lifted aloft
in tribute, and Alexis descended like an emperor,
drawing her with him, her fingers still clasped in his.
Mark slipped like a shadow in their wake, protectively
keeping Francesca within sight, though when the chance
had been given him to defend her, he had failed
miserably again. Gilda straddled a chair, her arms
folded along the back, eyes mutinous, her cronies
around her, that wild coterie with whom she roved on
Alexis' business. It was as well that looks could not kill
or Francesca would have been dead on the spot.

Alexis, wary-eyed, wanting peace between them,
thinking with male simplicity and singular lack of in-
sight that they could be reconciled, said, "Gilda, why
don't you talk with Francesca? Get to know her. And
Francesca, she can help you with your language . . ."
Then he fell silent, seeing that they were bristling like
two warring cats, giving a shrug and a wry smile, for the
atmosphere was fraught.

Try as they might to revive it, the party spirit had been dampened by the disturbance and the night was well advanced; guests began to drift away and those remaining were in a pensive mood. The gypsy violinists played on, their music dreamy, filled with glittering glissandos, the notes falling like drops of ice, clear and bell-like. The rich Rumanian wines had produced a mellow, reflective mood in everyone it seemed, with the exception of Francesca. She felt that she was going mad, horrified by the murderous thoughts which controlled her each time she looked at Gilda. True, Alexis was ignoring the gypsy, although she had tried to catch his eye several times. In fact, he hardly spoke at all, a thousand miles away, his eyes world-weary and smoldering. At length Francesca could endure it no longer, pressing a hand to her throbbing temples and leaving hurriedly, her only desire to reach the seclusion of the bedchamber. Her last sight of Alexis was of his tormented eyes set in a face of stone as he watched her go. Gilda moved to his side, a jeering smirk on her lips.

She flung herself into the middle of his bed, sobbing heartbrokenly. Her world had crumbled into small pieces, so she cried and raved, beating at the pillows with her fist. Oh, he might fancy that he wanted her now, presenting her to his people almost as if she were his chosen bride, but had he not done that with Gilda? They'd most probably shared this very bed! She groaned aloud in anguish at the thought, rolling to the very edge of the mattress, tortured by pictures of them lying there in each other's arms. She was about to jump up and flee to the sanctuary of the couch when Hetty came in, distressed to see her in such a state, insisting that she undress and allow her cuts and bruises to be bathed.

"Oh, my dear lady, don't weep so!" she begged, her

warm, motherly heart touched by her mistress's grief. "No man is worth it."

"I suppose he's with that brazen strumpet at this very moment, laughing at me!" Francesca wailed, sitting meekly under her ministrations.

"Not a bit of it, my lamb," Hetty assured her. "I've just come from the Great Hall, and she's taken herself off in a huff—very much out of favor, judging from his black looks. He's talking with Captain Willis and that gypsy Duke. Now don't you jump to silly conclusions. Get into bed and try to rest."

"I can't possibly sleep with him!" Francesca protested as Hetty laid back the covers, sliding a brass warming pan over the sheets.

"Of course you can," answered Hetty, briskly practical. "Lord love you, the bed is big enough. You can spend the night there easily without touching him. Not that I'd want to, mind you—he'd tempt the chastity of a nun!"

Francesca was too depressed and weary to protest further, obediently drinking the cup of hot milk which Hetty prepared, unaware that the maid had sprinkled a sleeping potion into it. Soon, her sorrows slipped away, swallowed up in slumber, and she relaxed with the ease of a child, waking drowsily in the middle of the night to feel Alexis' warm body molded against her back and his hand lazily caressing her. She experienced a very feminine stab of triumph over her rival and, pretending to be asleep, submitted to his searching fingers, his touch making her tingle and sending waves of delight rushing through her. He brushed his lips across her shoulders and his breath raised the down on her skin. Francesca quivered, caught up in wanton anticipation as his hand wandered down over her belly. It was as if she still dreamed, heavy with Hetty's potion, but she managed to gasp and pull away, only to find herself trapped by her own hair. Reaching out, he dragged her back, forcing her head down to meet his kiss. Her lips trembled beneath his burning mouth, and though she still struggled to free herself, she soon gave up the futile attempt as he pressed her back among the pillows.

She woke with a nervous start hours later, to find the room filled with daylight. Her body was uncomfortably wet, the sheets damp with the sweat which was pouring off Alexis. He was shivering violently, though his skin was hot to the touch, restless and muttering, his face flushed.

She sat up sharply, pummeling his arm. "Alexis? What ails you?"

His closed lids flickered and opened. Then he was staring at her, screwing up his eyes in the effort to focus. " 'Tis nothing, a fever which takes me at times . . . call Dinu, he knows what to do."

Francesca looked at him with growing alarm. He certainly seemed very sick. She rang for Dinu and hurriedly donned petticoat and chemise while waiting his arrival, though stiff and sore from her scrap with Gilda. Fragments of the night's events filtered through her mind, but she was too concerned about Alexis to give them much thought. She wrenched open the door and shouted down the hallway for one of the guards to fetch Hetty, who came at once and helped her into her gown. Francesca did not have time to wash or paint her face, she simply tied back her heavy hair and borrowed one of her maid's aprons to protect her skirt. Dinu answered the summons, cocking an eye at Alexis, recognizing the symptoms.

"He suffers these bouts now and again," he explained in his halting English. "They come on suddenly and lay him low for several days. He'll not heed me and take more care of himself . . . forever in the saddle in all weathers . . . gets a chill and neglects it . . ."

Francesca hung over Alexis anxiously; he was hardly aware that she was there. The sweating had stopped, though the fever was burning him up and he had developed a slight, dry cough. She swung round to Hetty, briskly ordering her to fetch the medicine chest from her baggage, frantically trying to remember what was needed. His illness resembled the ague from which her father suffered periodically and, when Hetty came back, staggering under the weight of the wooden, brass-hinged box, she fell upon her recipe book, thumbing through it while Dinu shrugged impatiently, saying that a concoction of brandy was all that his master would usually take. She ran an oval fingernail down the closely written pages, finding the one she wanted and rummaging through the contents, opening pots and packets, finally finding agrimony to lower the temperature and a decoction of the inner bark of alder for the fever. Dinu was briskly instructed to make himself useful, stoke up the fire and fetch hot bricks wrapped in flannel to pack round Alexis' feet, while she mixed a drink of the two ingredients. When he had done this, they stripped the bed and spread it with fresh linen. A difficult task which took all three to complete, for Alexis grumbled and swore continually, throwing off the covers as soon as they tucked them round him. The water in the skillet had boiled down and she added the medicine to it.

She took it over to the bedside where Alexis now lay prone, mumbling deliriously under his breath. The room was terribly hot and airless, but he must be induced to sweat freely and the potion would help this. With Dinu's aid, she hauled Alexis into a sitting

position, bracing his back against her shoulder and
reaching over to stuff another pillow behind him. When
she took up the pot he turned his face aside, flinging up
an arm and almost knocking it out of her grasp, but
Dinu seized his head and she poured the mixture into his
mouth. Then they laid him down and piled extra
blankets on him. Just for a moment he lay there looking
up at her, his expression miserable and humiliated. She
knew well enough that sickness would shame him, for
he would think it a weakness. She smiled encouragingly,
running a hand over his hot forehead, and his eyes
rolled shut as he slid back into unconsciousness.

The day passed quickly—a hazy time during which all
Francesca's concentration was fixed on nursing Alexis
and making him well again. She had little faith in Dinu's
haphazard methods and insisted on doing everything
herself. Alexis had a few lucid periods when he
demanded water, coming to himself long enough to
drink it down in greedy gulps. Dinu kept the fire blazing
and renewed the bricks. Soon Alexis started to sweat
again. This was a dangerous time, for he needed watching constantly to ensure that he remained covered. The
fever was at its height and he raved like a madman,
though she could not understand what he was saying.
Dinu, translating, said with a grin that he was cursing a
great deal and this she could well believe. He would find
it most frustrating to be helpless. Roger came in during
one of his more conscious spells, receiving his muttered
instructions, taking command—for there was pressing
business on hand and Alexis was extremely worried at
his incapacity.

"Where is Gilda?" Francesca kept her voice low as
she saw him to the door.

One of Roger's peaked eyebrows shot up and he
grinned impishly. "She's hanging around the vicinity

with a face sour enough to turn the milk. Not very pleased with life at the moment. But we've to ride out and scour the neighborhood. Word has come that some of the duchess's troopers are in the area. It needs investigation. I'll take her with me.''

By nightfall, Francesca felt stupid with fatigue, every bone in her body seemed to ache and there was a gnawing pain in the small of her back. She wanted to cry with helpless frustration, for Alexis' cough had worsened and there was no sign of the fever breaking. Trying to be sensible, she forced down some of the supper which Hetty had brought in, but it stuck in her throat. To strengthen herself, she drank the mixture so lovingly prepared by her loyal servant, which contained a pint of milk, white wine, the yolks of three eggs and a pinch of cinnamon. She sent Dinu off to rest and shed her own clothing, slipping on her loose, cool nightgown and brushing out her hair. Alexis seemed to be sleeping and she lay down on the bed beside him, watching the patterns of firelight shift across the shadowed room. The night grew very still and she propped herself up on one arm in the tent-like, canopied bed, unable to get her fill of looking at him. With those disturbing eyes closed under the fringe of long, curling lashes, she could take her time, lingering on every feature. He, usually so much in control, was as helpless as a baby, his face poignantly boyish, the frowning lines smoothed away, the lips pouting slightly, not compressed. Her heart ached with love as she pulled the covers more closely across his chest, bending to tenderly press her lips against his damp brow, brushing back a heavy lock of hair which straggled across it. With a contented sigh, she curled up, close to his side, and within minutes was fast asleep.

An odd sound woke her with a terrified jump. Gray

dawn was just beginning to lift the darkness, and she saw that Alexis was standing by the bed, unaware of her or his surroundings, in the toils of delirium. He was mouthing something in the gypsy tongue, his eyes starting with fear. Slowly, Francesca backed away, easing herself from the bed, never taking her eyes from him. He looked insane and she was horror-struck. Then he stumbled and crashed across the quilt where he lay sobbing convulsively, his hands digging into the mattress, shoulders heaving. He wept with deep racking sobs which seemed to come up from his belly and lungs; the effect was terrible and heart-rending. Francesca snatched up a blanket and covered him, for he was naked and sweating profusely.

"Alexis, my dearest love." She was on her knees beside him, her arms going round him, her fear swallowed up in pity. "What is the matter? Do not fear—I am with you."

With frantic annoyance she saw that he was still only semiconscious and tried to get him back on the bed; but he was over twelve inches taller than her and much heavier and she could not shift him. Swearing aloud and sobbing, she ran to where Dinu slept. She pounded on his arm and he shot up, his hand flying to the hilt of the saber which lay at his side. She rapidly explained while he dragged on his breeches. Together, they heaved the inert body of the big man into the depths of the four-poster and, while settling the coverings about him, she noticed that he appeared to be sleeping normally—his skin was cool, his breathing even.

" 'Twas the fever crisis which drove him mad," Dinu nodded sagely. "He'll quickly recover now, madame, thanks to your nursing."

Dinu was quite correct in his judgment. A day later, Alexis was so much better that she dared open the window a crack, letting in the crisp air and a shaft of watery sunshine. She had been busy all morning, tidying the room, making medicine, changing the sheets and washing him. Alexis lay and watched her, still too weak to move much, his face paler now that Dinu had shaved him, dark crescents beneath his golden eyes. Francesca sang softly, and came over shyly to brush his tangled locks, pushing in the waves with the palm of her hand. During his illness she had served him as devotedly as she knew how without thinking of the future.

"This seems to be becoming a habit of yours . . . saving the lives of Titus . . . and myself," he said haltingly, with something of the old mockery sparkling in his eyes.

Francesca could feel herself blushing like a schoolgirl, made suddenly awkward by his approbation, her heart leaping when he slowly turned his head on the pillow so that he might kiss her fingers.

In the days which followed while Alexis recovered, they knew a close companionship, an enjoyment of just being together, playing chess and reading, occasionally looking up to talk. Francesca clung to each golden moment, fearful of the morrow, knowing that it could not last. She was jealous of any intruder. Even Dinu or Hetty brought the outside world into this peaceful oasis and, in many ways, she dreaded each sign of his returning vigor, for soon she would lose him to his soldiers, his peasants. Once the pressing question of her ransom was settled she would have to go on to Govora.

She tried to put some of these sentiments into words one night as they sat in the firelit glow after supper. Earlier, Alexis had taken a turn round the castle, worried about his men, checking that there had been no slacking in discipline during his indisposition. In a flutter, bereft by his absence, she had changed into a gown and robe of purple silk, a purple so rich and dark that it appeared almost black in some lights, evocatively sensual against Francesca's creamy skin. It clung to her full breasts, displaying the rosy nipples shamelessly, swirling like a cloud to her feet. Two slender ribbons on each shoulder were the nightgown's only means of support and, with a tightening coil in the depths of her body, Francesca knew that it would take but one tug for Alexis to undo them. The dressing robe had long, billowing sleeves so transparent that the satin whiteness of her arms gleamed through the gathers. It was a deliberately provocative ensemble and she had put it on in a mood of defiance, weary of being dutiful and sensible. When he strode in he paused for a moment at the doorway, taken aback by her tantalizing beauty, and there was a look in his eyes which made her spine tingle. But he did not touch her—not then.

They supped almost formally at a table set for two before the fire, though Francesca was so excited she could hardly eat, fascinated by the long, lean man lounging in the cushioned armchair, legs stretched out to the blaze, Titus lying on the rug at his feet. There was something new about their intimacy now, the bonds of the flesh linking them, overwhelming her with delight. She felt herself to be on the threshold of love—a vast magnificent love which could be theirs, and which would keep them stretching out yearningly towards one another over time and space forever. Unable to sit still, she went to him, sinking down on her knees, head thrown back, looking up into his dark, almost sinister face, with adoration blazing in her eyes.

"Alexis, what are we to do?" she cried. "I must remember my duty and go to the margrave."

"And I must save my men. There has been no answer from the duchess and I fear for the lives of my messengers." His face was grave, but the perfume of her had a rousing effect on him and his expression changed, hardening into intentness. Bathed in crimson, the contours of her breasts rose above the silk, the deep cleft between in intriguing shadow. He reached out, running a finger around the low-cut edge of the bodice. "I like your dress," he said in a husky whisper which made her want to cast it aside. "Let us make the most of what little time we have."

He loosened her breasts from the low slipping gown, his thumb warm as it brushed her nipples. Francesca could not restrain a moan of sheer animal pleasure as he fondled her. She was so hungry for him, she thought she would scream if he did not take her soon. Her whole body was on fire. He lifted her up against him, holding her between his thighs and she sighed, pressing closer, mouth parting as his tongue flickered inside her lips. He took his mouth from hers, bent his head and softly nuzzled her neck, moving down to her nipples, circling first one, then the other. Unable to help herself, she buried her fingers in his curling hair, holding him there, not wanting him to stop. His hands moved over her bare flesh lovingly, as if he delighted in the texture of it, and then he was shaking, his desire seeming to scald through her every nerve. His lips clung to hers as if he wanted to suck out her very soul, and any of her fears which still remained were swept away. This was the man whom destiny had singled out to be her mate. With him everything seemed natural, simple and beautiful. To belong to him, to remain with him, helpless, possessed, was all that she wanted in life. The realization filled her with blinding delight.

With infinite care, he lifted her in his mighty arms and bore her to their bed, and she forgot everything as his hands and body played with her, drawing her ever deeper into a swirling well of pleasure. All through the night, again and again, Alexis roused her to a point of near delirium before taking her, and each time she experienced those exquisite feelings which heralded complete ecstacy. He was quite unable to leave her alone, allowing her to doze only slightly before possessing her once more. Francesca was as eager as he for that sweet conquering, answering the demanding fire in him with a blaze of her own.

It was day when she awoke, finding herself curled in his arms, her head on his chest. His eyelids lifted and he smiled sleepily, brushing his lips across her brow. It was a simple gesture, lit by warm affection and it wrung her heart. She freed herself from his arms and sat on the edge of the bed, dragging her robe about her as a shield against her own powerful desire to remain there, naked, with him. She pressed her two palms against her temples, trying to think clearly. It was difficult to maintain concentration with Alexis so near, even more hard when he reached over to lift a curling tress from where it lay on her breast, his fingers touching her nipple so that her heart jumped wildly. Summoning up her willpower, she rose and paced over to the window, gazing out on the dewy morning.

"Alexis, I have need of time to collect my thoughts," she began while he watched her indulgently, his bare shoulders and chest very brown against the white bedlinen, totally relaxed, the way men are after loving women. He was prepared to humor her.

"What would you like, little love?" he asked pleasantly.

What indeed! She wished that she knew. On the one hand, he was her beloved to whom she had now given herself joyfully; the deep commitment, for she was by nature a monogamous woman, was not moral or intellectual, but a physical, chemical reaction, holding a strange purity. Her nerves, blood and flesh would always respond to Alexis and to no one else. On the other hand, he was her enemy, though the last few days had seduced her from her purpose. His company was becoming hourly more tolerable so that she, so strong, willful and determined, had been weakened and brought low by a brigand who despised women. Now, to her further degradation, she had to confess to herself that she was madly in love with him and had become his very willing mistress. What was she to do?

She pushed open the casement and the chill, fresh wind struck her face, bringing with it the scent of pines, damp soil, a vivid recollection of the cathedral-like groves of the forest. She swung back to him. "Alexis, will you give me permission to ride for a while? Thus, I can clear my mind. I have not breathed clean, sweet air for days. Will you let me go?"

A strange, alien look stole into his eyes. "Will you promise to return? There are lives at stake. Can I possibly trust you?"

"Can you still doubt me—after last night?" She challenged, so clear-eyed and sincere that she won him over. He wanted to believe her, yearned to regain his faith. This would be a test. If she came through it, why then, all else could go to the devil. He would claim her as his own!

His amber eyes were riveted on her with an almost alarming intensity. "Very well. Go for your ride. Roger shall accompany you."

"Oh, darling, thank you!" Impulsively, she flung her arms round him, eyes bright like a child anticipating a treat. "You must trust me. How else can our relationship prosper?"

He gripped the white flesh of her shoulders, shaking her so that she stilled, holding his gaze. "I warn you, if you break parole, those left here shall suffer. Hetty, Lavinia, Mark, every goddamn one of them!"

Chapter Nine

THE DAY was cloudy, threatened by rain, but Francesca was as happy to be out in it as if it were summer. Her spirits rose as she jogged alongside Roger, on a sturdy, short horse prudently provided lest she be tempted by a swifter mount. It was cold, bringing a glow to her cheeks, invigorating after such close confinement. The air was like wine, fresh from the mountains and, as they clopped through the wildly beautiful terrain, she beheld fresh views of crystalline torrents dashing between granite cliffs clothed by firs as tall as the masts of ships.

"Can we not go there?" She reined in, pointing with her whip to a small hill topped by a shrine. It had been weeks since she prayed, and now, more than ever in her life, she felt the need of guidance, conscience-striken because she had shirked her devotions.

Roger gave her sidelong glance and his lean face broke into its usual merry smile. "A shrine, dearest lady? D'you feel yourself to be a sinner?"

Francesca blushed, annoyed with him. He was obviously well aware of what had passed between herself and Alexis. She surprised the horse by using her spurs, breasting the hill then slipping from the saddle. Her riding habit was superbly cut, fitting her neat waist and full bosom to perfection, and Roger admired her as he too dismounted. She genuflected, crossing herself before the small, weather-beaten niche which contained a faded statue of the Virgin and Child. Roger stood in respectful silence, the horses cropped the turf and, overhead, a flock of wild geese took their migratory path south. Very wise, he reflected, snuffing the air, experienced enough to recognize the signs of approaching winter. Suddenly he stiffened, shading his eyes and staring intently into the distance. There were horsemen on the skyline. Not wishing to disturb Francesca, he watched them carefully. They were coming closer and he felt in his bones that the two of them were the object of attention. As they approached, he became uneasily sure of it. They wore red and white uniforms, the colors of the duchess's soldiers. Roger cursed and reached for the pistols in his saddle.

"My lady! Mount at once, and ride for your life, back to Balvany!" His voice cut through her meditation and she looked up, startled. But it was too late, the troopers were already at the base of the hill, riding up it. She heard the menacing click of Roger's pistol and the singing of bullets from the intruders. Their leader shouted to Roger to surrender, and he lowered his weapon. Almost at once, they were surrounded by well-trained cavalry men, smartly equipped in scarlet jackets and white breeches, with shining black boots, glittering swords, and tricorn hats. There were twenty of them, forming a ring on their prancing steeds, and the officer addressed the astonished couple.

"Lady Francesca Ballinger, I believe," he bowed over his mount's chestnut mane. He was a fat, dark-skinned lieutenant with restless black eyes, narrow lips and heavy, scowling eyebrows. His troopers kept their pistols trained on Roger.

"That is my name," she answered, gloved hand on

her horse's bridle, totally thrown by this sudden turn of events.

"Madame, I come from the duchess," the officer spoke in quite good English. "It is my pleasant duty to rescue you from that saucy rebel, Le Diable. By happy chance we were in the vicinity."

"How did you know that I would be riding this morning?" She faced the men haughtily, unimpressed by their appearance.

He smoothed the thin dark line of his mustache. "I have my informants, madame."

Francesca bit her lip, not knowing what to do. The very last thing she wanted was to go to Govora; all other considerations apart, Alexis might think that she had broken parole and betrayed her word to him. She frantically racked her brains, seeking a way out. Roger moved nearer to her, though menaced.

"Damn it!" he muttered, furious. "I knew this to be a foolhardy jaunt, but Alexis was so insistent that you have your way. I should have followed my instinct and brought a few stalwart fellows with me."

"I have my instructions from the duchess," the officer spoke imperiously, motioning to a couple of soldiers to disarm Roger and guard him closely. "There is a message for Le Diable. Go you and deliver it, sir. No tricks, or his men now in her hands will die most painfully!" He pulled a letter from the breast of his uniform, a stiff roll of parchment, closed with an impressive seal.

"I cannot leave with you now," Francesca broke in, pale, lovely face upturned to him. "I am on parole, and my servants will suffer if I do not return."

His lips curled. "Fear not, Lady Francesca. The contents of that letter will persuade Le Diable to free your people and also hand over the dowry."

Roger glowered defiance, but had no recourse but to

obey. Francesca grabbed his arm as he turned to remount and be about his unpleasant errand. "Oh, Roger," she whispered urgently. "Tell Alexis what has taken place. Don't let him think that this was a plot and I part of it!"

The burly captain patted her hand. "I will speak up for you, madonna, though I must admit that I am puzzled. I was aware that the duchess's men were reconnoitering the district, but how they knew you would be here, practically unguarded, is a mystery." He shrugged and his firm lips turned down at the corners. "There are still those willing to sell information to her, and she pays her spies handsomely."

Events moved swiftly, an inexorable Juggernaut crushing Francesca's frail hopes of a happy future. Mute, despairing, she was escorted to an inn in a nearby hamlet, there to wait Roger's return. The quivering host and his menials, too scared to argue, hurriedly obeyed the officer's demand for food, while his men quartered themselves all over the building, using his hay for their horses, his wine for themselves. Francesca was taken to the parlor, seated like a frozen statue by the hearth, unable to partake of victuals. She could vividly picture the scene at Balvany, where Alexis would be possessed of a cold, blind fury, more terrifying than an outburst of rage, allowing hatred to engulf him, stifling any feeling he once had for her, convincing himself that it was a plot and that she came from the same callous, despotic mold as Renata, resolved to save his men at all costs. He would make no attempt to rescue her, thinking that she wanted to go to Govora, and all she could pray for was that her servants would be released unharmed, those innocent victims of this violent political struggle.

Hours passed, and she did not know what to expect. Numb with anguish, she ignored the lieutenant who was inclined to preen himself, full of his own importance, hinting of the reward awaiting him for his brave rescue of the beautiful future margravine. But at last the party arrived from Balvany, and she clung to Roger's hurried assurance that he would continue to plead her case with Alexis though, at that moment, he was too angry to see reason. She cried herself to sleep in Hetty's arms in the lumpy tavern bed, too weary to think further.

The mists of dawn shrouded the mountains and a thin shower of bright needle rain laced the air as the cortège left the village, winding down a twisting path through the shivering trees to a cleft which formed a pass cutting the towering range. A messenger had been sent on ahead to Govora so that they could be met outside the town walls and the prisoners exchanged. Roger and a small group of his men went with them to see the business formally concluded. Francesca huddled in the coach, staring unseeingly at the landscape, those fields of stones and boulders, the alpine peaks, the dense forests of fir, larch and beech. Lavinia and Ranby murmured together, well pleased to leave Balvany, planning what they would do when they arrived at Renata's court. Francesca was hardly aware of their existence, still seeing with inner vision the lofty turrets of the castle on its craggy pinnacle: dark, grim, yet holding all she wanted in life, its difficult and complex owner.

They traveled through the whole of that dreary day, stopping once at a shabby hostelry for food. She was given scant consideration; speed was of the utmost if they were to save the lives of those still in the duchess's clutches. She had threatened torture, and the imagination balked at what this might entail.

Riding through late afternoon drizzle, they finally came out on a narrow plateau in the center of which lay a small, walled town. Soon a group of horsemen appeared at the main gate, dragging with them a roped line of manacled men. Roger spurred his horse to meet them. Hetty, hopping excitedly at the carriage window and very nearly falling out, urged Francesca to join her and, listlessly, she watched him rein in as a tall rider on a bay mare broke from the main body. They exchanged frosty civilities, and she saw Roger unhook the money-bags from his saddle, handing them over. Her dowry, which had already caused so much trouble. The stranger clopped sedately along with him when he wheeled to return to the coaches.

Roger leaned across to open the door and, now level with the two mounted men, Francesca stared into the face of the stranger. He sat very upright in the saddle, an impeccably attired nobleman wearing faultlessly tailored black velvet. His jacket fitted his thin frame perfectly, his breeches were smartly cut, his boots highly polished. He removed his three-cornered hat, holding it against his chest as he bowed to her, his dark hair, winged with gray, confined into a braid. Then he raised his head and fixed her with most peculiar, agate colored eyes. It was a look which pierced her brain like an icicle. Warning bells clanged in her head. His face was long, narrow, with deep grooves carved by cynicism on each side of his ugly mouth. His right cheek was marked by a scar which ran crookedly from the corner of his eye, twisting his upper lip into a permanent sneer.

"Madame, welcome to Govora, at last. May I present myself? Baron Cezar Orlandos, at your service. The duchess had sent me to conduct you to the town, safely delivered to us." He spoke perfect English with just a trace of foreign intonation, but his eyes lingered on her face and figure for a fraction of a second too long, giving her a decidedly uneasy feeling. A pang of fear and loneliness shot through her as Roger made his farewell, gathering up the wretched, starved-looking prisoners, knocking off their chains and seeing that they had mounts.

Regretfully, she watched him out of sight, the last link with Alexis, who was probably at that moment already consoling himself in Gilda's arms. The thought filled her with such frustrated anger that she was at her most dignified as Cezar gave orders and they lumbered behind Renata's army under the ornamental gates and through the winding streets of the town. Francesca gained a jumbled impression of timbered, red-roofed houses, rich with carving, a large church with mosque-like spires, and a sullen throng who lined the route, their hostility like a living presence as the grim-faced troopers cleaved a path for the carriages. Sporadic scuffling broke out, and the vehicles were hit by a rattling rain of stones. A gaunt, ragged woman leapt in front of the horses, screaming and shaking her fist. She was brutally knocked aside by the soldiers, who were wielding the flat of their sabers without compunction.

Ashen-faced, Francesca turned to Ranby who was conversant with the language. "What did she say?"

Ranby fidgeted in his corner seat, mopping at his face with his kerchief, totally unnerved. " 'Death to the tyrants!' " He translated gloomily.

"What ails the peasants?" queried Lavinia crossly, having had high hopes that their entry into Govora would have been in the manner of a triumphal procession with herself waving graciously to an adoring crowd.

"It is a warning sign," commented Mark thoughtfully, eyes brooding as if seeing into the future and not liking what it held. "I was aware of it in Paris, a savage undercurrent of discontent. The lower orders of any country will take only so much—then they turn."

"Good Heavens!" exclaimed the chaperone. "I did not leave hearth and home to accompany Lady Francesca, only to be set upon by brigands and then attacked by a mob with staves and stones!"

"Let us pray that we shall receive a more cordial welcome from the duchess, dear lady," soothed Ranby as she rested her dimpled, beringed hand on his arm.

The cavalcade toiled by torchlight up cobbled inclines and across a square adorned with statues and a fountain, dominated by spires and towers. They were confronted by a huge building, its fantastic roofline silhouetted against the lowering sky. This was Castle Costin, their new home, a massive palace behind a fortified walled enclosure. Flares flickered and bobbed at the high double gates, reinforced with iron studs and bars, then they rolled under its archway, crossed a wide courtyard and swung to a standstill below a flight of stone steps.

With a sinking sense of doom, Francesca looked up at the dark hulk of the building, lit here and there at the upper and lower windows. In the smoky glare of the torches, shadows danced over its florid, outrageous grandeur and every surface seemed to writhe with carving, wildly distorted. As she hesitated, fighting her qualms, she was conscious of someone at her elbow—it was Baron Cezar. Dismounted, he was lanky and lean and there was an air of authority about him, but when he addressed the servants or troopers his demeanor suggested that he used the power vested in him quite unscrupulously. He carried his inches stiffly, and his reptilian eyes had a wary look, his mouth set in a disapproving line, accentuated by the livid scar.

"Come, my lady," he spoke in a soft, smooth voice, and held out his arm. Francesca rested the tips of her gloved fingers on his sleeve, holding the rest of her body as far away as possible without giving offense. On the whole, she did not very much like the suave Baron Cezar.

A highly ornamental doorway loomed ahead, its lintel surmounted by a stone dragon with a singularly

ferocious expression. The entrance hall was daunting,
very long and lofty, darkly paneled, and the mass of
yellow candles glowing in the branching holders danced
on the carved banisters of the great staircase. Soldiers
were posted at the entrance, armed and uniformed in
scarlet, and a number of flunkies in dark blue liveries
bustled about performing their duties. Cezar ushered
Francesca into a reception room, an even more overpowering apartment, baroque in the extreme, but with a
distinctly Eastern atmosphere too, suggested by arches
and grills, its upper walls bearing a spirited series of
warlike paintings, its lower half covered by an inlay of
semiprecious stones which reflected the light with a
somber glitter. The scene was one of gloomy, barbaric
magnificence.

It was very cold. The logs smoldering in the enormous
stone fireplace did little to diminish the dampness in the
air which struck into the very marrow. At the end of the
chamber there stood a dais with two thrones, and Francesca walked towards it, dumbfounded by the extraordinary tableau which met her eyes.

Cezar was bowing and introducing her but, though
she saw his lips move, Francesca was too bewildered to
grasp what he was saying. She stopped, fear grabbing
her throat, for Zoltan was standing just behind the
duchess's chair, clad in the bizarre uniform of captain
of the guards. He peered at her through slit eyes and a
mist of intoxication; Renata kept him well supplied with
wine. Recognition slowly dawned and his face split into
a drunken leer.

The brilliant, multicolored assembly packing the
room hushed as Francesca stood before the duchess.
She drew in a sharp breath, pressing her hands to her
thudding heart, as Renata rose to her feet, an imposing,
very alarming figure. She was a tall woman, queenly in
bearing, her strongly defined features betraying little

but an overweening pride. Though middle-aged, she was still very beautiful, her coloring suggesting an Italian origin. An oval face with pronounced cheekbones, a thin, high-bridged nose and full red lips, was framed by black hair caught back into a gold-meshed chignon. Her expression was impossible to read. Thirty years of turning a false face to the world had left their mark, molding her countenance into a mysterious, impenetrable mask. From head to foot, she was clad in amethyst velvet, and her gown was plain, almost severe, with a closely-fitting bodice, sweeping skirt and long, full sleeves. The high neckline was relieved by a circlet of the same purple gems set in solid gold. From her shoulders to the floor flowed yards of material of the matching, regal color, forming a cloak lined with white fox fur. In the other gilded chair huddled the figure of a man, but Francesca did not have time to scrutinize him for the duchess was addressing her imperiously.

"Welcome to Govora, Lady Francesca. I was indeed angered to hear that you had been abducted by that scurvy rebel, Alexis Romanesco." Her unusual violet eyes flashed, rage darkening that white brow. "He shall be caught and punished, I promise you! He and his ruffian crew are forever plaguing our vicinity. He rouses the peasants to insurrection! We have a score of long standing awaiting settlement."

Cezar placed the dowry on the top step of the podium. "I have not yet checked it, Most Gracious One, but I have Le Diable's word that it is intact." He spoke in a deferential voice, his manner part servile, part intimate.

"Can one trust that conniving vagabond?" snorted the duchess, staring down her nose at him.

"Madame, he well knows the swiftness of your vengeance should he attempt to cheat you," rumbled Zoltan, with a bold wink.

"You speak wisely, Zoltan," she gave him a smile which did not touch the coldness of her eyes. "I retained two of his men as a precaution. Even now, they are in the deepest dungeon of the Daliborka Tower, and if I find one penny missing, their heads shall adorn the spikes over the town gate by dawn."

Francesca could feel her reason tottering. The atmosphere was rife with oppression—it seemed to seep out of the very walls. In spite of the magnificence, the crowd of beautifully costumed courtiers, the obvious wealth and luxury, this castle was a barren wasteland of unhappiness. One fact shone crystal clear—Alexis was not just a mountain robber. Full of fire and force, he was dedicated heart and soul to helping the peasants throw off the yoke of the Pascaly tyrant, and she now knew him to be in the right. Her awareness was flickering, as if a flame was passing and repassing across her vision. The scene revolved, slipping in and out of focus. The thronged room, blur of silks and glittering uniforms froze for an instant, etched sharply like figures on a stained glass window. The duchess swung round, urging the man beside her to rise.

"Carl, my son," she held out her hand commandingly. "Come, meet your bride."

He stared vacantly for a moment, huge, hairy hands dangling aimlessly between his knees then, used to obeying his mother, the Margrave Carl lumbered to his feet. Francesca stood still, unable to credit the evidence of her own eyes, staring blankly at the man to whom her father had given her. His robes hung about him awkwardly, as if he were costumed for some monstrous play—a large youth with dull hair, and a massive head which hung forward as if too heavy for his neck to support. His great, mild blue eyes searched Renata's face pathetically seeking her approval, and he hung back, till she gave his arm an impatient jerk, forcing him to stand next to her.

Dreadful clarity sharpened Francesca's confused mind. The earl, her father, consumed by his fateful, overriding ambition for her, had promised her hand in marriage to an imbecile, mature in body, but with the mentality of a young child.

After the initial shock, Francesca came to her senses, fighting for her very existence, staunchly meeting the barrage of the duchess's bitter disappointment at her refusal to fall in with the wedding plans, for she had decided that the nuptials should take place the following week. It was hard not to weaken beneath the implacable wave of Renata's determination. Both she and Cezar brought every argument and threat into play, but Francesca dug in her heels, stubbornly insisting that they give her time to reflect and, for a while, they withdrew, though she had the uneasy feeling that they were planning some more telling means of persuasion. Battle-scarred and weary, Francesca welcomed the respite. It was as if her tired mind, unable to withstand further assaults, formed a protective layer round itself through which sensations were carefully filtered; it was a blotter which soaked up the wrong feelings before they could do any harm, and made her behave in every way like an admirable doll, sitting and standing when told, curtsying at the right moment, turning a blank, beautiful smile on those who addressed her. If she did not do this she was lost—wandering in a wilderness of desolation, prey to that most destructive of human emotions, despair.

She dared not even dwell on her father's part in it, making excuses for him, telling herself bravely that he could not have known of Carl's affliction, nor the enormity of the duchess's crimes and her lust for power.

Though Hetty's natural exuberance had been some-what subdued by the atmosphere of the palace, she had not been idle, infiltrating the servants' quarters, gossip-ing with the ladies' maids, valets and grooms, conveying information to her mistress. "They tell me that the duchess is deeply involved in witchcraft, ma'am." She would come out with these tantalizing snippets of hear-say while attending to Francesca's toilet, the only time they were granted any privacy. "She is known as La Sorcière!"

Her sparkling eyes were round with alarm as she chat-tered on in this vein one morning, her face appearing in the mirror behind Francesca's head, working on her coiffure, tucking a stray curl into place, securing it with a diamond-headed bodkin. "Her sexual appetite is enormous—and depraved! I am assured on the very best authority that she thinks nothing of bedding half a dozen lusty fellows during the course of a night!"

"Gossip, Hetty," Francesca replied languidly, in-clined to disbelieve backstairs tittle-tattle. She yawned widely, filled with the lethargy which always followed if she had been drinking wine served at the duchess's table the night before. More than once, it had occurred to her that it might be drugged, thus insuring that she would be apathetic and stop putting up opposition to the un-palatable marriage.

" 'Tis true, ma'am, I'm sure of it." Hetty was in deadly earnest. "And they say that she sleeps in sheets of black satin which give added luster to her limbs. That Zoltan now, I'll wager he beds her too!"

Francesca shivered, for Zoltan was forever lurking, following her like a grotesque shadow, grinning and pantomiming with his huge hands if she spun round and caught him. These disquieting suppositions were in her mind when she obeyed the summons and attended on

Renata later that morning. Hetty went with her, since
Francesca needed her moral support, for the palace was
an awesome pile, scene of many a dark happening in the
past.

The castle boasted a massive black tower, built of
blocks of lava. It was known as the Daliborka Tower,
and was rumored to possess a series of underground
cells into which serious offenders against the Pascaly
regime were lowered by ropes through trapdoors. The
duchess resided in outrageous splendor in an aerie at the
top of this gloomy turret and, to reach her, it was necessary to clamber up a perilous stone spiral staircase.
Zoltan mounted guard outside the studded door at the
top, wearing that peculiarly exaggerated costume in
which Renata uniformed her troops. He winked insolently at Francesca, eyes running over her figure with
unconcealed relish. She could feel her cheeks burning,
but outstared him and his eyes shifted away, opening
the door so that she might enter.

The room was fantastic. Renata was not a woman to
do anything by halves, and this intimate den with its
atmosphere of oriental decadence openly stated one
aspect of her diverse personality—that of extravagance.
Each item of furniture or rare, beautiful object, had
been carefully selected. There were mirrors and intricately wrought frames from Venice, carpets from
Oltenia, and great brass candleholders with their rings
of perfumed candles. It was very warm, almost suffocatingly so, heated by the log fire leaping in the
elaborate chimney, and there was a peculiar odor, sweet
and sickly, rising on the smoke from a chafing dish. The
great bed took pride of place; six feet in width, with
shallow steps leading up to it on either side, and silken
curtains of that deep, imperial purple so beloved by
Renata, who held court there, already busy with the
affairs of the day. There were several other persons in

the room; Cezar bearing a sheaf of documents for her signature; her grim-visaged waiting woman, and a footman carrying a silver tray on which were fragile china cups, a wisp of steam rising from each, rich with the aroma of hot chocolate.

"Come hither, child," Renata patted the place beside her, but Francesca declined to be seated. She watched, fascinated, as those long, pale fingers delved into the rosewood jewel cabinet balanced on the duchess's knees. A scintillating cascade of gems ran through her hands, as she held up first one gorgeous piece and then another to throat and ears, while gazing into a mirror held by a young hussar, vacant and amiable, who usually carried round her fan. Having selected an opulent necklace of fire opals, she subjected Francesca to the full, unnerving attention of her violet eyes. "When you marry my son, you will look marvelous. Your wedding gown is ready and I have chosen the jewels which you will wear. They will be a gift, of course, yours to keep. It will be a simple ceremony, conducted by Father Dietmayr, whom you have already met."

She nodded in the direction of the priest who was warming his backside at the fire, portly and prosperous-looking, wearing a brown soutane. Ears pricking at the mention of his name, he rocked gently on his heels, the light gleaming on his tonsured pate. His face was florid and a little too full, his eyes a shade too bright and protuberant. "I am honored to perform this pleasant duty, Your Illustriousness," he beamed.

The way in which that strong-willed woman had them all eating out of her hand was almost ludicrous. Even the priest turned a blind eye to the fact that Mark was lolling on her bed, leaning on one elbow, looking appealingly rumpled. Whether he had been there all night or had only just arrived was a moot point. From the start, he had warned Francesca that it was his intention to ingratiate himself with the duchess, saying that by so doing he could best serve her interests; but now she cynically wondered if it was selfish motives which were making him curry favor. Whatever the reason, it seemed that he had succeeded. The hussar and he were glaring at one another, making ill-natured jibes, while Renata treated them with scornful indulgence, and Father Dietmayr smiled his bland smile, pulling at his pendulous red lower lip.

Renata snapped her fingers at her maid, who brought a brocade dressing robe over to her, and with notable lack of self-consciousness, the duchess flung aside the silken bedclothes and stood up, attired only in a flimsy nightgown which displayed her voluptuous body. The hussar sprang forward and held out the robe while she slipped her arms into it. "Come with me, Francesca," she ordered, sweeping toward another door.

Annoyed by her peremptory manner, Francesca followed, finding herself in a dimly-lit apartment. It was obviously a study, filled with shelves, each one overflowing with books; mostly weighty, ancient tomes. On the circular table lay horoscope charts, cards and a crystal ball on an ebony stand. There were antique burial urns too, and a grinning human skull. This was Renata's sanctum to which none gained access without direct invitation. Francesca felt an icy shiver creep down her spine, for this dark, stuffy lair contained the accounterments of the necromancer.

Renata turned to her, eyes glowing. "My dear, I can understand that the prospect of being Carl's wife pleases you little. I have not bothered you for some days, leaving you to reflect on your duty. You must look upon me as a friend who wishes to help you. Believe me, if you cooperate, you will not find me lacking in appreciation. Honors and wealth will be heaped upon you, but it is imperative that you produce an heir as quickly as possible.''

Anger at this blatant statement made Francesca shake, and her chin set mulishly. ''Is that my function in life then—a brood mare giving birth to a succession of Pascalys?''

''What did you expect when you came here? Consideration? Love, perhaps?'' The duchess sneered, obviously thinking softer emotions to be a sign of weakness.

''I cannot think why my father committed me to such an alliance.'' Francesca spat out a grievance days old, discretion thrown to the winds. Her head was clear, her wits honed. Though she struggled in a web nigh impossible to break, at least they should know her true feelings.

Renata smiled, a slow, menacing curve of the lips, pacing to the table, picking up the cards, shuffling them with skill born of long practice, then spreading them into fans. ''The earl is no fool. He has business interests in Austria of long standing. Govora is rich in minerals, and there is much to be gained through trade with the Hapsburgs. It is all a matter of politics and finance. The arrangement has proved profitable for both families. Carl was but two when the contract was drawn up, no one knew that he would not grow up to be normal. Later, I saw no good reason to inform him.''

Francesca was bristling, every word the duchess uttered cementing her loathing and distrust. ''It seems that I am nothing but a pawn, a chattel to be passed from hand to hand, with no will of my own.''

Renata pursed her lips, looking down at the cards, a frown rucking her brow. ''It has ever been thus in the ruling class. Personal desires have to be sacrificed for the good of all.''

''How much have you sacrificed, madame?'' Francesca demanded with a sudden flash of maturity. ''Your lifestyle suggests that you have done naught but gain by your political maneuvers.'

"That is neither here nor there." Renata stabbed her a warning glance, gathering up the pack as if what she read there bothered her. "Your duty is to provide us with a male child."

"Is Carl capable of becoming a father?" Francesca whispered, shuddering away from the thought of sleeping with that slobbering, pitiful young man.

"I doubt it," replied his mother crisply. "But a child must be born, nonetheless. If he cannot do it, there will be others only too willing to assist!"

"What mean you?" the enormity of this suggestion took her breath away.

"Oh, don't play the innocent maiden, Francesca! You are a highly desirable girl, three-quarters of the men at Court are lusting after you, you must know that! I have no objection to you taking lovers, but be selective in your choice. I favor Baron Cezar as the sire. He comes from an old and very distinguished family. You should have little difficulty in giving us a lusty boy from such stock."

"I couldn't do that!" Francesca's voice rose an indignant octave, shocked to the core. "Would you really palm off another man's bastard as heir to Govora? D'you think you could get away with such deception?"

"No one would know." Renata leaned closer. "And if they suspected, they'd have the good sense to keep quiet or face the consequences! No one dares to cross me!"

It was on the tip of Francesca's tongue to shout that she intended to thwart her at every opportunity, but seeing the cold glint in her eyes and recalling the tales Hetty told of her skill as a poisoner, she bit the words back. If she was cautious and prudent she might be able to escape before long. And what then? whispered that thin, chill voice within her. D'you hope to run back to Alexis? He doesn't want you. He has made that very plain. He has Gilda.

Whichever way she looked at it, she was in a mess. So she dropped her eyes and assumed a meek, compliant pose, suffering the duchess's blandishments, for she became sweetness itself once she thought she had browbeaten her into submission, plying her with gems, painting a glowing picture of the wedding ceremony, promising a life of ease, pleasure and luxury. "I'm holding a ball in your honor," the duchess said, her arm about Francesca's waist while she tried not to cringe away in disgust. "To celebrate your betrothal and forthcoming nuptials. Carl likes you, and I suggest you spend much time in his company, even encourage him into your bedchamber. Who knows, a miracle can happen and he may react like a proper man."

Francesca slept very little, facing the dawning of the betrothal party. She climbed from the high bed, desperately alone, creeping to the casement. Below, the treetops floated in a white mist, like woodcombings, blowing up to the castle walls and billowing over the shoulder of the slope. The damp mystery of it added to her mounting terror; the window was fast shut, the huge building silent, even the guards seemed to slumber. It was as if the palace lay under an enchantment. A spell induced by Renata? Outside it was dawn and a distant rooster issued raucous challenge to the faltering sun not yet risen out of a raggle of night clouds, blackish over the eastern sky. Francesca turned and fled back to bed, terrified, drawing her rosary from beneath the pillow, grasping the familiar beads' solidness.

That evening, she behaved like an animated doll, walking stiffly, radiantly lovely in a gown of silver lutestring, the tightly laced bodice pulling in her waist and

thrusting up her breasts, narrow sleeves ending at the
elbow in a cascade of lace, the skirt puffed out on either
hip and swirling into a train at the back. The underskirt,
displayed by the swept-back over robe, was the color of
a raspberry, and had a center panel richly worked in
pearls forming a stylized pattern of flowers. The effect
was dazzling: the low bodice flattered her sloping
shoulders, and the careless glimpse of silken shift that
barely hid her breasts gave deeper color to her perfect
skin. Her face was waxen beneath the two spots of
rouge with which Hetty had dusted her cheeks to hide
her pallor, and she allowed them to move her from place
to place without protest, smiling until her face ached,
receiving the guests in the banqueting hall. And all the
time she was lost in a daydream in which Alexis suddenly rode into the midst of the celebrations, sweeping
her up on his great black charger and making off with
her.

But nothing happened. Mark came and went; he was
beautifully dressed and so was she—that was the sum
total of their conversation. He walked about the hall
talking to people, paying court to Renata, and laughing.
Francesca laughed a lot too—the wine helped. Hetty
saw to it that her glass was kept topped up, drinking
a good deal herself, surrounded by a circle of young
officers who guffawed loudly at every saucy remark she
made. She had a penchant for military men with their
twirled mustaches and dashing attire, while they could
not resist the trim English maid who rolled her eyes so
boldly, prying away their secrets without them being
aware of it.

The duchess outshone everyone, blazing like a comet
in a golden gown which flashed as she moved, a train of
spotted ermine falling to her feet, a diadem of pearls,
diamonds and rubies adorning her handsome head.
Carl's confused eyes lit up when he saw the feast, and he

spent much time at table, cramming food into his mouth
with grunts of satisfaction, oblivious of all else. Somehow, Francesca managed to survive the evening but,
when she sought the privacy of her bedchamber, it
seemed that her ordeal was not yet at an end. With grim
determination, Renata led her son into the room. Francesca stood frozen, in a white cambric nightgown with a
low neck, huge belled sleeves caught in at the wrists, and
skirts which whispered to the floor. Her unbound hair
rippled across her shoulders and down her back. Renata
touched it briefly, murmuring, "It is up to you now, my
dear. Try to get a response from him if you can, but if
not—there is Cezar."

Francesca shook her head. "What you suggest is
monstrous!" she grated in a low voice.

Renata shrugged, bending to give her a peck on the
cheek, one eye on Hetty and Carl's attendants, who
stood awaiting orders. "Suit yourself, child. You can
easily be replaced. No one will mourn your sudden
unexpected demise."

She patted her son on the head and shooed everyone
from the room. Francesca could hear their noisy progress fading in the distance. The silence which followed
was like having cottonwool stuffed into the ears. She sat
bolt upright on the side of the bed, arms clasped round
the hump of her knees, staring at Carl, wondering what
he would do. He was twisting his head from side to side,
peering into the shadows, a worried scowl on his round
face with those fleshy lips, bulging eyes and heavy
underjaw.

Over the days, motivated by an odd, aching pity,
she had tried to communicate with him, but it was very
difficult. He was not articulate, knew some English
phrases shouted at him by his impatient mother, a few
words of Italian, and a curious, babyish patois picked
up from the servants. She shut her mind against the

tormenting vision of how it would have been had Alexis been there in his stead. Brooding on such a theme was a sure road to madness, and she was fighting desperately not to break down. But it seemed that she had nothing to fear; Carl showed not a glimmer of interest in her as a woman. He was more terrified than anything else, having learned to fear the female very early on. As a child he was beaten and ill-treated by Renata, who never forgave him for being a shambling half-wit, a constant reminder that in spite of her wealth, her beauty, her knowledge of magic, she had been unable to bring forth the handsome, brilliant heir for whom she craved.

"Well, Carl, what are we to do?" Francesca said at last with a wry smile.

At the sound of her voice, the boy started, shrinking into a corner, hiding behind the curtains. He mumbled something indistinguishable, shivering and shaking his head. God! He's even more frightened than I, she thought, and continued gently, "Don't be afraid, Carl. I shall not hurt you. You know me, do you not? I am Francesca."

He was unused to soft words and sincere smiles, his childish blue eyes wide and wondering. "Fan-fan . . ." he brought out with a great effort.

"I want to be your friend." She enunciated the words slowly, and he nodded, giving an answering grin.

"Friend, my friend," he stammered, and the happy smile spreading over his face touched her deeply. With infinite care and gentleness, he reached out tentatively, expecting rejection. She remained passive so as not to scare him. His great, blunt fingers passed over her hair, a soft touch, full of hesitation. "Fan-fan, friend," he repeated, encouraged by this reception of his overtures. He fumbled in one of his pockets, pulling out a bag. "See, Carl show you."

The contents tumbled on to the coverlet. It was a

collection of lead soldiers and Carl excitedly tried to stand them in a row, baffled because he could not achieve this on the uneven surface. Francesca cleared a space on the tulipwood side table, and ranged the soldiers in orderly lines. Carl gurgled with pleasure, seizing an orange from the dish of fruit nearby, bowling it along and knocking down some of the members of the miniature army.

"Bang! Whizz! Boom!" he exclaimed, happy with his imaginery artillery. "Carl have cannon. Kill soldiers. Mama say, 'Good boy, Carl.' "

Later, when he wearied of warfare, she taught him simple card games. It was very quiet and companionable; the candles touched her hair with gold and glowed softly on his sandy head, bent close to hers in solemn concentration. A bronze clock on the mantlepiece whirred before striking midnight, and Carl suddenly put down his cards, and curled up at the foot of the bed like a faithful dog, falling asleep at once. Francesca eased down under the covers, her eyes wandering the room restlessly. Oh, Alexis, where are you? she cried in her soul.

It was almost two weeks since she had seen him, and the memory was beginning to fade, like the edges of some half-forgotten dream; she could no longer visualize his features clearly. She allowed herself the indulgence of recalling every incident of their brief encounter, brooding on each detail of their bitter quarrels, their frantic loving, torturing her mind by imagining him making love to Gilda, furious with her for not returning to Balvany, thinking it a plot. She felt raw, as if she was bleeding to death inside. All right, so he did not want her, hating her as he hated the Pascalys; yet it was pure agony to be parted from him, unable to know for certain where he was or even if he was safe from harm. He might be stranded in some ravine, fatally wounded or already dead! She clung to the hope that this was unlikely. Roger had told her that he seemed to live a charmed existence, taking the most appalling risks yet coming off unscathed though always plunging in where the fighting was thickest. His reactions were lightning swift, his aim unerring—a most competent commander.

In that desolate moment, she would have given anything to see him stride into the room, brushing all aside with his dominating presence, sweeping her into his arms. She wanted to lay her head against his chest and hear the steady pounding of his heart, remembering with aching longing the sweetness of his mouth, the knowing caresses of his strong hands. Those golden eyes would gaze deeply into hers, smiling at first, then changing, darkening with passion, and there would be that slight twist to his mouth, cynical and reserved, yet sensitive too, and he would speak to her with that quietness in his voice which still held the promise of suppressed violence. She thought of the last time he had loved her and her blood raced, fire running through her thighs into her loins. She tossed in the lonely bed, gritting her teeth against this longing for union with him, which was like a pain stabbing in her guts.

Chapter Ten

IRON FROSTS gripped the land, a bitingly icy cold. Francesca had never before known such low temperatures. It paralyzed her, making her huddle close to the fires during the short days and seek her bed early during the long nights. Then the snow came, blizzard-borne from the mountains blanketing the plateau from the outside world. Winds gusted round the palace, pasting white blobs to the windows, making Francesca a virtual prisoner within. If she was allowed out, there was very little pleasure to be gained, for the duchess's heavily guarded carriages drove through silent streets where the air was thick with hostility. In the great, gloomy castle she trusted none except Hetty. Even Lavinia had been won over, basking in Renata's favor, always elaborately gowned, dictatorial to the servants, filled with an exaggerated sense of her own importance. Ranby spent most of his time incarcerated with her resident astrologers and alchemists, learned men with flat, secretive faces. There were women too, and pretty pages whom Renata used as spies, setting them loose if foreign emissaries arrived. The ambitions of the day would be forgotten in the pleasures of the night. Next morning, these beguiling ladies or honey-skinned boys would come and present their reports to the duchess, who would listen, cold and unmoved, to the story of their conquests, using what they had learned in intimate moments to her own advantage.

Renata encouraged every vice and depravity, using blackmail and extortion, pandering to human frailties, trapping the weak and foolish in her web of intrigue. Cezar was deep in her trust, ruthless and cruel. They were constantly plotting someone's downfall, exciting the mutual jealousy of the courtiers, those time-servers and place-hunters, sowing dissension among them and, at the slightest hint of resistance, threatening them with the gallows. Gradually, Francesca began to understand the rottenness which seethed beneath the façade, realizing that it could well be herself who drank the fatal potion, or plunged down one of the trap doors placed so conveniently in the lower passages, with a shaft leading down into freezing, fast-flowing water. The duchess was growing daily more impatient with her prevarications— she would not be able to delay the wedding much longer.

Hetty was not quite her only friend, there was Carl, too. He had formed a strong attachment to her, only happy when by her side, vacant eyes following her, face alight with adoration, sad if they were parted. It was not love in the accepted sense, more a mixture of worship and utter dependancy. She was mother, sister and companion, blended into one lovely woman who was kind to him. In return, she found herself fiercely protective, cuffing cheeky pages who mocked him slyly and called him "loon."

"He can't help it, poor lad," sympathized Hetty. "He's one of 'God's babies,' as we used to call such unfortunates back home. 'Tis no fault of his. Admittedly, he was born with but half his wits, but that old bitch has addled what little he did have!"

The days passed in dreary monotony, with Francesca becoming increasingly apprehensive. There seemed to be eyes everywhere. At each angle of the castle, round corners, bends of stairs, she would come across one of Renata's minions; either Father Dietmayr pulling pensively at his several chins, lashless eyes alert, or Zoltan or Cezar, grinning knowingly and nodding as if biding their time. She grew almost accustomed to the shadowy figures trailing her when she and Hetty, swathed in furs, braved the ramparts for exercise, though the air cut the lungs like a knife. One day, she made the mistake of going there alone. Hetty was busy and she had been unable to endure the claustrophobic atmosphere of the palace a minute longer, almost running up the dangerous, rickety stairs.

She stood by the parapet, feeling closer to Alexis up there in the open, peering in the direction of Balvany. Snow powdered the roofs far below and, like white moss, crusted the steep pointed gables, thickened every twig and leveled empty wagons. It looked pretty and fairylike, until she remembered the unrest festering among the townsfolk. A chill, muttering wind gusted past her, bringing a flurry of snow. Francesca sensed that she was not alone, turning swiftly. Cezar was behind her, angular and gaunt in his beaver-trimmed cloak, a fur hat protecting his head.

"Lady Francesca," he said, bowing over her extended gloved hand. "So bleak a spot for a walk."

"I needed fresh, wholesome air," she replied meaningfully. "That palace stinks of corruption."

"Surely not, madame. The duchess is most particular about the cleanliness of the kitchens!" he fenced blandly.

"You know what I mean, Baron," she snapped, nerves stretched out unbearably thin.

"Dearest lady, you are oversensitive." He had not moved but it was as if he had stepped closer, so smooth, so menacing. "In time, you will enjoy our little court, playing them off, one against the other."

"I am not as practiced as you, who seem to live by lies," she retaliated hotly, her sweet, mobile face shrouded in the depths of her huge sable hood, green eyes flashing at him in the gathering gloom.

He gave a dry, mirthless laugh. "Soon you will be living a lie, when you are carrying my child and pretending to all the world that it is Carl's."

"Sir, let me pass. I would continue my stroll alone," she declared, refusing to add to his perverted enjoyment by showing fear.

Cezar did not move, the curl of his lips ominous. "Don't give yourself airs with me. I know that you were Le Diable's mistress. I have some very reliable informers on my payroll."

Francesca gasped, then her hand shot out and slapped him across the face. "You are insolent, sir! Renata's tool you may be, but you have me to reckon with! I am fond of Carl and will not wrong him!"

He turned white, the scar standing out lividly. "Such high principles from a bitch who has been whoring with the rebels. It is useless for you to resist the wedding plans. Maybe it is time you sojourned in the Daliborka dungeons. It is quite remarkable how a few days in its clammy atmosphere can change the mind of even the most stubborn."

"You dare not do that!" she cried indignantly. "I am a citizen of England!"

He chuckled evilly. "My dear, you are hundreds of miles from home. Who will stop me?"

"There are those of us who will try!" rapped out a clear voice. Mark had come up behind Cezar, and swung him round with a firm hand on his shoulder.

Cezar's mouth set like a rat trap, hand flying to his sword hilt. "Renata's poet lover, eh? Keep your damned nose out of this!"

"Francesca's welfare is my concern." All cowardice had been stripped from Mark by the burning rage consuming him at the sight of this brave, lovely girl threatened by such a villain.

"Go, crawl back to the feet of your generous keeper, lapdog!" Cezar was in a dangerous mood, itching to pull out his rapier and run Mark through.

Mark ignored this deliberately provocative insult. Love Francesca he might, but he was no knight-errant, he controlled his temper, remembering that he could help her in more subtle ways. Renata would listen to him, for the time being he was her favorite lover and she was tolerant of the men who pleased her.

"Watch your step!" Cezar snarled menacingly. "I'll not forget this!"

He turned on his heel and swung away. Mark put an arm about Francesca's shoulders. "Come, my dear. Let me take you back to Hetty. 'Twas as well that I listened to an inner prompting and followed you up here."

It was so bleak on the battlements. Snow had begun to fall silently, powdering their cloaks, but it was no colder than the chill which touched her heart with fingers of ice.

Late one morning, Hetty came rushing in, heavy with news which Francesca sensed involved her. She glanced up at her maid's sudden entrance, taking in the gray, snow-laden skies seen through the small-paned windows, laying aside her embroidery with a shiver, stretching her cold hands to the blazing logs. It was hot near the fireplace in her bedroom, but elsewhere in the high-ceilinged chamber the dark velvet curtains that hung across doorways and at casements, moved and trembled under the fingers of the wind.

The two women were alone. Francesca spent much time there, preferring it to the lavish entertainments where Renata ruled over her sycophants, attending only when protocol demanded. Cezar continued to bombard her with pressures, and she was always uneasily aware of Mark's wry smile and apologetic eyes as he paid lip service to the duchess. He was in a delicate position, knowing that were he to put a foot out of place they might both be in peril; for his mistress was a jealous woman, demanding possession of the body and soul of those on whom she smiled. She had once shown him a pouch, richly embroidered with pearls, which hung from her girdle. In it was the heart of a former lover who had betrayed her.

During those solitary hours, fraught with homesickness and misery, Francesca's thoughts dwelt constantly on Alexis. Had he ever really existed? Or was he just a figment of her fevered imagination, conjured out of loneliness and longing and that craving for something that can never really be? She was hemmed in on all sides by Renata's demands for an heir, the granite walls of the palace, the encircling mountains, the blinding storms of that harsh winter. Hetty brought a breath of life with her, always cheerful, bubbling over with irrespressible *joie de vivre*.

"Oh, ma'am—guess what's happened!" She managed to lower her voice, giving a quick glance round to make sure that no one else was there.

From the depths of the big, winged chair, Francesca

gave her a brief smile, and a pang shot through Hetty as she noted her beloved lady's pale, pinched face, the fragile, withdrawn air, the huge, sad eyes. "Tell me, Hetty . . ." even her voice was wan, no longer filled with laughter. "I pray that you bring good tidings."

"Indeed, yes, my dear! At least, I hope you'll deem it so. You remember Joachim?" Hetty added with a blush and a demure drop of the eyelids, though impishness peeped through.

Francesca nodded, amused, for he was the latest of Hetty's string of admirers, a coachman in the duchess's employ, a sturdy, broadshouldered young man with a sensual smile, and Hetty said she was in love with him. Maybe this time she was, although Francesca found it hard to take her affairs seriously. Her lighthearted insouciance allowed her to be constantly fostering some romance or other in which she always remained emotionally excited, mentally stimulated, but unscathed.

"Well, it turns out that he's in league with Le Diable," she confided, settling down on the footstool near Francesca, her brown taffeta skirt rustling crisply as she clasped her hands round her knees. "I was ignorant of this until today. It is a close secret, for Renata would kill him if she found out, but I have confided your unhappiness to him, my lady, and you have his wholehearted support. Joachim spies for the rebels, admiring Alexis above all others. He couldn't meet me last night, said he had urgent business, but he did slip into my room in the small hours. Knows his way round all the secret passages of the castle—what a man!" Her pretty face was aglow with admiration. "He had been with Captain Willis at a meeting place in the mountains, and was given this letter to deliver to you—from Le Diable!"

Francesca gave a strangled cry, the blood rushing up

to pound in her temples. The ancient tiled floor threatened to rise and knock her into reeling blackness. Hetty held her firmly for a moment until the dizziness faded, then she thrust a small screw of paper into her hand. Francesca stared blankly at the unfamiliar black scrawl. It was written in English and very concise. She scanned it once without taking in a word, and then read it through again to Hetty.

"Francesca," he had written. "I trust that you have not forgotten me. I cannot put you out of my mind and long to see you again. There is also business of importance which I would discuss with you. Meet me tonight at the Haldrenski Hunting Lodge. I shall wait there for you. The bearer of this message knows where it is. Alexis."

The harsh stone walls, the brilliant Gobelin tapestries, tottered crazily through a blur of tears. Francesca gave way in Hetty's arms, laughing and crying in turn. It was so easy to weep these days, even now when she was in an ecstasy of happiness. "Oh, Hetty!" she sobbed, "he doesn't hate me . . . he wants me to go to him. Your Joachim must be well-trusted to be the bearer of such a compromising note. Dear God, let us pray that he never falls into the hands of Renata's torturers!"

When the first wild rush of joy was over, she forced herself to be calm, drawing on her inner reserve of control. The next few hours would be perilous, and it was essential that she exhibit a bland exterior, no matter her inner turmoil. Nothing must arouse suspicion and, more than ever, she was thankful for the loyal, competent Hetty who would meet with Joachim and arrange every detail of the hazardous journey to the lodge. She consigned the precious letter to the flames, though longing to tuck it into her bodice between her warm breasts, a link with Alexis. She burned for the night to come, aching with desire, her heart leaping as she remembered his tenderness, his energy and controlled violence, his understanding of her needs, his eagerness to give as well as take pleasure. But even if they were not able to make love, just to see him, to hear his voice, would be sheer bliss!

The hours crawled by and it grew dark. Francesca and Carl supped with Renata, and Francesca did not fall into the trap of being particularly nice to her, this would have assuredly convinced the duchess that there was something afoot. Darkness thickened. The table with its white damask cloth, stretched endlessly between herself and the duchess. Two silver sconces, ablaze with candles, fought a losing battle with the encroaching gloom. Soft-footed flunkies waited on them. Renata was not in a pleasant mood, lying back in her carved chair, her face dark, brooding, slanting purple eyes watching Francesca. She had wreaked her vexation on the peasants brought before her that morning. The smallest misdemeanor had been savagely punished. Floggings and hangings had been the order of the day, yet this had done little to alleviate her general feeling of dissatisfaction.

She was drinking steadily, pawing Mark who lolled at her side, while Francesca wondered uneasily whether she had betrayed herself in any way. It would be just like the duchess to say nothing, letting her believe that all was well, and then suddenly pounce. The evening seemed to last for an eternity, until Renata finally got to her feet, her arm linked with Mark's, eager to retire to her chamber with him. This was the signal for them all to leave, and Francesca and Carl mounted the stone stairs behind them, armed guards jumping to attention as they passed, servants running ahead carrying torches.

In the dressing room, Hetty was waiting to help Francesca into her night attire, looking pale and strained. "When everyone is asleep, you can put on the peasant clothes which I've hidden in the wardrobe," she whispered urgently. "All has been arranged, my dear."

Carl was seated on the side of the bed, playing cards to hand. A grin widened his mouth as Francesca came in, and she knew how much he looked forward to the nightly ritual of visiting her. Her nerves were taut as bowstrings but, to please him, she obliged, though it was almost impossible to concentrate on the game. After a while, she indicated vast weariness and he, knowing his part, leaned forward for a goodnight peck on the cheek, then lay down on the couch, cuddling the old crumpled damask cushion which he insisted on having by him, smoothing the surface, crooning to it, soon dropping off to sleep.

Francesca watched him with mounting tension. The candles dipped and wavered and the shadows seemed alive with rustlings. She stayed perfectly still, staring at him until she felt that her eyes would drop out. He lay prone, a trickle of saliva running from the corner of his mouth, the upturned whites of his eyes showing in a glittering slit. She straightened her aching back. He would be asleep for hours; there was nothing to stop her going to Alexis.

She joined Hetty in the dressing room, stripping quickly and putting on the thick woolen, calf-length chemise with long sleeves, worn beneath an embroidered skirt of dark blue. A loose, warm jacket topped this, and Francesca sat on the stool to pull on thick knitted hose, then Hetty helped her lace stout wooden soled boots on her slim feet. Her hair was concealed under a veil, decorated with coins and kept in place by a small round hat. While they hurried, all fingers and thumbs with nerves, Hetty told her that she must pretend to be Joachim's lowly girlfriend if they were questioned at the gates. A coarsely woven cloak completed her attire, and Hetty disappeared for a moment, returning carrying a brass lantern with horn side panels through which the light of a candle streamed.

"Now for the tricky bit," she whispered, eyes enormous in the dull glow. "Joachim has told me how to open the panel. 'Tis the way to a passage, ma'am, and he says the palace is riddled with 'em. This one will bring you out at a corner of the garden and he will be waiting for you."

Her fingers were busy going over the paneling near the little corner fireplace, seeking a vital knothole. There was a soft, muffled click and a narrow door opened, a draft of cold damp air rushing from the dark aperture beyond. Hetty thrust the lantern into Francesca's hand, saying: "Go, my lady. I shall remain here to ward off unwelcome questions and await your return. God be with you."

It took every bit of courage, and all her love for Alexis, to make Francesca step over the gloomy threshold. She stood in a dank, narrow passageway, whispering farewell to Hetty, hearing the panel close behind her. Filled with terror, she crept along, the lantern light bouncing off walls which ran with moisture. The quiet was almost audible, clots of deafening silence pressing on her ears. She came to a steep flight of stone steps which wound down into the darkness. They were wet, slippery, treacherous, and she descended with utmost caution. At the bottom was a further twisting corridor which seemed to go on for ever. Francesca was rapidly losing her nerve, beginning to believe it a trap. She might be shut up there for good! Starving to death in the bowels of the castle, another of Renata's hapless victims! Sobbing, praying to a god whom she was almost convinced had deserted her, she rounded another bend and came face to face with a tiny door. She pressed it with trembling fingers—it creaked open, and she stepped beneath its low lintel, finding herself in a remote, overgrown corner of the grounds where the entrance had been cunningly concealed behind an ivy-covered buttress. Joachim was there, a wide, relieved grin splitting his pleasant features, reaching out to grasp her hand. She had never been so overjoyed to see anyone in her life! The night was very dark; it had been snowing earlier and there was no moon. Francesca shivered as the chill wind struck her. The cold fitted like masks to their faces and their breath hung on the air.

Joachim knew very little English, guiding her with nods and gestures, and she took his arm, walking boldly through the garden toward a gate where a guard was stamping his feet and flapping his arms against his sides to warm his frozen hands. As if shy at being caught with her lover, Francesca kept close to Joachim, face averted, while they exchanged pleasantries and he slipped a bottle of brandy into the sentry's pocket. With a final slap on the back and a bawdy jest, the soldier drew the iron bolts and gave Joachim a key, promising that he would neglect to bolt up after him, so that he might let himself in later.

Once outside, they sped through the narrow streets, reaching a shabby quarter of the town where, in the yard of a tumbledown inn, a horse-drawn sleigh was waiting. Joachim solicitously tucked a big fur rug about her knees and took the reins. They glided swiftly away from the sleeping houses, heading toward the dark mass of the forest. Francesca huddled under the wrap, the cold knifing her lungs, peering into the eerie gloom where the snow glistened and the gaunt trees loomed ahead. Joachim had a musket at hand. "Against

wolves," he informed her grimly. They were a continual
hazard, particularly at this time of year when they
roamed in starving packs, and few villagers dared ven-
ture forth after dark.

Deeper into the woods they went, the towering pines
lining the way like foe waiting in ambush and, overhead, star spears stabbed the dark, frosty vault of the
heavens. The horse kept up a brisk trot over the fresh
layer of snow, the sleigh sliding effortlessly behind him,
and they quickly covered the miles, soon reaching the
Haldrenski Hunting Lodge. Joachim knew it well, driving confidently under the archway of the gate built into
the high surrounding walls. It was a large, comfortable
building, designed by a prince long ago to accommodate
him when he rested after the chase. Renata sometimes
used it during the summer months, but now it was
deserted. Not even a caretaker was left to look after it,
and it wore a chill, empty air. Francesca shuddered, and
wondered yet again at the madness which ran in her
blood. Why was she not lying snug and warm in her
bed, instead of engaged on this lunatic assignation
which was quite likely to cost her her life?

Her feeling of unreality strengthened as they skirted
the grounds, seeking entrance at the rear. The courtyard
was thick with snow, and there were unmistakable
tracks scoring its surface—the prints of horse hooves,
and deep footmarks. Trembling anticipation banished
all other emotions as Joachim reined in. There were
heavy wooden shutters at the windows and, within
seconds, they stood at a solid oak door while he rapped
on the wood—three short knocks, followed by a longer
one. They heard the squeak of a bolt, the rattle of a
latch, and it opened a cautious crack, a thin ray of light
silhouetting the figure of a man. Francesca's heart
leaped then plummeted with sharp disappointment—it

was not Alexis but Roger who greeted them.

Thawing out in the warmth of the kitchen, Francesca's eyes darted around, seeking her lover. Roger beamed his delight at seeing her, grasping her hands, drawing her to him and kissing her frozen cheek. He was in high good humor, bluff and hearty as ever, stamping about in shaggy boots and a smelly goatskin jacket, peasant's gear adopted for the purpose of disguise, voice loud and hearty, as he said "Madonna! As beautiful as an angel! Even living in Castle Costin has not dimmed your glory! But I see by the stars in your eyes that you are expecting someone else, eh? Don't worry, sweetheart, he is here—that good-looking bastard who always captures the hearts of the wenches I most want to lie with!"

He was kindness itself, that burly, boisterous blade whom Francesca might have loved had he not been eclipsed by the overpowering attraction of his leader. He was never happier than when tricking the enemy, passing into their midst in various disguises, gaining information for the rebel commanders.

Joachim, grinning and gesticulating, unable to understand all of what passed between them but shrewd enough to catch the nuances, followed where Roger led, through to a further room with gleaming weapons and hunting trophies hanging on the walls. There, before a crackling fire in the gilded, heavily carved chimney, stood a tall, never-to-be-forgotten figure, handsome legs slightly apart to balance his weight, hands clasped behind the skirts of his coat. It was Alexis.

Francesca stood perfectly still, clinging to Roger's arm. Her head began to whirl, her heart pounding madly, and she was suddenly paralyzed, unable to move or speak. Roger came to her rescue, urging Joachim to relate the latest news from the town and, bemused, she listened to them talking, aware of nothing but the timber of Alexis' voice which scraped down her spine into her belly so that she badly needed to sit, her legs feeling as if the bones and muscles had dissolved. Then, as she recovered her balance, a tiny prickle of annoyance stiffened her pride. She had come miles and braved peril to meet him, and he was ignoring her! Her lower lip rolled out in a pout, and she subjected him to the blaze of her green eyes, compelling him to acknowledge her presence. Was this yet another ruse? In her angry disappointment, she almost expected to see Gilda come stalking into the room to mock her for her foolish gullibility. Yet, while she wrestled with these miserable thoughts, her body ached for him to come over and take her into his arms. Dear God! she cried despairingly within. It has been weeks since he held me, and I love him so much! Damn him!

Now the men had gathered at an oval table, looking down at the map spread on its surface. Alexis had stuck his dagger in one end to prevent it curling up, and Roger was tracing a pass through the mountains with one blunt fingertip. Thoroughly engrossed in planning their next move, they seemed to have forgotten her entirely. It was as if she did not exist. Francesca was not used to being ignored—she liked to exist, most emphatically, and for that damned stiff-necked Lord of Castle Balvany to know that she did!

She moved closer to the fire, the rough clothing and heavy boots feeling strange and uncomfortable. Maybe this country clothing was the reason for him appearing to be so cold and unmoved? She slid the cloak from her shoulders, letting it drop onto the back of a chair, and surreptitiously unfastened the top buttons of her woolen shift so that the deep cleft between her breasts was clearly visible. She seated herself, posing prettily, one leg crossed over the other—and waited for a response.

Roger was the first to surface from the deeply important conference. He ambled over and poured her a glass of wine, smiling into her eyes as he handed it to her. "We are nearly finished," he whispered, his eyes sparkling with laughter. "Then he is all yours, m'dear."

True to his word, within minutes he was clapping Joachim round the shoulders and taking him off to the kitchen, leaving Alexis and Francesca alone. The silence stretched out unbearably and Francesca had to break it. "Why did you wish to see me?" she asked in a tight, controlled voice.

He had been asking himself this very question, over and over. On the surface, his reason was that he needed her assistance. News had reached him of her unhappiness in Govora and her rebellion against the duchess when that lady had been expecting a compliant tool. He did not reply for a second, looking down at her. He was dressed in a pair of buckskin breeches and black boots, and white linen shirt open to the waist, displaying the dark curling hair on his chest, and lounged casually against the fireplace, his long legs crossed at the ankles, holding a goblet in one hand. In the saffron light of the fire, he looked extraordinarily handsome, and that strange, melting feeling was sweeping over Francesca, making all coherent thought impossible.

"I had several reasons for writing to you," he began, shifting position slightly so that she came under the full perusal of his golden eyes. "Firstly, they tell me that you would leave the court if you could. Is this true?"

His face was strong and proud, and her heart squeezed with anguish. How could he have even contemplated sending her away from him, knowing of Carl's affliction and the duchess's evil reputation? What right had he to question her now? With a militant gleam in her emerald eyes, she glared up at him. "If it is true, what does it matter to you?"

In clipped tones, he gave answer. "I could help you, but I shall need your cooperation. Can I count on it?"

Her chin lifted defiantly, though her fingers dug into the padded arms of the chair with the effort to appear composed. "Perhaps, it depends on your terms."

"You will have seen for yourself by now the injustice of Renata's regime. All over Europe, the peasants are stirring beneath the heels of their masters. Oh, admittedly, there are kindly landowners who have the welfare of their tenants at heart, as there are in England, but they are few and far between. I prophesy that, within ten years, France in particular will be plunged into a bloodbath the like of which has never been seen before." Alexis spoke very seriously, his eyes somber, and Francesca felt a thrill of foreboding running down her spine. She had been appalled by the duchess's greed and cruelty, her warm heart going out to the victims of her oppression, having attended her weekly court hearings, which were a travesty of justice. Yet, unfortunately, when the people did rise in rebellion, the innocent would suffer along with the guilty—good masters being slaughtered along with the tyrannical. She had never seen Alexis in such a mood of gravity, suddenly convinced that the stories she had heard about him were true and that he was indeed his people's savior, fighting the manorial barons not for his own gain, but for theirs.

"What would you have me do?" she spread her hands in perplexity.

With a lithe movement, he abandoned his casual stance and came to her chair. His hand reached down and gently tilted her chin, tipping her face up to him. Slowly, his eyes roamed her features, seeing the fire in her eyes, the determined set of her lips. Then his gaze went disturbingly to her throat and breasts, lingering on the smooth, rounded flesh exposed by the open neck of her chemise. "Can I trust you?" he mused. "Or will you prove as faithless as my wife, Maria, once was?"

It was like a violent blow in the stomach, and she jerked her chin from his grasp, leaping from the chair as if stung. "You are married?"

"I was, many years ago, but she left me for Baron Cezar, taking our infant son, lured by the luxury he promised. She died, the child too, and I fought Cezar, leaving the mark of my sword on his face which he'll carry for the rest of his life!"

His eyes were hard with remembered anguish, and she longed to hold him, to kiss away that look of baffled anger, make him forget for ever the woman who had wronged him. So many pieces of the jigsaw were suddenly fitting into place and there were more to come. At her expression of sympathy, he impulsively took her hand, holding it tightly, her pale, slender fingers entwined with his brown, powerful ones.

"I have seen Cezar's scar," she said with a shudder. "I hate him too, Alexis—so many horrible things have happened to me there. Renata is determined that I shall marry Carl and give birth to an heir, and the poor boy is quite incapable of being husband or father."

Alexis made a grimace of disgust, eyes flinty, but her face was soft, appealing, as she pleaded for mercy for her pitiable friend. "He is like a large, simple child, and has never laid a finger on me. He is quite harmless, fond of me because I am kind to him. You must not hate him, for it is his mother who is the wicked one. She is urging me to take Cezar as a lover so that I may become pregnant. She will pretend that the baby is Carl's and the rightful heir to Govora."

A look of pain twisted his face, but it was gone so

swiftly that she thought she had imagined it, replaced by haughty anger. "Of course Renata is anxious to secure an heir by any means," he sneered, his lips tight and hard. "She knows full well that she had no legal claim. She calls herself regent and her son margrave, but in reality they are usurpers—I am the true ruler of Govora!"

Astonishment robbed Francesca of her tongue, then she spluttered, "You! How can this be?" Yet, while disbelieving the evidence of her own ears, in her heart she knew that he spoke the truth. Every inch of him proclaimed that he was of noble descent: that narrow brow, dark as night, the proud, authoritative bearing, the force which flowed from him. He was born to lead men.

"It is a long, complicated story, my dear," a smile softened his eagle features. "We need another drink before I commence the telling." And, with great charm and courtesy, he filled two goblets with Tokay, leading her back to the chair, before pacing the floor like a caged panther as he told her his history. "Govora had belonged to the Romanescos for centuries, it was a happy land, wisely ruled. My father married an English lady of noble birth, whom he loved, and I was born to them. He had a cousin, Ivan Pascaly, a weak, though ambitious man, who had fallen under the spell of Renata and taken her to wife. They visited Govora and were impressed by its potential, its wealth, minerals and powerful position, and they plotted to make it their own. My parents, generous and good, were no match for the duchess, and one day, when they were driving out in their coach, the horses ran amok and it plunged down a ravine. Some said it was an accident, but many suspected that she had engineered the whole thing. I was but an infant and would assuredly have been murdered

too, had it not been for the swift action of my godfather, Ciprian Sahia, who took me to Balvany, his castle fortress high in the mountains, out of her reach, and
there he reared me. Renata tried many times to take me
captive, but she did eventually wreak her vengeance on
Ciprian. A gang of her bullies set upon him when he was
riding alone in the forest and beat him to death. Long
before this, her husband had met his end—I suspect that
she killed him too, thus becoming all-powerful.''

In a flash, Francesca understood that brooding
melancholy which sometimes absorbed him, making his
amber eyes those of a hurt child or a wounded stag. He
had so much cause for bitterness, hounded by cruel
twists of fate which would have brought a lesser man to
his knees. She said nothing, loathe to break their rapport; that sweet intimacy in which she was learning to
know him as never before. He had come to rest in front
of her, looking down, his half-empty glass held lightly
in those long fingers, watching her reaction.

''So you see, Francesca, I have much reason to hate
the Pascalys. Not only have they stolen my heritage, but
I have had to witness the persecution of my people,
helpless to aid them. I did what I could, gathering a
band of loyal fellows around me, calling myself Le
Diable.''

His words stirred a passionate loyalty and devotion
within her, both to his cause and to him. She would
follow him to the ends of the earth if need be. ''How
can I help you?'' she asked with a catch in her voice, her
lovely face aglow with eager life.

''We are arming, assisted by the rebel leaders who are
planning a violent revolt very soon which will sweep
across Rumania. This is but the beginning, and we
intend to attack Govora, but more arms are needed, and
for this we must have money. Can you smuggle out gold

and jewels to us? And spy within their very midst? It will take courage, but the end will be your own freedom as well as that of the peasants. If we can flush out that nest of vipers, I shall be their lord, seeing to it that justice and fair-dealing is reinstated in the land.''

She was swept to the heights by his enthusiasm. His words were like a trumpet call thrilling through her. He reached out his strong hands and grasped hers, pulling her up into his arms. He was like a god to be worshipped and her eyes shone as she looked at him, knowing why men were prepared to follow him into battle and die for him. ''Oh, yes, I'll aid you, Alexis,'' she cried, longing ignited by his touch. Yet there was still a small niggling doubt which clouded her rapture. ''But tell me, was this the only reason why you sent for me?''

Their eyes met and in his she read something which flooded her with joy. ''Oh, no, darling! Try as I would, I couldn't forget you, my little hellcat who led me such a merry dance!'' His voice murmured low, his hands gentle on her. ''Roger told me that you were innocent of breaking parole.''

''And Gilda? What of her?'' Francesca could not let it go, forced to voice her pent-up resentment and hurt pride.

He smiled with a sweet, ironic expression, pressing Francesca close to him, remembering how he had found the gypsy's blatant advances repugnant, unable to put from his mind the memory of Francesca's silky, alabaster skin, her soft, pliant body and exquisite face, that fusion of minds which had sometimes happened between them, the feeling of belonging impossible to explain. Oh, he had angrily told himself not to be a fool! She would undoubtedly betray him, having been clever enough to charm him into an almost besotted state! Through many a long night since, he had examined his own emotions closely, grudgingly admitting to himself that he had been enchanted with her. If she had not been taken by Renata's soldiers, he might have committed the unspeakable folly of falling in love with her!

Now, with her slender form in his arms, those supple curves molding sensuously against his body, he whispered into her hair, "Gilda means nothing to me. I swear that I have not touched her since meeting you. She's mighty angry with me for it, too!"

Francesca was lightheaded with happiness, her senses swimming at the feel of his hands on her body. Perhaps this time, this time they might break the web of misunderstanding and quarrels which marred their relationship. He had confided in her, and her heart swelled with pride. She needed no prompting to wind her soft arms about his neck, pulling his mouth down to hers. It was a gentle, questioning kiss as well as a demanding one which suddenly hardened into passion. Francesca opened her lips under the onslaught of desire, her tongue probing his . . . seeking . . . seeking . . . while the hungry, throbbing pain stabbed deep in her womb. They were both trembling when he released her, saying, "Wait, beloved, a moment only. I must prepare a couch for our loving."

He moved about the room swiftly, while she sat and watched him as he gathered up great sable covers and heaps of brocade cushions, spreading them out on the hearth, making a snug bed fit for a queen. He threw additional logs on the fire, the blaze dancing on them as they lay among the furs, the ruddy glow crimsoning her body as he carefully undressed her. He took his time, kissing and caressing each area of flesh as it was uncovered to his hungry gaze, his lips and hands like a trail of fire moving over her throat and upthrust breasts, which seemed to beg for his touch. She wanted him so badly, letting him know it, her hands exploring him with growing confidence, losing all reticence, abandoning herself to the mounting feeling. And all the while, his brown, strong fingers were moving gently over her skin, sliding down over her belly towards the softness between her thighs. She moaned when he touched her there and he played with her as on a finely-tuned instrument, so that she was engulfed in a series of wonderful sensations.

Once, she nearly stopped him, as his head went down so that his lips might follow the caressing of his fingers. She was overcome with a confused bashfulness, and he paused to say, "Darling, don't be shy, I want to show you all the ways a man can please a woman. Believe me, the sweet taste and perfume of you drives me crazy with desire. Let me do it, please, my love."

Then she could deny him nothing, her legs falling open weakly as she enjoyed the new, amazingly sensual feeling produced by his tongue licking her gently, persuasively, until she was almost mad with ecstasy, and her body convulsed with fulfillment. He moved up to lie with her cradled in his arms, while she came back to earth from that languid cloud of supreme pleasure. She felt him rumble with quiet laughter, and he said, "And now, dearest, you can do the same for me."

He released her and lay back among the furs so that she might undo the small pearl buttons on his shirt and strip off his breeches. She was only too happy to perform this service, leaning across him, her coral-tipped breasts brushing him as she moved. She was stunned yet again by the magnificence of his body, tanned by exposure to wind and sun. Her hands wandered over his firm flesh, wondering at the fine texture of his skin which she had almost forgotten. He was tough and very masculine, used to hard riding, rough living and fighting, and she admired strong men above all others, the animal grace of his movements delighting her. She felt she would never tire of looking at him, and loved him with her whole heart, eager to please him so that she might become as indispensable to him as breathing. He embodied everything she had ever longed for, and she gripped him tightly, digging her fingernails into his shoulders, wanting to mark him—to put her seal on him. He belonged to her! Almost delirious with joy, she ran her lips over his face and throat, sinking her teeth into his neck.

After that outburst, she was more gentle, while Alexis lay there like a lazy lion, and let her do what she would with his body. She nuzzled his chest, tasting his skin, her tongue traveling slowly down to his navel, circling it, the black hair of his belly brushing her cheek. He took her head in his hands, fingers firm amongst the disarray of her curls, urging her lower. She felt his hardness against her breasts, rubbing her nipples on it, then bending to cover it with her mouth, using skill to give him the greatest enjoyment, bringing him to the edge again and again, then holding off before the pressure became too great, power flooding her as she felt his flame shudder and buck.

Her own loins were on fire and she could wait no longer, straddling him, sinking down, head flung back, throat arched, whimpering with pleasure to feel him penetrate deep into her vitals. She moved in a leisurely fashion, savoring each sensation, feeling the urgent thrust of his hips beneath her. Then he told her to roll over, and she lay on her stomach, face buried in the sweet-smelling sable, knees drawn up while he mounted her like an animal, his movements becoming frenzied, his gasping breath against her ear as he held her in a tight embrace.

"Do you like it?" he panted. "Is this what you want? Shall I give you more, more?"

"Oh, yes . . . yes!" she gasped, hardly able to speak as the fury of his climax shook them both. He lay prone for a moment, then eased his weight from her, turning on his side. They were silent, each too shattered by the shared experience to speak, but there was no constraint between them. He pulled her closer, and her rounded body was as one with the tough hardness of his own. Her fingers played with the hair on his chest, still heaving from his recent exertion, and he captured it in his hand, raising it to his lips, kissing the fingertips.

"My darling," he murmured, eyes half-closed, watching the pattern of firelight sleepily. "D'you realize that we've been together for over two hours and we haven't quarreled yet? What a miracle!"

Francesca stiffened, sensing mockery, but he laughed and rolled over, lying half across her, holding her head between his hands, looking deeply into her eyes. "No, don't start now. Let us not spoil this moment of enchantment. We have come a long way tonight along the stony path of understanding one another. Pray God that we have further opportunity to make something good out of this blessing vouchsafed us."

Fighting him was the very last thing in the world she wanted to do, and her arms closed tightly about his body. Once more the magic began between them, and they forgot everything except the burning desire which consumed them.

A while later, Alexis got up and commenced pulling on his clothes. Francesca was warm and sleepily content, but he said it was time for them to go. The night was wearing on and it would be dangerous to remain longer. Joachim was waiting for her, and they drove off into the blackness. The stars had disappeared and snowflakes, like wisps of wool, meandered down from blue-black, bloated clouds. The air was motionless, leaden with cold. Francesca crouched beneath the warm wrappings, numb with misery. The change from radiant joy to the bleak prospect of returning to the palace was too sharp to be endured. She hugged to herself Alexis' promise that Joachim should carry messages to her, and his assurance that her ordeal would soon be over. She, in return, determined to gather together as many valuables as she could without rousing suspicion, and send them to him by that faithful courier. But every step the horse took, each gliding forward of the runners beneath her, put space between her and her lover. It was as if her lifeblood was slowly draining away, pumping out with every agonized beat of her sorrowful heart. She felt maimed, as if one of her limbs had been cut off, yearning for the happy day when they might never be parted again. But did he really want this too? Doubts began to torment her as the trees flashed by and they came to the fringe of the forest where the dim scattering of cottages told her their journey was nearly at an end. He had murmured endearments in her ear that night, but did they mean any more than the things men say to women in the glowing aftermath of passion? Tears stung her eyes. They had spent so little time together, and the barren spaces between their meetings were so long. It was in a tired, dispirited mood that she saw the dark spires of Govora looming up out of the darkness.

Chapter Eleven

FRANCESCA DROPPED into bed just before dawn, putting off Hetty's eager questions, just assuring her that all was well. She had not been missed, no one had come to the bedchamber, but even so, she had the nagging feeling that there was something wrong. The warmth thawed out her chilled limbs and she dozed fitfully, then awakened with a start to hear the clatter of armed men running down the passages, excited shouts and sergeants barking orders. At first she lay trembling, waiting for them to hammer on her door, certain that she had been betrayed, but no one came to arrest her, the sounds disappeared to the courtyard and the soldiers moved away, riding out of the town. Carl came running in, watching them from the window, his confused mind thinking them his toy warriors come to life.

"Soldiers! Soldiers!" he pointed eagerly when she joined him, fastening her dressing robe over her nightgown, the cold tiles of the floor imprinting themselves on her warm, bare feet. Snow drifted down from an iron sky, and she was glad that it had continued, covering their tracks.

Hetty came in, white to the lips, but kept silent until Carl had been taken off to have his breakfast, then she poured out her ill tidings. "Someone has betrayed Le Diable, ma'am. They know about his hiding place in that cave near the Turnu Pass."

Francesca stood as if turned to marble, every vestige of color leaving her face. "But how?" she whispered, while Hetty shook her head in dumb anguish. Francesca moved to the window again, dragging herself there like an old woman, pain and fear like a living thing within her, threatening to rip her apart. Somewhere, out there, those callous brutes of Renata's were hunting Alexis down. Blindly, she stared out over the silent white courtyard.

All day she waited, racked with suspense, filled with an ever-growing premonition of disaster. Yet, to all outward appearances she was calm, no one must suspect that she was half-dead with terror. Not for herself, though God knew, her life would be forfeited were she implicated in any way with Le Diable. It was for him she feared, her prayers were for his safety alone. In the late afternoon that summons she had been dreading finally came. With her head held high, beautifully gowned and coiffured, she obeyed the duchess's command to attend her in that ostentatious room where she had been taken on her arrival at Castle Costin. It was the place where most of Renata's public business was conducted, be it an evening of music and dancing, or a council chamber where she dispensed that mockery which went under the name of justice.

Renata was seated on her throne, backed by her guards, surrounded by her courtiers. Carl occupied his place beside her, restless and unhappy until he saw Francesca, then he quieted. The duchess's loud, imperious accents reached her as she walked down the length of the hall. "This is a day for rejoicing, my dear. Le Diable has been captured. Does that not please you? Will it not be satisfying to see the rogue who abducted you brought here in chains?''

Francesca forced her stiff lips into a smile, taking the chair reserved for her on the dais; but she felt as if she was struggling in the thrall of some terrible nightmare. Renata was watching her, lynx-eyed, enjoying every moment of the charade. She more than half suspected that Francesca was involved with him, but had been unable to lay hands on proof. The duchess felt a thrill of sadistic pleasure at the thought of the girl's present suffering if her suppositions were correct. Vengeful in the extreme, she had been infuriated by her stubborn refusal to take Carl as her husband, and now, like a cat playing with a mouse, she was exercising her cruel, agile mind, seeking ways to trap her.

She gave a brusque order, and one of the soldiers went to the door, shouting for the prisoner to be brought in. Francesca sat transfixed as the voices of the crowd swelled and Alexis entered, jostled on either side by heavily armed men. He still bore himself proudly, though bloody and disheveled, his eyes ablaze with fury, a contemptuous smile lifting his lips.

Zoltan gave him a savage punch in the back, jerking him forward until he stood below the dais, forced to look up at Renata. She rose to her feet majestically, violet eyes narrowed in gloating triumph, but beautiful —killingly, ruthlessly beautiful—wearing a stunning dress with great sleeves of cloth of silver trimmed with leopard. "So, Le Diable—you are my captive. Long have I awaited this moment."

Blood was trickling from the corner of his bruised mouth and his hands were bound behind his back, yet his eyes were still heavy with disdainful superiority as they flickered over the duchess. "I had no notion that you were so desirous of seeing me, madame," he replied smoothly. "Had I but known, I would have paid you a visit ere this. It has long been my intention to do so, though accompanied by musketeers and swordsmen.''

Her lips curled dangerously. "Don't try to be clever with me! I'll have your tongue slit!''

One of Alexis' curving black eyebrows shot up, his sardonic expression deepening. "I am quite powerless to stop you, lady. This would be in character, would it not? Torturing the helpless!''

Zoltan snarled out a filthy oath and smashed into the prisoner's face with a gauntleted fist. Alexis's head snapped back with the force of the blow but, though he staggered, he kept his footing. Francesca fought for control as never before in her life, unable to believe that such horror was taking place. She saw Alexis' bloody features swimming before her: the courtiers smirking their approval of Zoltan's cowardly action, the fire and torches crackling, light dancing on their rich clothing, velvet and silk and furs, striking rainbow shards from jeweled rings and sword hilts, a conglomerate of colors that shimmered like sunrise, blurred by her unshed tears. Francesca wanted to scream at him. "Keep silent, my love! Don't provoke her!'' But she was forced to sit there silent, as if she had never met him, never experienced shared moments of deepest intimacy.

The tumult thundered round her head, and through it she tried to communicate with him in some way, to let him know that she loved and supported him, but he deliberately avoided looking at her. Her heart contracted with tenderness, thinking, He will not endanger me in any way. That is why he ignores me!

Renata paced down the steps from her throne, her magnificent train whispering behind her. She paused before Alexis, her eyes running over his handsome face and going down his long-limbed, powerful frame. The throng were making so much noise that few heard what she said to him, but Francesca caught every word and was sickened to her soul.

"A fine, strong stud," she said slowly, musingly, reaching out to feel his biceps and run her hand over his broad chest, exposed by his torn shirt. He stood quietly, enduring her insolent handling, his eyes narrowed to glittering slits, lips clamped shut." 'Tis a pity that you have to die, my friend, a wicked taste of such outstanding virility."

She was looking at him now with open lust, her tongue peeping out to lick over her full crimson mouth, eyes hooded, heavy with invitation. Her body seemed to ripple as she pressed close to him, rubbing her heavy breasts against his side, buring to seduce him. "We owe allegiance to none, you and I," she purred silkily. "What care we for causes? We are out for our own gain. Come, be my consort and we can rule the land together. What a combination! La Socière and Le Diable! I'll teach you my magic arts, and in my bed I'll rouse you to such ecstasy as you have never dreamed possible. What say you? Agree, and I'll save your life."

Had it been a sword, his look of pure hatred would have killed her outright. "Filthy witch!" he snarled, shrugging her off violently. "Were you the last woman on earth, I'd not touch you!"

Renata recoiled like a striking snake, face working with fury. "No man refuses Renata and lives!" She spat out the words venomously. The crowd fell silent, well-trained to recognize her dangerous fits of rage. "You have condemned yourself, sirrah! I need information concerning the wherabouts of your associates. Where do they meet?"

"Go to hell!" Alexis stared arrogantly down his aquiline nose at the blazingly angry woman, balked of her will.

"Be sensible, my lord," put in Cezar, who had been watching the scene with his chill, sardonic smile, his eyes shifting from Alexis to Francesca, trying to read her shuttered face. "Why suffer needless pain for something which we shall drag out of you in the end?"

"Crawl back to your kennel, lick-spittle!" roared Alexis, his control snapping at the sight of the man who had stolen his wife, straining at his bonds, blind to all save the force of his desire to take Cezar by the throat and throttle the life out of him. It was he who poured posion into Renata's ear, conniving with her to sell their country to the Hapsburgs. He, who wanted Francesca. Pain knotted his guts as he remembered how, with a green-sick boy, he had trusted her last night. It must have been she who betrayed him! The bitch! If anything, she was a more formidable enchantress than Renata. So pretty, so dainty and, when it pleased her, so gentle! Oh, she'd fooled him right enough. In fact, she was the deepest little baggage in the whole corrupt Court! In that moment of supreme disillusion, he firmly believed that she would have sent half of Rumania to the gallows without so much as a tremor!

He glared at her with such bitter accusation in his flashing golden eyes that she shrank in her chair as if scorched, all her hopes crumbling into ashes, bewildered and dismayed.

Renata had recovered her composure, cool and hard as ice, and those who knew her trembled, for in such a bland, suave mood, she was at her most deadly. She leaned on Mark's shoulder and played with the diamond pin which fastened his cravat. He smiled into her eyes and stroked her fingers. Francesca wondered dully what emotion he was experiencing at the humiliation of his rival. Was it satisfied revenge? The justification of a wronged lover? Or did he fell compassion—for herself, if not for Alexis?

Cezar was stammering out a retort, but the duchess silenced him with an impatient gesture. "Stop blustering, Cezar! And you, Le Diable, for all your damnable pride, will be treated as any other rebel dog. I'll give you tonight to dwell on't. A few hours in the deepest dungeon of the Daliborka should give you food for thought. But, if you still refuse to tell us what we want to know, I shall turn you over to my torturers, then when they have torn the information from you, there will be other treats in store. Don't imagine for a moment that you will be given the release of a merciful death. Oh, no—that would be too easy. I shall order your tongue to be cut out, and then . . . yes, then I think I'll have you castrated and sold as a eunuch slave destined for the harems of Constantinople. The Turks would appreciate the jest. These punishments shall be carried out in the marketplace, for all to witness how Renata deals with insurgents who dare question her authority!"

Her voice rang out under the vaulted rafters of the hall, while Alexis stared at her stonily, and her sycophants laughed and applauded. Tired of the game, Renata dismissed him, and he was marched out. She turned her attention once more to Mark, smiling, her eyes full of voluptuous, almost oriental languor, while he listened to the witchery of her voice. Quite shamelessly, she slid her hand over his groin and between his satin-covered thighs, oblivious of her followers who had begun to indulge in their own perverted forms of entertainment.

Sickened with disgust, Francesca slipped away unobserved to her chamber, quite alone, without even the solace of Hetty's company. She reached the hearth and sank down, drained, into a nearby chair. Could it have been but a few short hours ago that she lay in Alexis' arms, weaving improbable dreams of his loving her one day? Her mouth twisted with a fresh shock of pain as she remembered the undisguised glare of hate that had burned in his eyes in the hall? Could he really believe that she had sold him to his enemies after their closeness of last night?

She dropped her head into her hands, wanting to weep, biting hard on her lower lip to control its trembling. No, tears were for weaklings! Even if he did hate her, she must try to save him. The thought of him tortured and mutilated nearly drove her to the brink of insanity. Her brain was working furiously as she examined the courses open to her. Joachim sprang to mind, and she jumped up, tugging on the bellrope, summoning Hetty.

Hetty had already consulted her lover, both of them eager to help Le Diable. So far, they had escaped suspicion. Rumor had it that he had been betrayed by a woman, but no one knew her identity. A message had been slipped to Zoltan at dawn, telling him of the cave near the pass. Alexis had been caught unprepared and alone. It had been impossible for him to escape, outnumbered by Renata's hand picked troops.

"Don't fret so, ma'am," Hetty kept repeating, scared by the wasted look on her mistress's face. "His men won't let him be tortured. Rest assured that by now all have been alerted. The whole countryside around will be arming and coming to his rescue, so Joachim says."

Francesca shook her head dolefully. Darkness had already swooped like a smothering pall. All too soon it would be dawn. What hope had they that his men would reach there in time? The difficulties were immense, hampered by bad weather and lack of arms, their chances of success were minimal. Her depression was spreading to Hetty, even that normally buoyant girl was finding it almost impossible to bolster up hope. She had seen Joachim briefly, then he had slipped away, and she could only assume that he had gone to join the rebels, taking his considerable knowledge of the castle and its surroundings to aid the rescue plans. It was an endurance test to pretend unconcern, they were only too aware that their every move would be reported back to Renata.

"Dear God! We've got to do something!" Francesca hissed, driving her fist into the palm of her hand, while Hetty attended her in the dressing room. Her own reflection in the pier glass was that of a stranger with a stark, white face and huge, tormented eyes. She changed into a cream silk nightgown which fell clear to her feet from a frilled yoke, with full sleeves drawn in by ribbons at the wrists, and slipped her arms into a green over robe, lavishly trimmed at collar and cuffs with silver fox. Hetty had fixed her hair which tumbled about her shoulders, shot with wildfires of gold. It was the only thing about her which seemed to have any life left. With a groan, she clenched her fists, pressing them to her forehead in agony. Alexis, her beloved, was languishing in some stinking dungeon, and God only knew what they were doing to him at that very moment. The duchess had promised him until dawn to reconsider, but she very much doubted whether Zoltan would be able to keep his hands off him until then.

There was no recourse but to sit with Carl until he slept, dispatching Hetty to the servants quarters in search of news. When she had gone, Francesca crouched against the silken bedhead, wide-eyed with apprehension, starting like a frightened doe at every small sound. Never had she felt more helpless and inadequate. She tried to pray, twisting her rosary in her icy fingers, but God and all His saints had deserted her. Very well then, she must face it alone, muster her shrinking reserves of strength—this quaking cowardice would certainly not help Alexis. She battled with the awful imaginings which were like vipers in her brain, gaining the upper hand, cool counsel prevailing, and lay back against the pillows, her eyes closed, willing a calmness into her body.

She was disturbed by someone rapping softly on the door. Heart in mouth, she crept across, pressing her head against the polished wood and whispering: "Who is it?"

" 'Tis I—Mark," came the instant reply. Wondering, distrustful, she let him in. She had never seen him so serious. He had abandoned his foppish pose, along with the blue satin suit which he had been wearing earlier. Now he was clad in plain, dark clothing, as if ready for action.

"What do you want?" she questioned, pale hands clasped against her breasts, almost in entreaty, wanting to trust him, yet knowing him to be the duchess's creature. She had seen him using his wiles on her often enough and been nauseated as, daringly, careless of observers, he had kissed, flattered and cajoled that powerful despot.

His handsome face was set in a kind of wry determination, though with a hint of amusement in his hazel eyes, as if he could not fathom his own uncharacteristically noble impulse. "I think I can help Alexis to escape."

Francesca swayed towards him, hands groping, fluttering, as if trying to pluck support out of the air. His arms came about her while he soothed her like a hurt child and, head pressed into his chest, she missed the wistful, pensive expression which softened his eyes as he caught the sweet fragrance of her hair.

"Oh, Mark—please aid us. I love him so. I shall die if he is tortured!"

" 'Od's life!" he answered shakily, lips against her temple. "Would that some charming lady loved me with such devotion."

She released herself a little so that she could look up

at him, trying to probe his expression. She had learned
to expect barbed teasing from him, that sophisticated,
worldly buck; but now his eyes were wide and clear,
shining with unusual sincerity and honesty. "But Mark
. . ." she remonstrated," there are so many ladies
swooning over you. You are quite the *beau garcon*, high
in Renata's favor."

He grimaced. "Bah! That witch, smothering me with
caresses which make my flesh creep! My God, to what
depths have I sunk, pandering to her lust!"

Tears of pity filled her eyes, and a faint echo of that
love she had once felt, an ache for the gaiety they had
shared in London. It was as if it had happened to two
other people long, long ago, before her world had
turned topsy-turvy, hurling her into dark and dangerous
events.

He gave her a gentle shake. "Come, we must act at
once. There is little time. Joachim will be here in a
moment."

Astonishment widened her eyes. "You know about
him?"

He gave a grin and nodded. "Oh, yes! I've made it
my business to find out a great deal of what goes on
behind the scenes. Fortunately, Renata missed out on
this one, else she'd have strung him up weeks ago. She's
not always as well-informed as she imagines. I told you
that it was my intention to encourage her patronage in
order to help you, did I not? I may be a bounder, but I
hope that I have a few principles left."

She was totally perplexed by this attractive rogue
who, despite everything, had an endearing charm,
although at a certain point he put up barriers. No one
could ever claim to really know him. A sound from the
dressing room startled them, and then Hetty and
Joachim came in, arriving via the secret passage. Francesca stabbed a quick glance at Carl, but he was sound

asleep and snoring. She envied his innocence, blissfully unaware of the lives balanced on a razor edge.

A shadow crossed Joachim's squarish, rough-hewn features at the sight of Mark, and his hand flew to his dagger. "It's all right, Joachim," she said quickly. "He is a friend."

"The duchess's paramour?" He seemed doubtful, eyes alert for any false move.

Mark's cynical smile deepened. "Don't forget that I am English, my dear fellow, and would aid Lady Francesca. I owe her that much. With my knowledge of Renata's apartments, I can show you a way down to the dungeons beneath. I have not spent all my time in debauched idleness and decadent luxury, you know. I was able to gain admittance to that closet of hers, where most of her darkest deeds are planned. There I found a most useful map, which even she did not know existed, showing the labyrinth of hidden ways which honeycomb the walls of the palace. I made a copy of it."

He drew a folded paper from an inside pocket and spread it on the sofa table, bringing across a gilded candlestick. They leaned over it eagerly, whilst Joachim nodded and exclaimed, recognizing landmarks, ways which he knew well.

Francesca's palms were sweating with excitement, though the night was icy, as the men pointed out how the secret stairway which she had used was connected with other winding passages, a spidery network of lines intersecting one another, built as escape routes and hiding places during centuries of wars, religious conflicts, rebellions and uprisings. Their existence had been kept a close secret; Joachim had discovered them by dint of his own shrewd conjectures and continual ferreting. Now, they found one they could use, leading to the Daliborka Tower.

Francesca was already snatching up her fur-lined

cloak, flinging it over her nightwear. "Let us go at once."

"A moment, madame," Joachim cautioned, tracing a line on the paper with his finger. "If we reach him, then we must be sure that he can get away by a passage which leads beyond the walls. If he breaks out into the grounds, there will be the guards posted on the gates to contend with. I have contacted his followers through sympathizers in the town, and they are gathering from all points ready to attack. It is essential that he joins them." He folded the map when satisfied, and took up the lantern. Mark paused, a hand on Francesca's arm.

"Are you sure that you want to come?" His eyes were anxious. "It will be dangerous, my dear."

Her face blazed, courage flooding her veins. "Of course! I must play my part. There must be something I can do!"

"Very well," he agreed reluctantly, drawing a knife from the sheath concealed beneath his jacket and giving it to her. "But you must be armed, and for God's sake, don't hesitate to use this if the need arises."

It fitted into her palm most comfortingly, light and beautifully balanced, a pretty, deadly toy, and gripping it firmly, she stepped into the dark tunnel behind Mark and Joachim. Hetty was ordered to remain, as she had done the night before, to allay suspicion. She clung to Joachim for an instant, kissing him warmly, sending him away with a jest on her lips to cover her deadly fear.

It took a few seconds for their eyes to become accustomed to the gloom. The walls dripped with moisture, and the cold advanced from the shadows, a clammy creeping tide. Francesca shuddered, following Joachim's bobbing light, a prickling like icy daggers probing her flesh, rising up through the soles of her slippers, sucking the warmth from her. They took a path to the right which wound ever downward, twisting, turning, here a slippery passage, there a flight of steps treacherous with moss. Once, she almost fell, giving a cry, but Mark's strong arm was there to pull her back from the jagged hole into which she might have plunged, guiding her feet back to the broken, narrow stairs. Fearfully, she peered down into the hollow darkness beneath, a darkness traversed by fitful streaks of light from the lantern.

It seemed that they could go on descending for ever, until they reached the very pit of hell, but at last the steps ended and they crept along a further way, coming to a blank wall. Sharp dismay lanced her. Had they come all this way to find a dead end? Tears scalded her eyes; she was shaking with cold. It had become almost tangible, a part of those gray, damp walls which she had the most horrible conviction were about to close in and crush them. But Joachim, ever resourceful, was shining the lantern around, penetrating the relentless gloom. He came upon an ancient winch and began to strain at it. For what seemed like an eternity, it stuck fast, corroded by the disuse of decades, then, slowly, agonizingly, it began to turn. A tiny aperture appeared among the solid stone as a brick slid smoothly to one side, revealing a spyhole. Mark put his eye to it, whispering that it gave him a view of the chamber beyond, and that it was deserted, though lit by a flare. It appeared to be a guard-room. Joachim turned the cogs another notch, and a narrow door opened with just enough space to squeeze through.

They realized that someone must stay behind to operate the mechanics, so Mark and Francesca crept into the empty room, silent as shadows, hardly daring to breathe. It was grim and cheerless, deep in the foundations of the tower. There were signs of recent occupation: a brazier, glowing sullenly, did little to dispel the chill, spluttering torches made the atmosphere smoky, gleaming dully on the racks of guns, the tall pikes. Cards and dice were scattered on the plain boards of a trestle table which had benches each side of it. It was obviously inhabited by the soldiers from time to time. Francesca wondered why they were off duty now. A door with an iron grill stood ajar at the further end. Mark went towards it and she pressed close behind him. There was a light beyond and they peered through. Francesca could barely repress her gasp of horror at what she saw.

Stooped at the waist like a bent old man, Alexis hung from the rafters, suspended by his wrists which were tied behind his back. His toes just touched the ground, one foot at a time, never both together—that was Zoltan's cunning—his helpless enemy scrabbled the floor to cushion the pain, but never succeeded in achieving the solace for which his screaming muscles craved. Zoltan lounged on a stool, back against the wall, picking at his blackened teeth and watching the torture with an experienced eye. A grin of intense satisfaction twisted his thick, coarse features. For years a red ember of hatred and envy had scorched within his stupid, blustering head, and his defeat in the gypsy encampment had cemented this emotion, making him offer his services to Renata, hoping to be revenged on Le Diable. Knowing that they would obey her to the letter and leave the prisoner in his cell until dawn before turning him over to the torturers, Zoltan had dismissed the guards, saying that he would keep watch, determined that Alexis' ordeal should begin long before that, with himself as the executioner.

"Are you ready to kneel at my feet and beg my forgiveness?" he said lazily, one hand resting on the handle of the pulley which controlled the rope.

Alexis was almost unconscious. His eyes were shut as he fought the agony which tore like white-hot pincers.

The sweat trickled down his face and dripped from his chin on to his naked chest. Pain whipped his wide shoulders, bunched so unnaturally, and flamed through the joints. He groaned, his teeth clenched, the room spinning dizzily and, mingled with the roaring in his ears, the torture which mauled his body and deafened his mind, one thought bruned like fire: the dread urge to kill Zoltan and the woman who had betrayed him— Francesca!

Zoltan was getting impatient. "Well?" he shouted, big, hairy fist ready on the handle. "Speak! I'll break you yet! Damned highhanded aristocrat! Thought you could best me, did you? Me, Zoltan the Gypsy!"

He gave a sudden twist to the pulley. The rope creaked and Alexis rose higher, twirling slowly. Mark flung open the door, sword in hand. Zoltan spun round, his mouth gaping in surprise. The winch spun, the rope ran free, and Alexis crashed to the floor. With a savage roar, Zoltan seized a pike from the wall, closing on Mark who had taken up a fencer's stance. His slender blade met the wood of the long stave, steel thudding dully. With a supple twist of his wrist, he freed it, bending in swift, graceful movements, pinking Zoltan, his rapier flashing sparks of flame, blooding him in a dozen places, while the gypsy feinted with his ungainly weapon, bellowing in frustrated rage, unable to break that sparkling barrier which pricked him so daintily. He backed off, tiny eyes shining dull red. Mark paused for an instant, and Zoltan rushed him, bracing for the thrust, the pike slamming into his chest. He dropped his sword with a grunt, skewered like a butterfly, blood gushing from between his lips. Zoltan yanked the pike free and Mark crumpled slowly to his knees, hands clawing at the wound, blood seeping through his fingers. With an oath, the gypsy stood over him, the weapon raised high, preparing to bring it down in a vicious blow which would have ended Mark's life, but Francesca who had been standing, terror-striken, suddenly sprang into action. She hurled herself at Zoltan's back and, before he had time to swing round and seize her, she had struck deep with her knife. Her aim was true for she knew that she had only one chance to catch him off guard. It was an awesome thing, killing a man, and she was astonished by the ease with which it happened.

Zoltan did not even cry out. He dropped the pike and pitched forward onto his face. With every other consideration banished from her mind, she ran to Alexis. He was curled on his side while the agony in his arms throbbed and died, his head hanging forward, his tangled hair wet with sweat. Francesca mopped his face with a corner of her cloak, murmuring endearments, only half-aware of what she was doing, nearly mad with anguish. She sliced the rope which had been drawn brutally tight, scoring his wrists with deep, red weals. She took each one in her hands, chaffing them to get the circulation moving. His eyelids flickered and lifted; for the first time he seemed conscious of his surroundings. A frown crossed his brow as his eyes opened and fastened on her face. They focused, sharpened, blazed in violent anger. He jerked his arm away from her touch as if it were poisonous.

"Bitch!" he grated hoarsely, and struggled to sit up. "I trusted you, and you betrayed me! What a fool you must have thought me! How much amusement it must have given you and that witch-queen, Renata!"

The contrite look in her wide-spaced eyes left him cold. Simmering with rage, frustrated by the pain which made him flinch as he tried to straighten his shoulders, he noted the whitening of her cheeks, and his lips curled into a cruel, wolfish smile. The shameless little whore had better try her tricks on someone else. He did not intend to be cheated again by a pair of ravishing green eyes or that soft, vulnerable expression which even now caused a tightness in his throat. Angered anew by this feeling, he struggled to his feet, jerking his head to where Mark lay.

"There's a man dying over there. Save your false sympathy for him. Another poor dupe who fell for your lies!"

Her hot temper was rising. Love him to distraction though she might, his lack of faith in her was appalling. How dare he judge her without letting her speak? She glared at him, and ran to drop on her knees by Mark who turned his head to look at her. It cost him much effort and he coughed, bringing up a great crimson clot.

"Oh Mark . . . Mark . . . dearest friend . . ." she sobbed, the hot tears welling to run down her cheeks. Slowly, he raised his hand so that he might touch hers. That odd, impish smile lifted his lips.

"What's that? Tears, tears for me? Gad's life, sweet thing . . . I'm not worthy of them." A spasm of agony shook him, his face contorting, his breath coming in great, painful gasps. The sweat stood out on his forehead in drops. It passed, but his cheeks were ashen and he could hardly speak. She leaned low over him to catch the words. "You must not tarry here, go now. I'm done for, darling . . . save yourself . . . and him."

Francesca opened her lips in denial, then saw that his breath, which had been stirring a tendril of her hair, had ceased. She straightened up, staring down at him, shaking her head as if by so doing she could ward off the truth. He still wore his slightly whimsical smile, but his eyes were glazed. They were looking directly at her, as if he had been seeking her face, even at the last.

She freed her fingers from his and rose to her feet. She was numb, as if her brain had protectively cut off all feeling, lest she should start raving and rending her garments, driven completely insane. Alexis was struggling into his shirt and fur coat, bending to pick up Mark's sword. He refused to look at her. She could feel their chances of escape running away like grains of sand in an hourglass. Facing his fury, she moved closer.

"Follow me, Alexis—I know the way to a passage which will take you far beyond the castle."

His eyes were crystal hard, his mouth sneering in spite of his battered lips. "Leading me into another trap, are you, sweetheart? You surely cannot expect me to believe that you and your lover, lying dead at your feet, really intended to free me? I don't know what the devil is going on, but this seems totally illogical."

"It's true, sir," Joachim was at the door and had overheard the conversation. His eyes went from Zoltan's corpse to that of Mark. "There is no time to explain. Come away, I beg you. It is nearly daybreak."

Alexis gave him a piercing glance, then followed him. Francesca was forced to run to keep up with their long strides. They reached the tiny opening in the wall, stepped inside and it rolled shut behind them. Joachim wiped the sweat from his face. He fumbled in his coat and found a tallow candle, lighting it from his lantern and thrusting it into Francesca's hand. "Can you find your way back, madame? It is best that you return. I don't think you are under suspicion, and we can travel faster alone. Our men are about to attack, and then you will be free. Have courage."

Disappointment was smothered by utter weariness and despondency, a desire to have Alexis out of her sight as quickly as possible, unable to bear the silent condemnation which emanated from him. If he thought her a traitor, refusing to believe her sincerity, then it was best if they parted. She looked up, seeing his face for the fraction of a heartbeat, seared by the bitter anger there. Then the men melted into the darkness and she braved the long ascent alone. Fear lent wings to her feet as she fled through the Stygian gloom. The shadows seemed solid, the feeble light from her candle struggling bravely against that quenching fullness. Sobbing with terror, she hammered on the door hidden by the paneling. Hetty's voice swelled and faded like music borne on the wind, and Francesca collapsed into her arms. Soon she was in the big chair by the fire, swaddled in blankets, while she tried to tell her what had befallen, in confused, disjointed sentences.

They had no idea of how long it would be before the peasants attacked, or even if they would go unharmed should they succeed in taking the palace. Carl was still sleeping on the couch, and the two women kept watch by the dim glow of a solitary taper weeping its waxen tears, though the sky was lightening, and chilly sunrise lurked behind snow clouds. Was Alexis already out there in that crippling cold? Or had he been recaptured and was even now undergoing extremities of pain? Against her closed eyelids, Francesca saw him swinging on the rope as she had in the torture chamber, and wanted to gag. To exorcise this ghastly vision which haunted her, she watched the dawn paling the candle, with wild, feverish eyes, recalling the hatred and revulsion contorting his face when he looked at her, believing her to be instrumental in his torment. She felt her heart bleeding, a gaping wound within her. There was no hope of sleep—that had deserted her for ever. Dully, she listened to an inner voice which whispered longingly of death.

Chapter Twelve

SOMEONE WAS shaking her shoulder, rousing her from the lethargy which had overcome her exhausted mind. "Ma'am, wake up! You must dress quickly!"

Hetty stood before her, a sensible traveling dress over her arm, a hooded cloak dumped on the bed. She had changed into a dark blue woolen gown, though still retaining her neat silk apron and frilled cap, the uniform of the personal maid of which she was inordinately proud. The mists rolled back, and clear, terrifying remembrance filled Francesca's brain. She started up, flinging aside the blanket covering her knees.

"What is wrong, Hetty?" she gasped, tossing back the long hair which fell forward into her eyes. Hetty handed her some undergarments and she dressed rapidly, forgetting the cold, hardly aware of Carl stirring sleepily, his nightcap over one eye, sitting up and gazing at them owlishly.

"Listen!" Hetty stiffened, head raised. The castle shook with the force of a terrific explosion from outside. Pandemonium broke out—cries, screams, the pounding of feet, the rapid staccato of gunfire. " 'Tis the rebels, ma'am!" Her face was a picture of alarm, mingled with excitement and hope. "They attacked at dawn, and took the town. It fell easily for the citizens are all for them, but the castle has been fully manned, and the duchess will put up a struggle. They've lugged cannons to the walls and are blasting away, but the palace guns are giving hot answer."

"Jesus, how could I have been so sunk in misery that I didn't hear it?" Francesca wondered, pulling on her riding boots, settling her claret velvet skirt around her hips, clumsy with haste, backing up to Hetty so that she might lace the bodice. Carl, fully awake now, had a worried, puzzled expression on his face.

"Noise!" he quavered, clutching his cushion against his ungainly body. "Bang! Bang! Too much noise!"

"Don't be alarmed, Carl," Francesca tried to instil confidence into her own voice, though her heart was drumming wildly. She brushed her unbound hair, so that it fell like a shining, wavy curtain about her shoulders. Carl crept close to her as she sat on the stool before the mirror, burying his face in her lap. "They are playing soldiers, my dear," she murmured, feeling him quiver, patting his head kindly.

"Get up, you great booby!" came a sharp command from the door, and Renata stalked in, followed by Cezar. Men at arms brought up the rear. Carl staggered, tripping on the hem of his nightshirt, nearly falling. His mother stared at him with distaste. "God, why was I cursed with such as you!" she hissed, while he cringed away from her, blubbering. "Had I but a strong warrior for a son, I should not now be threatened by that lawless scum!"

"Our men will quickly quell them, Your Grace," Cezar put in hurriedly, darting a glance at Francesca. She drew herself up to her full height, haughty and defiant, remembering that it was he who had robbed

Alexis of his bride, soured his nature so that he had a deep, immovable distrust of women. Cezar had been the forerunner of her misfortunes, and she found him more despicable than ever, hating him with all the vehemence of her fiery nature.

"That dolt, Zoltan—letting Le Diable escape!" stormed Renata in a towering rage. "And Mark too, how was he implicated?" She spun round on Francesca who stood her ground, chin lifted stubbornly. "Do you know anything about it?" Renata stabbed a long finger at her.

The door burst open before she could reply, admitting Lavinia, heavy breasts heaving, clothing pulled on anyhow, wig askew. Ranby trudged wearily behind her, saying crossly, "My good woman, control yourself. I've never met such a one for the vapors! Get your smelling salts out of your reticule and take a long sniff!"

"We're going to be slaughtered by that mob out there! I know we are!" wailed the chaperone, while in the corridor beyond, there came the sound of panicky feet and upraised voices as Renata's courtiers roused to the fact that the castle was under assault.

Francesca grudgingly granted that Renata did not want for courage, half-expecting her to leap on a horse and lead her men herself. As it was, she swept up to the battlements, there to view the fighting and consult with her commanders. Francesca did not miss her quick order to the guards to remain where they were. The duchess was highly suspicious of her and intended to keep her under surveillance. Carl's attendants were admitted, carting him off, ignoring his noisy lamentations at being parted from Francesca.

She ran to the window with Hetty at her elbow. It was a gray day, the sky heavy with the promise of more snow. Frost sparkled on the roofs; icicles transformed every guttering to lacework. A black column of smoke rose from where part of the town was burning. The weapons of the rebels belched forth fire, bombarding the stubborn walls of the palace. Hetty whispered that those heavy pieces of artillery had been dragged through the night by teams of oxen from their hiding places deep in the forest. The attack was only slightly premature; they had been planning it for the very near future, and Alexis' untimely capture had merely accelerated events.

"But will they succeed, Hetty?" she almost implored, laying her hand on her maid's sleeve.

Hetty gave a quick glance behind them, but the guards were talking heatedly together at the far end of the room. "They are fierce, desperate fighters, ma'am, and they know only too well what dire fate awaits them if they are defeated. The duchess will be ruthless in her revenge."

This was the grim truth, and Francesca broke out in a cold sweat as inner vision painted horrible pictures. Every one of those reckless, brave men would die in the most awful manner which the duchess's ingenuity could muster, and she would be betrayed too, suffering harsh punishment and probably death, and every member of her household would be silenced, lest word reach England of her fate.

The fighting at the walls was fierce and desperate, the rebels advancing with order and resolve, dragging scaling ladders into position. The defenders fought grimly, the air split with shouts of command, the booming of round shot, the shriek of steel and whine of bullets. Francesca and Hetty clutched at one another, half-hidden by the protective stone of the casement, eyes glued to the courtyard, seeing the red uniforms of Renata's men as they hurried to their posts, the musketeers ranged along the high parapet, many to tumble from this lofty perch, picked off by Alexis' marksmen. Soon shouts from below told them that the attackers had entered the fortress, pouring over the wide breach blasted by the cannons in the massive thickness of the walls. The deadly strife of hand-to-hand fighting rent the air. It was but a matter of moments before the advance party overpowered the guards at the gates. Wild, savage horsemen thundered in, and all was over—save the slaughter.

Francesca's guards rushed away in an effort to save their skins. In the entrance hall, the courtiers were panicking, while men struggled to gain admittance, wounded, bleeding, desperate. The women ran about hysterically, their terror infectious, knowing that they would be put to the sword by the vengeful insurgents. After one terrified peep down into that maelstrom, Hetty and Francesca ran back to the deserted bedchamber, followed by the screams of those who were now being cut down. Flames roared from the direction of the Daliborka Tower which had already been fired. Francesca snatched up her dagger, and Hetty armed herself with a heavy brass poker. If Alexis and Joachim did not come to their rescue, they might well be massacred with the rest. They were about to bolt and bar the door, and Hetty had already started to shove a heavy chest towards it as an extra barrier, when Cezar pushed his way in. He was battered and bloody, a gun in his hand, a terrible mad light flashing in his baleful eyes.

He caught Francesca by the arm, wrenching her up against him. "Get your jewels. We are leaving."

Murderous rage shook her as she tried to drag her arm away, but his fingers bit like talons. "Leaving? What mean you?" she spat at him.

"I know a way, but you are coming with me." There

was a strange glint in his black pupils as he looked down into that wild, lovely face, her disgust enflaming him. "I've always wanted you, and now you shall be mine. We will ride to my castle, deep in the mountains, and no one will ever find us. Come . . . hurry!"

He pushed her toward the dressing table, armed, vicious and determined. Francesca flung a glance at Hetty, but he kept his pistol trained on the maid, a cold smile lifting his scarred mouth. Francesca moved slowly, very conscious of the knife hidden beneath her bodice. She had already killed once—why not again? But opportunity was not presenting itself. Could she but distract him, give Hetty the chance to rush in with the poker? She picked up the jewels and moved to where her furs lay on the bed, her walk undulating, throwing him a sultry look.

"Give me a moment, Cezar. There are other valuables which I would be loathe to leave for the rebels," she said, her voice low and conspiratorial. He lowered his pistol and Hetty sprang at him, bringing the poker down with a savage swish but, too quick for her, he gave it a vicious twist which tore it from her grasp, following this with a smashing backhander which connected with her chin, knocking her across the room.

Like a wide-clawed cat seeking freedom, Francesca went for his face, nails biting deep into his skin. He snarled and grabbed her wrists, pushing her down onto the bed. "Bitch! Bitch!" he was shouting, mad with rage. "By God, but you shall come with me!"

He tangled her in the sheets, laughing at her muffled, furious demands for release, smashing a pillow down over her face. Francesca panicked. She bucked and kicked, but the pillow was pressed harder and she could feel the imprint of his hand through it, fingers pushing into her eyes, over her nose and mouth. Her chest was nearly bursting and she knew she was going to die. Fear gave her savage strength, her arms flailed and she kicked again, connecting with some part of him for he cursed in pain. She could feel him trying to throw a rope about her, taking her prisoner, and screamed into the suffocating pillow, sparks and spirals dancing against the blackness, her energy ebbing, her lungs clamoring for air.

For an instant, she did not register relief as he was plucked from her by a great, strong hand. Fiery pain filled her chest; circles and stars swirled madly; her eyes felt as if they had been gouged out. Someone knocked the covering from her face. She sat up whimpering, moaning, the room dazzlingly bright. Cezar was backed into a corner by the bed, snarling at Alexis.

Towering and formidable, Alexis eyed him for a moment then, "Draw, you dog!" he challenged. Bathed in the crimson glow of the burning buildings, the two men circled warily, blades glittering as they feinted. This was no gentlemanly fencing bout; they were fighting to the death, senses honed, reactions lightning fast. Then, with a sudden, searing clash of steel, their blades met and engaged. Parry, riposte, lunge—they moved with the grace of dancers in some death ritual, both expert swordsmen, old adversaries who knew each other's tricks. Cezar was as agile as a serpent, and Alexis, for all his size, moved lightfooted as a cat. Francesca was dazed by the flashing points of fire as the rapiers darted swiftly, each seeking a careless move, a break in defense. She was panting heavily, hardly daring to believe that she was alive, bewildered by the uproar in the room where Roger was dueling with two of Cezar's henchmen, stepping lightly over the bodies of others shot down by some of Alexis' musketeers.

Hetty, regaining consciousness from Cezar's blow,

crawled to the bed, face already puffing and one eye beginning to close up. Watching with mounting horror, Francesca could see that Alexis was suffering from the wrenching of his arms during the torture, *and* he had already been engaged in heavy combat for some hours. He was running with sweat and she could hear the harsh rasp of his breathing. When Cezar lunged unexpectedly, slashing his thigh, she screamed at the sight of the dark blood spreading through the ripped fabric of his breeches. She was about to leap from the bed but Roger, having killed his opponents, threw an arm about her and pulled her firmly back.

"Break his concentration now, darling, and he's a dead man," he said tersely.

The ringing and clashing of steel on steel echoed through the room, their shadows flung grotesquely in the wintry gloom by flickering flames outside. Back and forth they moved, slashing and hacking, desperately fighting for their lives. Suddenly, Alexis lost his footing in a pool of blood pumping from one of the prone guards. He fell to one knee and Cezar sprang upon him, tangling with his blade, sending it spinning off to clatter to the tiled floor. He hung over the disarmed man for a second, his face a diabolical mask of jeering satisfaction. Francesca tore herself from Roger, leaping between the two men, the tip of Cezar's sword pressing into her throat while she glared up into his insane eyes. Events moved so swiftly that she was not certain what happened, for the next moment Carl materialized, giving a bellow of anger at seeing his beloved friend threatened, lumbering across to knock Cezar to one side, giving Alexis time to leap to his feet, whip out his dagger and drive it with all his strength into Cezar's chest. He gave a surprised yelp, then buckled slowly, trying to speak through the bloody foam which filled his mouth as he crumpled to the ground.

Francesca had her arm about Carl, but his wits had gone completely, leaving him a gibbering, sobbing hulk, unable to comprehend anything. The hubbub from outside increased. Someone was being relentlessly pursued. Renata burst in, eyes wild, splendid gown in ribbons, for they had very nearly captured her. She had not accepted being vanquished, a pistol was rammed into the back of the person she had taken as security for her own safety—it was Gilda.

"Stand back, sum!" The duchess's voice rang through the room, her aura of debased majesty still awe-inspiring. "One move and this slut dies! And she *is* your slut, is she not, Le Diable? Even though she betrayed you to me!"

"What!" Alexis' eyes snapped as he stared at the gypsy girl. "I don't believe it! Not you, Gilda, not after fighting by my side for so many years?"

Those oblique eyes in the olive-skinned face were turned imploringly towards him, an expression of anguish on her features. In her soldier's garb, bloodstained and travel-worn, she looked more than ever like a handsome stripling. "You no longer wanted me once you clapped eyes on her." She stabbed Francesca with a blasting hatred. "I knew you were meeting her at the hunting lodge, and I hated you, Alexis, because you had deserted me! I preferred to see you dead than belonging to her!"

A black scowl brought his brows swooping together. "And you call that love? You traitor! How could you do such a thing?"

On her knees before him, Gilda pleaded for forgiveness, broken by guilt. "I *did* love you, Le Diable! I love you still!" she cried and clung to his legs, her face rubbing against the leather boots which reached halfway up his thighs. He reached down, an expression of loathing on his dark face, jerking back her head so that she was forced to look up at him, her eyes slanting oddly, dragged up at the corners by the hold he maintained on her black hair.

"I should kill you for this," he grated.

"You'll kill no one, Le Diable! This is for my comrade, Zoltan!" a voice shouted from the confusion at the open doorway. Arpad stood there, directing his pistol at Alexis. There was a roar, a searing flash of powder, and his bullet exploded in Gilda's back as she flung herself over Alexis, a human shield. Arpad went down beneath a rain of blows, the rebels rushing in, trampling over him. Renata made for the dressing room, dragging Carl with her.

"The secret passage!" warned Hetty, dancing with excitement, injuries forgotten. "She's going to escape!"

By the time they reached the little room, the panel had shut, but Hetty showed them how to open it, and men scrambled through. Alexis could not prevent them, for they were borne on a red tide of bloodlust, hunting out everyone who had been implicated in the duchess's crimes. Francesca was thunderstruck, compassion for Carl aching in her heart. Then she felt Alexis' hand on her shoulder, turning her to him. Very gently he held her, and they stood for a moment amid the turmoil, hardly daring to move, listening to the pounding of their hearts beating so close together. She yielded to the delicious feeling of having found a refuge, of being protected and defended. She fumbled for words as he said, "My darling . . . I am so sorry . . . I thought it was you who told the duchess where I was hiding."

She nudged her head against him happily. "It doesn't matter, Alexis. It's all over." Then she perked up at him, mischief dancing in her emerald eyes. "You can be rid of me now. Send me packing back to England!''

His grip tightened possessively. ''The devil I will! You belong to me. That's what you want, isn't it?'' He gave her a hard shake, staring steadily down into her eyes with a look which was like fire and wine to her. She nodded breathlessly and, the sensuous curve of his mouth more pronounced, he pulled her closer to his sweat-soaked body, his lips taking hers in a dominating kiss which left her in no doubt of his intentions. Her arms crept up to cling about his neck; she was almost swooning with rapture, such incredible joy after so much unhappiness. Roger was at Alexis' shoulder, face faintly apologetic, eyes crinkling with laughter.

''Sorry to interrupt you, sir, but there will be time aplenty for that later. The duchess has retreated to the Daliborka Tower.''

Alexis released Francesca reluctantly, already making for the door as he spoke. ''But it is on fire!'' he exclaimed. Roger nodded grimly.

They stood on the battlements in the freezing wind and a clear view of the tower met their horrified gaze. It had been fired from below, but Renata must have entered it from one of the maze of passages. The courtyard was thick with people, stark against the trampled snow, every face upturned, an ominous hush held them still. Two figures were clearly discernible at the topmost window of the tower, outlined by the raging inferno. The duchess stood there defiantly, screaming curses and abuse. Francesca cried out as she saw the squat, bulky shape of Carl, his huge head turning this way and that, seeking one face in his confusion and terror—that of his sweet friend. His eyes came to rest on her, so far away on the opposite rampart, but he recognized her and stretched out his arms. She shrank against Alexis, burying her face in his chest, sobbing bitterly.

That horrific tableau hung for an instant, as if
suspended in space, then the flames, funneling up
uncontrollably through the old building, reached out to
lick at them hungrily. The walls crumbled with a noise
like thunder, and they disappeared into the heart of the
fire.

After the initial chaos, Alexis and the rebel leaders held
a meeting in the hall of the palace. Commands were
allocated and order restored. Francesca rode out with
him, passing through the breach and past the dead who
still guarded it, into the town where the streets were
lined with a cheering populace gone mad with joy at
their liberation. She sat her mount proudly, Alexis
having insisted that she ride with him at the head of his
forces. There was a brilliance radiating from him and
she was deaf and blind to all save the light in his face,
overwhelmed by the savage thrill of pride in the
achievements of her man—pitiless and primordial.

Francesca was only too eager to leave Castle Costin,
now a scene of destruction, piled with dead, half-
destroyed by fire. Those of Renata's supporters who
had not died in the conflict were already hanging from
the walls, on the hooks usually reserved for flags and
banners. The stench of death pervaded the atmosphere
and she shudderingly wondered if she would ever be
able to bring herself to live there again, though knowing
that, as margrave, Alexis would be bound to use it as the
seat of government.

Before setting out, they had talked quietly of their
future, fingers entwined, walking in the snowy garden,
pressed close together while the wind thrashed the walls,
flapped at her skirts, gusting snow and whipping tattered clouds across the glowering sky. Sadly, she

recognized the sense in his words—it was necessary that they be parted for a little longer, after which they would be together forever. He would be fully occupied for the next few days with Grisan Giorg and the other leaders, sweeping the country clean of the vipers who had gorged on it for too long. Justice must be done, cases judged and assessed, righteous men reinstated in positions from which they had been ousted by Renata. He promised to put the wedding preparations in hand at once and she was swept along by his enthusiasm, clinging to his strong hands, heart racing at the tenderness in his eyes.

He took her to the Convent of St. Denys, which was situated just beyond the walls. A dedicated order, whose mother superior had kept it unblemished during the duchess's regime, caring for the bodily and spiritual needs of those who sought refuge in the peace of the ancient cloisters, refusing the temptations of Castle Costin. Hetty and Lavinia joined her, and she rested and recuperated, letting the nightmares slip away, returning to her old self, a spirited girl, filled with happy optimism and an innate faith in human nature.

She found it impossible to sleep the night before the marriage, and roused Hetty early, setting about her preparations. She bathed, seated in the big wooden tub carried in by three of the smiling nuns, who had entered into the excitement of having a bride in their midst. After she had soaped herself thoroughly, she wrapped a soft fluffy white towel around her and, seated on a rug before the fire, slowly, caressingly, began to brush her heavy hair which had been washed the night before, the flames on the hearth bringing to life the fiery glow of the wavy mass. For a while she was lost in a sensual dream, longing for Alexis, then Hetty, Lavinia and a gaggle of waiting women were there to attire her for the ceremony.

Standing naked in the firelight, she rubbed lotion over her skin, shivering at the thought that, in a few hours, Alexis' hands would be caressing that satin smoothness, then she sprayed her body with a heady perfume which reminded her of spices and roses. A silken shift went on first, and she enjoyed the luxurious feel of the material, then she sat on a stool, pulling up fine white stockings, kept in place by garters with sparkling paste buckles, and Hetty brought over a pair of high-heeled satin shoes. Petticoats were fastened round her waist, and then came the gown itself.

At last she was ready, pausing before the pier glass, hardly daring to believe that the radiant bride in the mirror was really herself. The wedding dress was the same one which had lain in readiness for her at Castle Costin, but then she had refused to even look at it. This was different—she was to wed the man of her choice, the man she adored above all others. Only now could she appreciate the great beauty of the gown with its yards of white satin worked with flowers in silver thread, its tight bodice and heart-shaped neckline trimmed with Brussels lace, as was the deep flounce which finished the sleeves. A veil covered her hair, which was loosened about her shoulders, a rich, abundant fall of curls, and her face needed little additional cosmetics to enhance its loveliness on that happy morning. The tiring women stood back with a sigh to admire her, while Hetty put final fussy touches to the perfect picture which she made. But Francesca knew that she would have been transported with the same feeling of joy had she been clad in rags to meet her beloved bridegroom.

As in a dream, she was transported to the very old church which stood in the center of Govora. Although it

had been snowing, the townspeople had been standing
for hours, waiting to catch a glimpse of her and, peering
from the window of the great state coach, she could not
help being reminded of her first entrance through the
gates when she had wanted to die with unhappiness, cut
to the quick by the hostility which had surrounded her.
Now, seated between Lavinia and Hetty, both magnificently gowned, she literally had to keep pinching herself
to make sure that she was awake and this was not some
lovely dream from which she would be roused to harsh
reality, still in the clutches of the duchess. When the
coach rocked to a halt she took a firm grip on her
emotions, allowing belief to rush through her in a
glorious flood, stepping down to be greeted by a gray-
bearded, very upright old nobleman who came forward
and made a speech of welcome. She entered the church
on his arm, her trembling fingers stilled as he smiled
down at her, dark eyes twinkling encouragingly under
tufted white brows, like some benign uncle. Later,
Alexis told her that this was precisely his relationship to
them—he was one of his father's brothers who had been
exiled for years.

The church was very beautiful, its sanctified gloom
punctured periodically by shafts of weak sunshine
which made warm patterns on the flagstones—red,
mauve, green, shining through the stained glass windows high under its fan-vaulted roof. The well-dressed
congregation shuffled and coughed, a gasp of admiration at Francesca's loveliness rippled through them
as she was led towards her bridegroom. She smiled
serenely, though her knees were weak, keeping her gaze
fixed on the priceless treasures which surrounded the
golden, jeweled shrine of one of the patron saints which
stood near the altar. She was achingly aware of Alexis'
tall figure at her side, sneaking a quick glance at him,

petrified by sudden shyness for he looked every inch a
ruler, very fashionably attired in a green velvet jacket
with an elaborately embroidered yellow silk waistcoat,
black satin breeches, silk hose and buckled shoes. The
finest lace frothed at his throat and wrists, and his hair
was glossy, smoothed back and tied with a ribbon. He
wore a dress sword at his hip of cut steel which caught
the light of the candles, and a wide blue insignia across
his chest, bearing a jeweled order, and more than ever
he exuded that mysterious, compelling force which
made him the center of attention at any gathering. He
reached out and took her icy fingers in his warm ones
and she relaxed as the ceremony began.

It was a moment of high emotion, and Francesca
could hardly retain a sob as the final vows were taken
and a thick golden band placed on her finger. The scene
was fractured across by happy tears—the glittering company, the white-robed choristers with their innocent,
well-scrubbed faces attaining the heights of musical
perfection, the priest in splendid regalia performing his
sacred duty of binding the young couple together.
Alexis lifted her veil to kiss her, gazing for a moment
into that perfect face, the eyes glowing with love, her
mouth of an exquisite beauty, a little parted with excitement, and he was almost awed, unable to believe that
after all their trials and tribulations, she was really his at
last. He lowered his dark, handsome head, and his lips
brushed hers. Francesca closed her eyes under that
tender salute, her heart jumping, longing to be alone
with him, away from the crowds, locked in his arms.

This was not to be—not yet. They were swept up in a
whirl of celebrations, while the cannons thundered their
tribute and the bells pealed a wild, joyous carillon, then
they were borne off to a feast in the banqueting hall of
Castle Costin. Francesca found that she could endure

the palace now; with Alexis at her side the evil memories were vanquished. When they had performed this pleasant duty of entertaining nobility and dignitaries, they managed to escape at length, riding away to the Haldrenski Hunting Lodge. Servants had gone on ahead to prepare it, light fires and throw back the shutters. Even the weather seemed to smile on the lovers, pale sunshine sparkling on the snow, fingers of warmth touching their faces as they traversed the woodland paths. They were accompanied by friends—gypsies and fellow soldiers. Their followers sang cheerful bridal songs, the jingling bells on harness adding a merry accompaniment.

The lodge was magnificent. The views from the spacious windows on three sides were of whispering, snow-covered woods, and westward the ground sloped sharply, revealing a wide vista of untamed beauty— ravines and tumbling water and huge mountains. Francesca knew that she would always love this place and look upon it as home. There, Alexis would rest with her, temporarily forgetting the cares of rulership; there her children would be born.

The Duke of Little Egypt and Elvire officiated at the celebrations, conducted in gypsy style. Although they might have preferred to be outdoors, the *tziganys* adapted happily, the huge logs roaring in the chimney representing their campfire. They threw themselves into the lively festivities, the potent red wine adding its own witchery as toast after toast was drunk both in honor of the bridal pair and also to celebrate the recent victory over oppression. Violins and tambourines made the air vibrate with music as Francesca joined her husband by the fireplace where he was talking to the Duke. He had discarded his formal suit, much more the man she had originally known, wearing a buff leather waistcoat laced across the front, and sleek beige breeches meeting the tops of high black boots. The white silk shirt with its ruffled cuffs was open at the neck, and a bright sash girdled his slim waist. A lock of blue-black hair fell across his forehead, and there was a glitter in his amber eyes which caused a stab of yearning to grip almost painfully within her. The gypsies stamped and cheered, their music becoming wilder as they feasted and drank, their maidens and young men whirling into dance.

It was deep in the night when Francesca at last found herself alone with Alexis. She felt again that curiously odd little spasm of shyness. Then he came to her, holding her in his arms while they solemnly studied one another. Calm happiness washed over Francesca in a warm flood. They were here in this safe, paneled room, rich with candleglow and firelight, and would remain there undisturbed for hours. There was no need for haste, no unwelcome intrusions, thoughts or quarrels to disrupt this perfect harmony. Sighing with joy, she laid her head against his chest, hearing the steady pounding of his heart, feeling the warmth of his flesh beneath her hands. He pulled her closer and her soft body molded itself unconsciously to the leaness of his. She had never doubted his desire for her, but was that all he felt? Dear God, she prayed. Let there be more!

With a catch in her voice, she said hesitantly. "D'you realize, darling, that you have never told me that you love me?"

Capturing her wandering fingers in one hand, he kissed the tips lightly, rumbling with laughter as if he considered her question to be superfluous. "Haven't I, dearest? How very remiss of me!"

She waited, only too aware of his hands running up and down her spine, which was covered by a thin shift. "Well, do you?" she asked at last, greatly daring.

"Of course I love you!" He jerked the words out and

it was his very impatience that convinced her, for Alexis would never be a humble lover with pat phrases springing to his tongue and, her throat choked with happiness, she flung her arms about his neck. "Oh, and I love you so much too! I don't know how or why it happened, but I can't live without you!"

Her eyes flew to his, and the sudden unexpected tenderness that lurked in those golden depths caused a quick flutter of excitement in her stomach. "We have spent so much time fighting, you and I," he said softly, "I, with my damnable pride which refused to admit that I needed anyone, and you—such a fiery madame, determined to think the worst of me. And all the time I acted from motives of jealousy, unable to bear the thought of you married to someone else, or dallying with Mark."

At the mention of that name, she sobered, staring into the glowing embers of the fire, seeing a pair of humorous hazel eyes and a slightly wry smile which seemed to bless her union with Alexis. "He died to save you," she reminded him softly, and he reacted as she had hoped he would, giving credit to that one noble act of Mark's life.

"I know it," he said seriously, seated in the chair by the hearth, reaching out to pull her onto his knee. "He was obviously misguided, and could I but have had him as a comrade, giving him a purpose, I would have encouraged his better qualities."

This was the time for confession and opening their hearts to one another, and Francesca wriggled against him, whispering into the warmth of his neck, "I could have easily killed Gilda, thinking that you despised me."

She stole a quick glance at him; a smile curved his mouth as he answered. "I'm sure you could have, my dangerous little darling! I'd best beware, lest you stick that pretty knife of yours into me again! Gilda was a strange girl," he went on thoughtfully, frowning slightly, vexed by her death, yet relieved too, for he would never have been able to trust her again. "She loudly and frequently protested her passion for me, yet was consistently unfaithful. This I'll not tolerate, so don't you try it." He was suddenly fierce, his hands bruising her arms with the force of his grip.

"I want no one but you, Alexis," she soothed, running her fingers lovingly over his face, smoothing out the worried lines, exploring the contours of his beloved features with soft fingertips. His eyebrows felt coarse, and her touch slipped down to his bold, proud nose; then she traced the firm outline of his sensual mouth longing to feel it close on hers.

"We have been fortunate to find each other in time." His breath was warm against her hand. He moved his head and nuzzled her ear, his teeth gently nipping the lobe where a diamond earring gleamed. "Dearest, you are my world, my moon, and stars and sunlight. You will rule wisely as my margravine, just and kindly to our people so that they will love and bless you. We will train our children to follow our example—our tall, straight sons and beautiful daughters." Then an intent look crept into his eyes which shortened her breath and made her heart pound. "But their mother must never neglect me for them. I expect her undivided attention, always."

This was her cue, and she let her body show him how much she loved him, for the first time free from any restraint, confident and happy as his wife, knowing that they had the whole of their lives before them. They lay in the great marriage bed, her mouth blossomed under his, all her love and longing crying out as her body ground into his hard-muscled strength, and her hands sought to tell him of the fire which consumed her. A long shudder coursed through him at her touch and, in answer to his throbbing need of her, he slid gently between her thighs, lifting her hips with his hands to crush her even closer as he drove deep into her rejoicing flesh. She responded with every fiber of her being as he swept her along with him to the heights of ecstasy—her body and soul aflame with adoration as he roused her as only he knew how. Alexis, her husband—the man who loved her!

Later, replete and satisfied, they lay locked in each other's arms, and she suddenly hugged him tightly, saying fiercely, "We must never be parted again. Never stop loving me, Alexis!"

He shifted his position, pushing her down in the silken pillows, looming above her, twining his fingers in the dark red hair splayed out about her face. There was such a warm flame of love in the depths of his eyes that joy sang in her heart. "Never fear, darling. We shall spend the rest of our days together. But don't think that it will be a bed of roses. I am still a soldier and there will be demands on my time which you won't like. We shall still fight, I expect." There was a thread of laughter running through his deep voice as he captured her head between his hands, drinking his fill of that lovely, wayward face. "I am as overbearing as ever, and your temper is as hot as hell!"

Francesca snuggled contentedly against him, knowing that there were bound to be difficulties ahead, yet nothing mattered but the love of this one man. The earl would have to be told and his reception of the news was bound to be stormy, then there was Alexis' important work in the reorganization of his country, but that was tomorrow. Now there was only the night—and their love. They had blissful hours till dawn when the sun would rise over the mountains, illuminating their lives.